1

ISBN-13: 978-0615944210 (John Martin)

ISBN-10: 0615944213

John Martin

The Mythology of Sylphs/John Martin

Table of Contents

For Moira and Jenny

I remember the day I heard her name for the first time. Second grade, it is our first day back from summer vacation. It is the end of a supposed age of innocence. We ourselves are innocent. The day is bright and blue. It is the kind of day on which we believe eternal innocence is possible. It is a day near the end of days before our handsome prince is murdered, before the ragged fab minstrels shatter our perceptions. It is the days before we knew the content of our character and before the streets turn to fire. It is before we break our mighty sword on a small yet unbreakable rock called Vietnam. I see her for the first time on this day as I can still see her even now, near the end of this golden age of innocence, a time I can't recover.

My homeroom teacher, Sister John Patrice is calling the attendance roll. I'm in the middle of the most vivid of my vivid daydreams. I see the world through the eyes of one of the birds flitting back and forth over the church roof opposite. I'm a fast and acrobatic flier. I turn as the other birds turn. I wheel and caper across the sky among them, I'm one of them. I climb up one side of the steep roof, clear the ridge line and burst into the wide open sky. Joyously I revel in the freedom of the sky. It is so real, it must be real, it is real.

One day I lost the gift of seeing the world through the bird's eyes. It may have been that very day. On that day I discover a new and more exhilarating distraction. Flying, half listening, when Sister, calling the attendance roll, says; "A real liar ling hi."

These words pull me from the sky. I land with a thud in my chair. Why should such a strange-sounding string of letters interrupt my flight? Is this someone's name? If so, it is a singular appellation signifying in itself the difference, if not the total uniqueness of the person so named. It isn't a pleasant sounding name. "Areal"? Is that the first name or is it "Arealliar"? Who in their right mind would name their child "a real liar"? I immediately become curious, as does the rest of the class, about the unusual creature to whom such an unusual name must belong. It crosses my mind that whoever possesses this name might have three heads, or perhaps an arm sticking out of their back. They might even be Chinese, with a name like ling-hi (or liar-ling hi, depending on where the first name ends and the last begins) it's possible. I find myself leaning towards three heads as more likely. Nobody out of the ordinary jumps out at me unless you count Charlie Doyle. Charlie Doyle seems to have an unlimited supply of snot, some of which remains suspended between his nose and his impetiginous upper lip. Everybody has one head, everybody has only two arms. There is no one who appears Chinese.

The name belongs to a skinny pretty girl with long black hair, who occupies the seat diagonally in front of me. She raises an expressive hand at the end of an elegant arms and says, "Present." She then surprises everyone by standing and saying, in the most mellifluous speaking voice I would ever hear. "Sister, excuse me, but you pronounce my name R-EE-L LEER-a-LING-EE." What dash, what elan to stand up to Sister and dare tell her how to pronounce her name, and to do it in that most mellifluous of voices. R-EE-L adds, "I don't wish to be rude, but I'm proud of my name."

What a name too, Ariel Lirilinghi. It sounds like poetry to me. I begin trying to write poems about that name starting right then. Sister, who is generally believed incapable of doing so, smiles.

"Of course, you are dear, as you should be." Sister says, "I apologize." Wait a second, where is the fearsome sea-hag that the previous second graders warned us about repeatedly? "Would you please say your name again, child, so we can all know how to say it."

"Yes Sister, it's R-EE-L LEER-a-LING-EE." She doesn't have to wave a magic wand over my head. The spell is cast.

"Thank you, dear, it's very beautiful the way you say it."

Ariel resumes her seat, and in so doing turns to me and smiles, blushing profusely and twisting her hands up under her chin. I sit dumbfounded, caught in mid poetic composition. Who knew that poetry was so hard and that the distance between feelings and words could be so wide. The poem I'm composing is driven from my head along with every other word in my vocabulary. My mouth is agape, the first of many times she will catch me in this attitude. She must think I'm an idiot.

I try desperately to conjure something poetic, or at least mildly UN-idiotic to say. I can't stand that she might think me stupid. I rack my brain to come up with something that will dispel the idiot image I've projected.

Sister continues calling the roll to which I have become oblivious. My mind is fully occupied with the task at hand. I finally settle on what I will say. At the very moment when Sister says my name, I blurt out in Ariel's direction, "Nice name!". The class erupts into laughter with the exception of Ariel herself. That is, she doesn't laugh out loud, but her eyes laugh. Her big amber eyes are beautifully happy. She smiles broadly and the dimples on her cheeks have made their first appearance, these hidden harbingers of happiness that make her even prettier.

She is the only one smart enough to realize I'm talking about her name and not mine. I'll admit what I've said is neither clever nor witty, but it serves its purpose in that it makes her eyes laugh, this makes me feel less stupid. I intend to see those laughing eyes and dimpled cheeks as often as possible. The road to hell is paved with good intentions.

"Yes Mr. M____ you have a very nice name," Sister says in her most sarcastic voice. "Would you in the future just say present." It is a very mild rebuke from such a widely reviled cast iron battle-ax.

"Yes, Sister." I sink down in my chair, red-faced.

Ariel has already turned back and is ready to pay attention. She is a serious student right from the beginning. Her seriousness is matched by her daunting intelligence, which leads me to the highlight of my early academic career (alright, my entire academic career).

The highlight of my academic career comes when I defeat her in the second-grade spelling bee. Three of us are left standing after a grueling two-hour slugfest. It is Ariel, a girl named Melinda Wrobels and I. It is Ariel's turn. The easy words have long since been used up. Sister chooses the next word no doubt to accelerate the end of the contest with which she is getting bored. The word she chooses is Antarctica. Ariel, being the smart girl she is, and having no idea what a difficult word this is for your average second grader, confidently proceeds to spell it. Capital A-n-t-a-r-t-i-c-a. She finishes and gives Sister her confident little smile.

At the time I had a deep interest in the doomed Explorer Robert Falcon Scott (I wish I had his name) who died while trying to return from the South Pole upon reaching it after the Norwegian expedition led by Roald Amundsen. I admire Scott, preferring his romance with doom to Amundsen's well planned, well executed, uneventful and extremely successful mission. If anyone in second grade can spell Antarctica it is me. Ariel and the rest of the class await Sister's verdict. I already know the verdict.

"Oh, I'm sorry Ariel," she never calls her Miss LEER-a LING-EE. "That's incorrect." Shock registers on Ariel's face. She is not wrong very often. I triumphantly spell it correctly, turning the metaphorical knife by accenting the 'c' she had missed.

The feeling of triumph dissipates immediately. I'm panicked that she will hate me for beating her, and I have ruined my chance at love! I hatch a hare-brained second-grade scheme to go out on the next word. Somehow this will prove I'd spelled Antarctica correctly only by accident. This would, therefore, restore my chance for love. My logic is impeccable.

The next word is "trudged". Interestingly, "trudged" is a word used more than once to describe Scott's progress across the ice. "Scott and his men trudged across this frigid desert to their doom, to their permanent Antarctic night." There is no doubt in my mind I know how to spell "trudged", that sentence is etched in my brain. I can't remember exactly how I misspelled it. I'm sure it must have seemed sufficiently stupid that it could only have been luck that brought forth from my mouth the correct spelling of Antarctica. That she would be upset not that I beat her, but that she had promised her father she would win didn't occurred to me, living as I did in the "me-centric" universe.

11

Melinda Wrobels wins the spelling bee by default. She spells "trudged" with ease. She is so proud of her first place ribbon that she wears it pinned to her uniform for a week. She makes me sick.

Not everyone forgets how Sister had at first mispronounced Ariel's name. Devlin Flynn tortures her at every opportunity by repeating "who's a real liar, ling hi" over and over again or some variant thereof. She asks him to stop. This only intensifies his desire to torture her.

He will never tire of torturing her, at least not until he breaks her. This is his goal as he stated it to me. "I'm gonna make her cry." Devlin is a sadist. Devlin and I live across a 'courtyard' from each other in the projects. He, like me, comes from a large family. His brothers are Brady, Bryan, and Brendan. His sisters are Bridget, Brenda, and Killeen. Brady Flynn is in prison for beating a wheelchair-bound veteran of the Korean war, and taking his money. Certain traits run in families.

I guess you'd say Devlin and I are friends. At least we "play" together. Being Devlin's friend is an iffy proposition. He can be a lot of fun to be around. He can also become extremely violent in the blink of an eye, violence brought on usually by an indiscernible provocation. He may not be the most effective fighter, but the level of violence to which he seems willing to raise any confrontation and his determination to do real harm make me cautious.

12

He has thrown baseball bats and large auto springs at my head. I have been lucky so far. I've seen his attacks coming. I flinch every time he comes up behind me unexpectedly. I tell myself; be more watchful.

At Devlin Flynn's hands, I have been bent backward over a waist high chain link fence. On that occasion, he tried gleefully, with all his might to break my back. I kicked him in the nuts to get out of that one. One day, in a murderous rage, he repeatedly banged my head off the brick wall of my building, trying savagely to bust it open like a watermelon. I can't remember how I got out of that one, maybe I passed out.

Devlin, when he can't restrain himself will compulsively attack anyone he perceives as weak. Ariel fits the bill; she exudes the fragility of the beautiful, small, and meek. That she is no less meek than I am, I fail, of course, to recognize because she certainly looks as if she must be. I have such cathartic dreams of protecting her and being her hero.

One day in the sixth grade. We are in the playground for lunchtime recess one of Devlin's compulsions strikes. His eyes roll back in his head, like he is having a seizure. He corners Ariel and screams in her face; 'Who's a real liar? Ariel is!' He keeps her boxed in. He screams until he turns blue in the face. He pauses, takes a deep breath and does it again for about another three minutes.

13

It isn't funny or amusing in the least. The sheer maniacal ferocity of this attack alarms us all. It is so bizarre, so out of the blue, so without warning, so uncalled for. Boys just don't attack girls. It is a serious violation of the unwritten rules.

Flynn grabs Ariel by her upper arms and squeezes, all the while screaming in her face. Ariel fights against crying, confused about how to make him stop. She tries to push him away, but he is right on top of her and too strong. She doesn't have it in her to sock him in the face or kick him in the nuts. She couldn't have hit him with her hands anyway because he has them pinned to her side. She would later display a ring of bruises on each arm. She looks around for some help from anybody. She looks beseechingly at me.

I have good reason to fear Devlin as I've said, more so than the others who don't have to live with him. As much as I want to act heroically, at the moment of truth, my courage fails. I hesitate. I learn it's not easy to be a real hero.

There is a boy who is not afraid. He was until this very day a quiet kid with a goofy smile and a cowlick. His name is Coleman Curran. He surprises everyone by telling Flynn, just as Flynn is drawing another breath to continue his crazy tirade, "Shut up or I'll shut you up, you loudmouthed faggot! Let her go, or I'll kill you." Everyone present gasps at his bravado. I feel sorry for poor Coleman, sure that Devlin will kill him. Sure enough, Devlin tries his best, but it doesn't take long to see that

Coleman is already a trained fighter. His blows are short and sharp and carry a sting, while Devlin's are long telegraphed affairs without the force behind them sufficient to deter Coleman from defeating him in short order. Unfortunately for Devlin there are no baseball bats or auto springs handy.

After soundly thrashing Devlin, Coleman, by way of marking his victim, consummating his victory, or just because he is as crazy or crazier than Flynn, hocks up the contents of his lungs and spits a huge gob of mucus on Devlin's chest. Then he turns in Marine Corps lockstep and walks away. His friend Dennis pats him on the back saying, "Nice job Cole." Devlin sulks against the fence, trying to get the clod of mucus off his shirt with no success. It isn't so much the beating, but the lungy that sticks with me. It seems so much like a kick to the head of a man who is down. If there is something wrong with Devlin, there is something very wrong with Coleman too.

Ariel apparently doesn't see it the way I do. I can see in her eyes as she follows Coleman's back that she has found her hero and protector, and has little use henceforth for me. I have missed my chance to be her hero.

Coleman has no particular interest in Ariel. He would have done the same thing if Flynn had picked on any of the girls. His interest is strictly in beating up Devlin to advance his reputation as a fighter. Word spreads about who has beaten up who, and soon everyone knows. Coleman has one foot in the demi-monde of street fighters. My brother is involved in this world too. If you keep your eyes open, you will sometimes see two groups come together on the street, in the park, or if the fight were expected to be particularly violent, in the basement of the building adjoining my own. Each group supports the fighter in their midst, terms negotiated, blows exchanged, last man standing wins. Later it becomes more organized, and rumor has it money is made and lost.

Devlin Flynn, however, is back to his old tricks in short order, at least as it pertains to me. I decide I'm not going to take it anymore. Coleman's thrashing makes me believe I can beat him. I fight him as hard as I can, exchanging punch in the face for punch in the face, moved to tenacious fury by his ruining my chances with Ariel.

I hit him with a good roundhouse right on the left side of his head. He falls to the ground and doesn't get up. I believe for a moment that I've killed him, but he doesn't die. I'm not sure how I feel about that. It would be nice to have him out of my life.

I am eleven years old, so I probably would not have been punished by the law. At that time there are more clearly delineated divisions between adult and juvenile offenders. I'm too young to even be considered a juvenile offender. Besides, all the witnesses say he had started the fight, as he always does, and that I was just defending myself.

The doctor says I couldn't have possibly hit him hard enough to cause what had happened. Instead, they find something wrong in Devlin's brain (tell me something I didn't know). However, we didn't hear about this. I benefit for a while from being the kid who put another kid in a coma. Fortunately, he comes out of it eventually anyway.

I'm not punished by the law, but by my father. He wouldn't accept my contention that Devlin deserved it, at least not while he whipped me about the arms, abdomen, back and shoulders with his belt, while I defended as best I could. It ended as it always ends with my mother wailing for him to stop and me lying in my bed, rigid, tears of anger pouring down my face promising myself that I would one day get that fucking bastard.

I'm getting a little bit ahead of myself, back to second grade.

I have such intense and confusing feelings for Ariel from the beginning. An objective observer might say that she isn't perfect and neither am I blind to her imperfections. The paradox is that this aggregation of minor yet endearing imperfections makes her somehow more than perfect. There are girls in the class, who arguably are more perfectly formed, but none is more beautiful in my eyes, which is the only place that counts. I'm not trying to downplay how pretty she is, and assert that I'm someone so noble. But there is something about Ariel that comes from inside her. Perhaps a harmony of grace, brains and beauty in perfect balance that resonates against the sounding board that is me. I couldn't say.

I am so smitten that I try when standing near her to compress myself so that I won't be so much taller than she. I also unconsciously develop the habit of holding my pen with the same grip as she does. Sister John seeing my grip raps me on the knuckles with her ruler and chides me; "Hold your pen the way I showed you." (Oh, there's the Sister John we'd been warned about). She restrains herself, however, from rapping Ariel's knuckles even though Ariel is holding her pen in the same way. Instead, she draws in a deep calming breath then raps me on the knuckles again. She fills her quota of knuckle rapping without having to hit Ariel. I'm not mad that I get rapped and she doesn't. I would rather Sister hit me again, I'm used to getting hit. For my sake, she earnestly tries to grip her pen correctly. She reverts to her natural grip, well, naturally, and I follow suit, until the next knuckle rapping.

These early days of second grade are some of the most beautiful days of my life. Because of where we sit in relation to each other I get to study her freely. She is mostly unaware. She does, however, on occasion, catch me staring, and at those times we both turn red. She doesn't seem annoyed and never expresses displeasure.

That first day of second grade, I don't think I learned anything. I spend the day staring at Ariel's slender, soft, fuzzy arms. I dream of touching her to feel how soft she is. My little pee-pee gets so hard just from thinking this thought, it feels good. I no longer need to daydream of the birds to feel like I'm flying.

2. Home and Work

Ariel is the second child of Enzo and Kathleen. Their first child, David, had been born eight years earlier. While neither Enzo nor

that bringing a child into the world isn't just about love; it is also about money, so they work and wait until their circumstances improve before having Ariel.

Kathleen is a stay at home mom, that's the way it is, and that's how Enzo wants it. He hustles his ass off to make money as a man should. By the time Ariel is ready to be born, he is steadily established in a job that pays the bills, lets them enjoy some luxuries, buys the house in Brighton Ariel grows up in, and leaves a little left over to set aside every week. While this job isn't Enzo's dream job, he remains relatively happy, and Kathleen loves him for working so hard. Enzo supplements his income by running a canteen truck two days a week.

David had been delivered C-Section, as many children were at that time. Both Kathleen and Enzo wanted to try to do a natural childbirth with Ariel. The doctor, a Korean named IL Kim, fought them (he had better things to do, like play golf). Enzo, and more importantly Kathleen, were insistent. On that fateful day, while Kathleen struggles, legs enstirruped, to push Ariel out into the world, Doctor IL makes an episiotomy incision just after Ariel's head crowns. Enzo manfully keeps his face calm so as not to frighten Kathleen. He counts the vision of his wife's vagina being sliced as the most disturbing thing he's ever seen. The incision and Ariel's cataclysmic torpedo like entrance into the world happen in such rapid succession he doesn't have time to dwell on it. Doctor Kim is surprised himself by the speed with which Ariel breaks forth into the world. He drops the scalpel so he can catch her. After a second or two of juggling the slippery newborn, he stands up and shows Enzo his baby girl, announcing in his singsong English. "Wow, she wants to be here and here she is."

Enzo, to his surprise, lets out two very distinct sobs. His lip quivers and a tear comes to his eye. He masters himself quickly (men don't cry even at the birth of their beautiful daughters).

He'd prayed silent, fervent prayers for a baby girl since Kathleen found out she was pregnant again. He could feel his heart soften as he looks with tenderness at little Ariel lying on the table. The nurse quickly administers the Apgar test, the first of many Ariel will pass with flying colors. She is sponged down and swaddled.

Enzo picks her up and cradles her in his arms. Now he does cry. He brings her to Kathleen and lays Ariel next to her. The doctor delivers the placenta and asks in his singsong English, "You want the placenta?" Enzo politely declines.

Her face, while scrunched up like all babies' faces, exhibits one of the characteristics that would distinguish her in people's minds for her entire life. You had to look closely to notice. She could not smile yet, but almost imperceptibly the right side of her mouth curled up, as though she were trying to smile.

In later years, it always seemed to me that when she smiled, she kind of led with the right side of her mouth just a little, as though she'd had a mini-stroke. You had to look closely to see this. I did look closely, I knew her face better than I knew my own.

The first years of her life consisted mainly of being smothered in love from her adoring family, so much love, really it was almost enough to make you sick. The charmed circle she'd been born into was so different whatever circle of hell into which I was born.

As soon as she was old enough, Enzo would read to her. She loved it when he did. She graduated from picture books to stories quickly. She especially loved it when he read his own stories. Enzo, while riding on the back of the trash truck passed the dull hours by dreaming up stories to amuse his daughter. Yes, Enzo is a trash man. He isn't proud of it, but it pays surprisingly well. It is a job that no one aspires to, but absolutely must be done for the sake of civic order.

Thinking up silly stories with titles like Ariel Rides the Pink Pony and Down on Muffin is what occupies his mind during the mindless, hours working. Down on Muffin is about a young swan that sheds its gray down to become a beautiful black swan. One day Muffin flies away. Kathleen made a little black swan rag doll out of the down. That's what she told Ariel. Ariel, of course, believed her. Enzo told Ariel that Muffin comes every year on one magic night. Ariel fell asleep many a night waiting for Muffin's return. Ariel never noticed that her father, even if unconsciously, had plagiarized a number of stories in writing Down on Muffin. Ariel Rides the Pink Pony is the story of Ariel and her little magic pink pony's quest for the national equestrian championship.

Ariel's personal favorite is called The Little Mademoiselle. She requests it often. In the story, the little mademoiselle gets into all sorts of trouble. Most of the trouble is caused by the unseen but sinister Guilliame. She escapes from trouble time and again with the help of a mysterious and laconic guardian angel who always appears just in the nick of time.

"Daddy, are we, French. Because I think I want to be French can we please be French!"

"Honey, I'm Italian and so you are half Italian, always be proud of who you are."

"So Mom is French?"

"Why don't you ask her."

"MOOOMMM are you French?"

Kathleen comes out of the kitchen rolls her eyes, and In the thickest Irish lilt of her girlhood says, "Dearie, of course, I'm French, can't you tell by the accent!" Then she ducks back in the kitchen to finish stuffing the canoles

"So, daddy, that settles it, I'm French because I really want to be French."

Enzo laughs, although he is hurt that she would choose to be French, and feels ridiculous for being hurt over such a silly thing. "I suppose you can be whatever it is you want to be," he says, acquiescing as he always did to her whimsy.

"Please daddy, please tell about the part where the giant spider monkeys swing the little mademoiselle through the trees again." She begs and begs. Sometimes she holds her hands in the air, running around the room, making swooshing and monkey sounds. She jumps over David as he does his math homework. She feels like she is flying. Enzo laughs and laughs. Kathleen comes into the room and with just a hint of a lilt asks "What are you two up to?"

Ariel stops in mid-flight, "We're up to the part when I swing with the monkeys," in her mind she is the little mademoiselle, "can't you tell." She resumes her flight through the trees.

"I tot it were something like that," Kathleen says. "David, if you erase, clean it up, please don't just sweep it aside." It was Kathleen's job to keep order and try and keep everyone's feet on the ground.

"Yes, Ma."

No matter how tired he was, Enzo would always comply with Ariel's requests that he read to her because it was truly the single great pleasure of his life that his beautiful daughter should so appreciate his silly stories that were composed while hanging on for dear life to the back of a trash truck. It was for him the saddest of sad days when she no longer wanted to sit in his lap and be read to.

"Bonjour, père, comment ca va, c'est une belle journée, n'est ce pas?"

"What?"

Ariel, never forgetting her wish to be French, took it upon herself to learn the language. She was so smart and had a natural ability, but she never saw herself as a linguistic genius. She got her start by listening to Edith Piaf, and from there it was all the dreamy Jean-Paul Belmondo films. Soon the subtitles disappeared. She'd accomplished this linguistic feat by the time she was in the fourth grade. "C'est une tres belle!"

"Yeah sure honey, whatever you say."

"Ciao, papa, come stai, è una bella giornata non è vero?" Hey dad, how are you, it's a beautiful day, isn't it?

"That's better, but let's speak English, my Italian's rusty."

"Nessun, Papa, prega di." No Dad, please.

He relented, and they spent the day speaking Italian to each other. He didn't really mind, in fact, as the day wore on he enjoyed it more and more. Kathleen wasn't there, she had stayed home pleading tiredness, no need to run the constant translation.

They are out for a walk in the woods early on a Saturday morning. The air is still cool. The grass, saturated with dew, soaks her sneakers. Her father tells her to keep her eyes open, so as not to walk through a spider's web. She doesn't like spiders. She has a recurring nightmare about a giant spider sewing her into a cocoon so tightly she can't move. Then a giant straw breaks through the wall of the cocoon to stick into her and

25

suck her dry. She wakes up terrified. Enzo comes and comforts her.

"Spiders aren't bad," her father tells her, "really they are good. If it weren't for spiders we'd be overrun by bugs, It's, well, spiders and other things like bats and birds."

"I don't like bats either daddy, they have ugly faces. Birds I guess are OK, except they poop on you from the sky. I hate that."

"Me too.", her father agrees.

They come across a near perfect orb weavers web. It is easy to spot because it glistens with dewdrops. The spider sits next to one of the drops apparently drinking it. Ariel stares in wonder, marveling at the geometric intricacy of the web and the spider as it drank. She watched in fascination as the dewdrop disappeared inside the spider. She didn't know that spiders drank. Enzo stares in wonder too, not at the spider, but at her, He's pleased to see the effect of curiosity overpower her natural revulsion, As always, he is amazed and sad to see her grow. She's growing so quickly. He wants in his heart of hearts to stop time, and freeze this moment, He feels silly thinking such a thought because he wants to see the fine woman he knows she will become. Every step of Ariel's growth is bittersweet to poor, innocent Enzo.

Soon, it is she who is teaching him, pointing out the various flora, and showing him the anatomy of a flower. It seems to him that she is a vast storehouse of knowledge. As far as Enzo can tell, she retains everything she's ever read, heard or seen.

He feels a feeling so irrepressibly powerful, so immensely joyful, so fulfilling, that he can't resist the temptation to share his joy with his trash collecting co-workers. He is one of those guys whose main topic of conversation is his children, but especially Ariel. In the lunchroom, between the morning and afternoon runs, he finds ways to work Ariel into the conversation.

When his co-workers are talking about the Red Sox, and how awful they are, Enzo's contribution to the conversation is; "Oh yeah, Ariel loves that Tony Conigliaro." Tony Conigliaro is a tall, handsome, local kid from Revere, and a rising superstar. It was one of the most tragic days in baseball history when he was struck in the face by a fastball, effectively ending his career. Enzo went on and on about how hard Ariel took it. He has no inkling that his co-workers roll their eyes at all his talk of Ariel.

He lines his locker with pictures of her, while his co-workers line theirs with pictures of the recent playmates, or in some cases, especially the lockers of the two men on either side of him, Paul and Lewis, with truly disgusting pornography. One day, Enzo gave each of them a picture of Ariel, in her first communion dress, praying in the light of heaven. As a joke, both

27

men enshrine Ariel's picture amidst the pornography. With every opportunity they razz Enzo.

Paul and Lew are burly young men, given to drinking and whoring to the end of their paychecks. Enzo, in his innocence, believes Ariel's picture will transform them.

"Hey Enzo, it looks like your daughter is posing with Miss October," Paul says, pointing to Ariel's picture next to Miss October.

Lew adds, "Hey Enzo when will your daughter be old enough to give us some nice titty pictures instead of this first communion shit!"

Randall Hugh Witt, or Randy Hugh, as his wife calls him, is the day shift supervisor. Generally speaking, he likes the job, although sometimes he wishes he were an English professor at an all-girls' college (wouldn't that be fun?). He does look more like an English professor than a trash foreman, with his tweed and his bookish squint. His favorite part of the day is the lull after he's finished all his paperwork, but before the collectors return from their routes, and the sorting begins. One man's trash is another man's treasure.

His wife is a beautiful woman, fourteen years his junior. She keeps the lead in his pencil, as it were. He prides himself on keeping a woman so much younger than he satisfied. Just last night he'd made love to her. She wore only a pair of thigh-high, gray, soft felt boots. Oh, those boots are such a turn on. She looks like the sexy D'Artangnon of his fevered boyhood dreams when swordplay was all the rage. He calls her Puss 'N' Boots and she purrs. She calls him her loving Doctor Autodidact. He'd entered her from behind. He lectures her from back there, professorially, about the ways in which she can please him, using her body bent over in front of him as a lectern, his hands on her hips. He gives her the occasional gentle smack or drives himself in a little extra hard to emphasize the cogent points he makes, as he would if he were a real college professor (at an all girl's college).

The lesson for today is to reach back and stroke him exactly where, and exactly how he's instructed, at exactly the right moment to maximize his pleasure. If she does the lesson incorrectly, then she will have to take a "surprise" oral exam and thereby taste the salty tang of knowledge for which he knows she is so thirsty. He "lectures" in a funny, pseudo-Viennese accent, and makes air quotes when he says the word "surprise". She, of course, performs the lesson flawlessly, driving him to the heights of ecstasy. "Oh, please let me take the oral exam anyway and then spank me for being so naughty!" She begs. They are happy together.

It is this scene that he is reliving (and embellishing) in his mind during the afternoon lull. So immersed is he in his thoughts, that he doesn't realize the collectors have returned. His office door flies open and Maurice Mastrapasqua, toady, and all around company rat, bursts in to report with a little too much enthusiasm that Enzo Lirilinghi has just now decked Lew Thomas down in the lockers.

This is the part of the job Randy Hugh hates, having to arbitrate peace between the lowlifes. Plus, Enzo is his best and most reliable worker, and yet he will have to let him go if Lew files a complaint. This is the company policy; they have zero tolerance for violence. Randy Hugh hates Lew because Lew calls him Hugh Witt-less. Enzo is suspended (per company policy) until the following Monday at which time his fate will be adjudicated.

The little hearing takes place in Randy Hugh's office. Enzo squirms in his seat, fighting the impulse to beg for his job. He has not told Kathleen. He spent the days of his suspension hustling the canteen truck. He concludes he can't adequately support his family on the proceeds from the canteen truck alone. He has visions of Ariel starving to death in rags. A thing he had seen often enough immediately after the war when everything was destroyed. Kathleen might have to go back to work. He shows none of his worries to his family. He keeps it to himself as a man must, despite the churning in his stomach. He chides himself relentlessly for being so stupid as to be drawn into Paul and Lew's game. As he sits in the chair, awaiting his fate, he wrings his Red-Sox cap in his hands.

"I don't really see what I can do," Randy Hugh says at last.

"Enzo summons all his dignity, and says, "I understand, should I clean out my locker?" The horrifying image of his ragged starving daughter dances before his eyes.

Randy Hugh turns to Lew.

"You and I both know you provoked this whole thing. Why don't you think about letting this go?" Randy Hugh pops an antacid tablet. "If you sign this paper I have to fire Enzo."

Lew turns to Enzo, "You know Enzo, there isn't a single man in my life who's hit me, and walked away unscathed. The only thing that saved you that day was that you knocked me out, no one's ever done that before either. I respect that. If I had handled it in my usual way, we'd both be out a job and you'd be in the hospital." Enzo was going to dispute that contention but thinks better of it. Lew turns back to Randy Hugh. "I don't settle my disputes this way, I prefer to settle them like a man." He balls up the paper and takes aim at the wastebasket.

That was good enough for Randy Hugh. "You guys can settle your little disputes any way you like, just not on company property." That was all Randy Hugh would say. The 'hearing' was over, and Enzo retained his job. How long he would keep his health was a matter up in the air. Lew storms out.

"Have a nice weekend (it was Monday morning), Hugh Witt-less." he says in parting.

Enzo is in his locker to grab his gloves and hard hat for the morning run. He is about to close his locker when it is slammed shut, almost crushing his hands. Lew's meat hook presses squarely in the middle of the locker door, bowing it inwards. A sinister smile cleaves his face.

In a threatening tone, he says, "Enzo, let me show you something." He pulls the already open padlock out of the metal hasp on the front of his locker and lifts the hasp. Enzo is sure Lew is going to show him the gun with which he plans to kill him. This bit of drama is a way to heighten Enzo's fear and his own enjoyment.

Lew opens the locker door. Enzo isn't sure what he is supposed to see. He sees Lew's lunch, hardhat, goggles, and his gloves.

"What are you trying to show me, Lew? Wait I see you brought a lunch, you're not going out for drinks at lunchtime?"

"Can't you see? Are you blind?"

Enzo sees, Lew has cleaned all the pornography out of his locker, leaving only Ariel's little picture stuck in the door frame just above the hasp.

"Enzo, you can talk about your daughter anytime you want to, I don't mind."

Enzo is slightly befuddled. It had never occurred to him that anyone minded. "Thanks, Lew."

Paul came up just then, and opened his locker, revealing that he too had cleaned house, except for the small picture. Lew, from that day, became a better person. He stopped drinking and whoring and decided he wanted to settle down and live the life of a simple man. He too, in the coming years, proudly showed anyone mildly interested pictures of his own children. He perhaps bragged less than Enzo, but he still bragged. He never told anyone, but he believed it was the image of that little girl, praying in the light of heaven, that and that alone that kept him good for the rest of his life.

Paul had a tougher time with it, backsliding frequently, but he always tried.

Enzo sometimes thought he was the father of a real angel.

My chance to be her hero came just a few days after Devlin Flynn's attack on Ariel. It happened during Sister Homunculus' history class. Sister Homunculus is the worst history teacher in history. She reads from the textbook in a droning monotone while mining her ears for wax. Occasionally she hits the mother lode. I wish I were lying when I say this, but she will then stick the nugget on the end of her tongue, and draw it into her chitinous ma9ndibuli. History class is just before lunch, my mother puzzles over why I can't put on weight.

My seat in the class is near the middle, four seats back from the front. Ariel sits in front of, and to my right. Her friend Nancy Turner sits behind, and to my left. The reason I say this is that I'm in the direct path of all the urgent notes that constantly pass between them, through me.

Nancy is a red-haired, green-eyed girl covered with a wild bloom of freckles. She is as good a friend to Ariel as Ariel could ever hope to have. I base this observation strictly on the volume of notes that pass between them without cessation during the course of any given day. They are so eager that each should know the other's thoughts they can't defer the telling. Nancy, despite her wonderful singing voice, strikes me as mean. Ariel could find a nicer best friend. That she should willingly be friends with Nancy causes some confusion in me. I try not to dwell on it.

At times, I think perhaps I should charge per note, and thereby make my fortune. At recess one day I nervously proposed this idea to them as a joke (sort of, I could use the money). I called my little idea the pony express in reference to the fact that they both frequently wore their long hair in ponytails. I reached out and touched Ariel's ponytail. Nancy slapped my hand away. "Don't touch her." she hissed. I found this odd because Ariel didn't seem to mind me touching her ponytail too much. Nancy acted like she owned Ariel. I chalked the slap and the attitude up to Nancy's meanness. "We don't need your stupid pony express," she added. I flushed with rage and embarrassment, that my good-natured joke should be met with such vicious resistance. That Ariel seemed fine with Nancy standing between us was lost on me.

Nancy is right of course they don't need to pass notes through me.

I'm not the only conduit for notes, every boy in the class is expected to obligingly pass these stupid notes back and forth. Ariel is, like Dr, Moriarty, at the hub of a vast if not necessarily criminal network.

I say they are stupid notes, but I really don't know, I never opened one to see what it was. One time I pretended I was going to. Ariel gave me a super dirty look. I didn't open the letter; I didn't want her mad at me. I couldn't imagine what was so important they needed to write so many notes. I let my imagination run wild. I imagined they said things like; [gratuitous juvenile joke warning: those who feel they possess a refined sensibility or for whatever reason have their nose in the air are instructed to proceed forward one sentence. Don't say I didn't warn you.] "my tits are tingling," or "I have to scratch my ass really bad." Sometimes I chuckled (I couldn't help it) thinking of a raunchy or funny message as Ariel hands me a note to pass. She would scowl. I'd pass the note.

Note passing, while pandemic among the girls, is strictly verboten. I risk as much as they by playing mailman. They don't appreciate me one iota. My opinion in the matter hasn't been disregarded so much as never considered. Neither Ariel nor Nancy ever once deign to share the treats they had in their lunches as payment for services rendered.

They always had ring-dings or Twinkies; oh my god I love Twinkies. I mean they come two to a package they could have given me one. I had my peanut butter and jelly or my cheese and tomato sandwiches, but almost never had a treat. When I did, it was usually half a stale jelly doughnut leftover from after

36

church on Sunday. Sometimes I felt used, and would refuse to pass a note.

Notes I refused to pass would have to take the more circuitous route and be handled by at least one extra pair of hands, thereby increasing the likelihood of detection.

One day just such an incident occurred. I refused to take the note from Ariel, feeling particularly put upon by a recent and excessive spike in volume. The note made its way across the Northern route and was in transit between Ed Herlihy, who sat in front of me and Melanie Hawthorne. Melanie is a pathologically shy, plump, possibly octoroon girl who wouldn't say "shit" if she had a mouthful, and it was on fire. She sat to my left, in front of Nancy. Ed had just relinquished possession when Sister Homunculus raised her voice, and in a loud monotone said;

"Miss Hawthorne, bring that note to me." The note was dangling in Melanie's right hand, easily within my reach. Melanie froze, because of the unbounded terror caused by the idea of getting up, and showing her rather broad behind to the class, better to freeze and play dead, so to speak. Sister Homunculus, who was born exasperated, had no patience for Melanie's reticence.

"Miss Hawthorne, get your fat ass moving. Bring me that note." I thought that this was a bit of the pot calling the kettle black and I chuckled (I am prone to spontaneous chuckling).

37

Sister Homunculus was used to Melanie Hawthorne freezing like a squirrel in the path of an oncoming car. Melanie wasn't moving that ass unless she came down the aisle and lit a fire under it said;

"Mr. Maxwell, since you think It's so funny, you bring me the note."

"Sister, perhaps you didn't know, but I've already refused to deliver this note once, why would I do it now?" I said. You would never have guessed that Sister Homunculus had a better arm than most of the Red-Sox pitching staff. She fired the piece of chalk she'd been holding just for this purpose right off my forehead. I would normally have ducked out of the line of fire, but I was mesmerized by the speed with which she'd thrown the chalk. I'm emblazoned with a chalk mark on my forehead. The residue of James Dean like cool I'd displayed with my cavalier remark shattered along with my dignity as the class roared.

I glance at Ariel to see if she is as amused as the others are at my expense. Instead, she is staring at the note dangling from Melanie's clammy paw (how do I know it's clammy? You just have to trust me on some things). A look of abject horror? disgust? is etched on her face. It is plain to see she doesn't want that note read to the class, which is what the Homunculus will do in her best blathering monotone.

"Mr. Maxwell, bring me that note now, young man, before I get really angry," a terrifying prospect indeed. I seize the day; grabbing the note from Melanie's hand I stuff it in my face and force it down before the Homunculus can get down the aisle.

I have ruined her fun so I must pay. She whacks me on my back with the blackboard pointer. She chips my scapula with the second blow, the next blows hurt mightily. It is everything I could do not to scream, I lose count. I bite through my lower lip drops of blood dot my desk and I struggle not to faint. On the edge of my consciousness, I hear someone yelling "Stop, Stop, Stop! in a loud shrieking voice. The blows stop. I don't know who it was who yelled for the Homunculus to stop, my world had narrowed to the blows and the interval between.

I hold back the tears, and don't feel very heroic. I'm afraid to look at Ariel in case she is looking at me with that look of sort of benevolent toleration which was about as far as she ever went in terms of appreciation for the delivery service. I don't know what I would have done if I saw that look. Homunculus isn't finished, not by a long shot.

She returns to her desk and plops into the seat sweaty and out of breath.

After many moments of suspense where the only sounds in the pin-drop silent room are my pathetic sobs and her pathetic wheezing.

With her breathe regained and the sweat wiped from her brow Sister Homunculus announces with the glee of someone who senses final victory, "Since Mr. Maxwell has seen fit to eat the note, we are all going to sit here after school until the author comes forward and reveals its contents."

This is a favorite and time-tested Gestapo tactic found enormously efficacious for extracting information through years of use. She pits those blameless among us against the one or ones who are to blame.

Homunculus resumes reading as though nothing has happened. My pain recedes to tolerable levels. I wipe the blood from the desktop with the raggedy cuff of my shirt, leaving tiny rings and trails of coagulated blood. I lick blood from my lower lip, it stings. My lip is swollen. I try to move the floating chip in my scapula back into place by wiggling my back against the chair. It hurts to do so, but I bear the pain with a certain fascination about how much pain I can bear. My back is the first place my dad is going to hit me.

Ariel is squirming in her seat too. I think for a second in my cloud of pain; about time you goddamn goodie two shoes, about time you found out what it's like. I quickly bless myself and plead for god's and Ariel's forgiveness.

The class broke up for lunch. Those with stronger stomachs, worse eyesight, or impaired short term memories wolf down their sandwiches and milk, better able to disregard the mental picture of the Homunculus chowing on ear wax than I am. I gag down my cheese and tomato sandwich, then head out to the playground. My enemies all take a swipe at my back. I'd say their names, but I've decided that I don't wish to enshrine them here or anywhere. I shall carve their names from the stone. I call them by the aliases I've given them Lothar, Gorgon, Xerxes, and Attila. Each takes a whack. None of them knows I have a chipped bone in my back, but each is aware of the pain their whacking causes. They like this. I turn from one only to be whacked by the next as they surround me on the four points of the compass. East side, whack west side, whack all around New York, whack. Round and round I spin, pushing, yelling, fighting back. whack, whack, whack. Round and round, the world becomes a monstrous merry-go-round of pain. Tears will only make it worse.

"Stop." A single word, spoken moderately brings the Merry-go-round to a halt. She doesn't say anything

 else. They stop and hang their stupid Neanderthal heads, put their hands in their pockets, and drift away, grousing about how I let a girl fight my battles for me. I back up to the fence and lace my fingers through the mesh and hold on for dear life. No one is going to come up from behind me for the rest of lunch, and I'm determined to be at the back of the line when lunch is over.

"Are you alright?"

41

"Yes, thanks." I lie through clenched teeth.

"Good," she says.

She turns to walk away. "Hey, why don't you just say what the note said, or make something up, that's what I would do."

She gives me a look I can't quite fathom. "I can't lie, not about this." It seems for a second she is going to say something else but stops before she does seemingly distressed, like on the verge of tears from a different kind of pain.

"What? Don't worry about it, everybody lies. It's all lies."

"I can't lie about this."

"OK," I say. "Suit yourself. Listen, let me give you a piece of advice."

"You, give me advice." she says

"Well if you're gonna be that way, forget it." I say more sharply than I intended. "Thanks for helping."

There was nothing more I could think of to say that would keep her there and keep her talking. While I rack my brain for something she turns and walks away.

"See ya." she says

"Yeah, see ya."

I puzzle over how she'd been able to stop the gang of four so cold. It made no sense. She has a new-found authority like there had been an election I'd missed. It dawns on me, that she must be Coleman's girlfriend. Her new-found authority flows from him, it has to be that. Since his annihilation of, and excessive expectoration on Flynn, no one wants to fight Coleman. My elation at talking to her evaporates, as the pain in my back again returns to tolerable levels. I wonder why would she exercise her new-found authority to help me. I can really twist myself in knots.

The afternoon passes slowly. There are three classes after lunch: math, reading and music. The music class takes place in the basement. I have to pee badly after music class. I thought as I was relieving myself that if I had gone to the detention without draining the vein I'd be pissing my pants in a few minutes. I look around the boy's room, all the usual suspects are clearing their bladders for the long haul, including the gang of four. Refreshed and relieved we climb the stairs to the history room, only a couple of taps on the back luckily no of these hits my chipped scapula.

We resume our normal seats, and Homunculus announces that we will remain here until the person who wrote the note reveals its contents.

Thanks for the refresher, asshole.

We sit in silence for about ten minutes or so, everyone with their hands folded on the desk. This is particularly hard on the ADHD kids who are undiagnosed. The only diagnosable learning disability that we knew of is called stupidity! You can tell who the ADHD kids are. They have a foot going like a jackhammer or drum the desk like Keith Moon on crystal meth. The girls with ADHD move their legs apart and bring them together rapidly and incessantly. I suppose this feels really good. Sitting still is torture for these kids.

Me, I could sit there until the Homunculus fossilizes, assuming this hasn't happened already. My bladder is as clear as my conscience, and I don't have ADHD. Ariel also it seems can sit still forever.

After about fifteen minutes, the Homunculus leaves the classroom. This is all part and parcel of the Gestapo tactic, leave the room, and let everybody attack the culprit. Which is exactly what happens.

"Melanie, just tell her what was in the note, stop being a fat jerk we want to go home."

Of course, most people think that Melanie wrote the note. Only Ed and I know otherwise. People chant; Melanie, Melanie, drawing out the word MEL-A-KNEE, repeating it over and over, progressively louder.

Melanie starts to shake. I think she is going to have a seizure. This is an interesting development. I look at Ariel. A bead of sweat trickles down her temple. She is also squirming in her chair. She is either overwhelmed with guilt that Meanie is being subjected to the razzing she deserves or she has to go to the bathroom, Maybe that's it. That is the other part of The plan. If the guilty party doesn't break under the invective or at least opprobrium heaped on them by their fellows, then the pressure of having to urinate will do the job. Ariel, being such a GD goodie two shoes, and therefore unfamiliar with pre-detention bladder clearing protocols already has to go. She didn't want any advice from me, though.

My perverse nature kicks in, and I start chanting Melanie, Melanie, along with everybody else, only I chant it in Ariel's direction, completely disregarding what she'd done for me earlier. Ed follows my lead. He knows who the real culprit is. Melanie was about to die but was so pathologically shy she couldn't defend herself. Everyone else is so pathologically stupid they never think to ask the question; just who was Melanie passing a note to, she has no friends.

Ariel isn't faring any better, she is in an absolute torment.

"Oh for god sakes, this is ridiculous already, tell a lie, tell the truth, who cares, how bad can it be?" I offer my advice unsolicited. The Homunculus reenters the room and the commotion dissipates.

"Be quiet, hands on desks." We sit quietly for about two hours. I have to give Ariel credit for toughing out having to go to the bathroom. People are really angry. Melanie is the focus of death looks from everyone. If looks could kill, she'd be a smoking pile of ash. She couldn't bring herself to say it was Ariel and neither Ed nor I was gonna rat. It didn't seem possible, judging from her obvious discomfort that Ariel could hold out too much longer.

I have a brilliant idea. Why hadn't I thought of it sooner? I stood and said, "Sister Demetrius (her real name), I wrote the note."

"Really Mr. Maxwell, come up front and tell the class what it said. "

I made my way up front. Pretending to be nervous I said, "I'm really reluctant to say what I wrote sister, it's pretty embarrassing."

"Out with it."

"Alright, the note said, my balls are bigger than yours." I couldn't keep a straight face. Everybody roars.

Without missing a beat Homunculus says, "Bigger than whose, Mr. Maxwell?"

"What is bigger than whose, Sister?"

"Mr. Maxwell, you said yours are bigger than someone else's, whose are they bigger than?"

I said "My what is bigger than whose? Perhaps if you could tell me Sister what it is of mine that I said was bigger than whose, then I could better answer your question." I'm trying to exasperate her into saying the word balls, which will be hilarious. It isn't working, she maintains an icy composure.

"OK Mr. Maxwell, we all know what you said. You handed the note to Melanie, so we know you were passing the note to someone in the two rows to her left. In those two rows, I see...." as she says the names I check them off mentally; Lothar, Gorgon, Xerxes, and Attila. "So it seems you wish to let one of these boys know that you have two somethings that are bigger than their two somethings."

"Ahhhhhhh." Oh shit, the Homunculus has outplayed me, she's set me up beautifully. If I had actually written the note, and passed it to Melanie, then one of those boys would be the most logical intended recipients, me and my big mouth.

I have two hopes, my first is that none of the aforementioned is bright enough to know what is going on. This would be a reasonable hope if there were just one of them to fool. This hope dissolves when I see the "I'm gonna kill you" look on Xerxes evil rat like face. I wouldn't just have to face him, though. I would have to face all four of them. That's how they roll, especially Xerxes, who never fights alone. How does a rat like him acquire such loyal allies?

47

The Homunculus has scheduled my execution for just after detention on the street outside the school. First, they will beat the name out of me, then they will beat it back into me. I have to do what I have to do to save myself. I have to name someone who can't kick my ass, or at least wouldn't try. In my present state I'm pretty vulnerable and in no shape to take a beating.

"It was Julius, sister." Everybody laughs, except Julius, even the gang of four. I hate using Julius this way, I like him and have even been to his house, but I have saved myself, and I breathe a sigh of relief.

She sees through my ruse completely. "I can see your earlier assertion isn't true is it, Mr. Maxwell?" This stings, it is true, I have not behaved heroically. She has won again. "Sit down Mr. large trousers." Everybody laughs again, only, this time, they laugh at me. I and my not so big balls skulk back to my seat.

Ariel squirms for a couple more minutes. She raises her hand and implores Sister to allow her to go to the bathroom. "Not until you come up here and tell the class what was in that note." Sister says. She'd known all along and let me make a fool out of myself. I feel myself turn red with rage and humiliation.

Ariel goes to the front of the class. She stands with her legs crossed at the ankles, knees pressed tightly together, obviously trying desperately not to go on the spot. I'm clenching my own legs together in sympathy. "Sister, I wrote the note," There is fear bordering on panic in her voice.

"I know dear, what was so all fired important that it couldn't wait until lunch for you to tell Miss Turner? Do you think I haven't noticed that you and she pass notes back and forth using poor red-faced Mr. Maxwell as your chief mailman? How stupid do you think I am?" I turn even redder at getting used as a humorous prop.

Ariel, in her distress, doesn't realize it is a rhetorical question, and she answers "Not very, sister." The whole class laughs. Ariel's visible distress increases, she has never been the object of a class wide laugh.

"Oh I'm glad to hear it. Now would you please tell the class in a nice loud voice what was in the note. Ariel wrings her hands together, twisting her fingers under her chin.

'Just get it over with, tell a lie, say anything. Say something funny.'

Ariel either refuses to or can't say another word. She whimpers and the little jig she is doing becomes more urgent by the moment. Unable to hold back any longer after what must have been an ordeal of terror, knowing that she wasn't going to speak, and knowing this was the likely outcome of that decision, she ceases her little samba and freezes in a rigor of intense

49

mortification. She empties her bladder. While doing so, she stands still in an attitude of prayer, no doubt asking sweet Jesus to spare her this humiliation. The hissing sound of rushing urine is the only sound to be heard. With no help from Jesus forthcoming. She empties her bladder, a praying, peeing statue. When she done she turns to run from the room in utter humiliation, but god is unkind and she doesn't escape one final grand humiliation. As she turns to run she slips and falls. At least she gets her hands down and doesn't slam her head off the floor, but her long hair dips into the puddle. As she gets up it drips from her hair. The girls let out a collective chorus of disgust.

"EEEEEWWWWWW."

The puddle spreads outwards, causing those in the front seats to move down the rows to the back wall so as not to get their shoes wet. The smell of urine is strong. This comes as a shock to me, I guess I thought in some recess of my mind that her piss would smell like rosewater. Ariel's shoes make squishy sounds as she runs out.

We all sit in stunned silence. The tension is palpable. The Homunculus puts her head in her hands. I'm so angry I for one want to kill her.

You torture us and when someone cracks you're going to pretend now you didn't mean it, you fucking cunt.

50

My friend Owen leans over toward me, and behind his hand says, sotto voce; "Wow, she really had to go!" I was o wound up I can't help it I laugh hysterically. The Homunculus jerks her head out of her hands and looks right at me

"Mr. Maxwell you little bastard, this is all your fault. You think this is so funny, you clean this up, the rest of you can go home."

4. Tough Talk

The class has filed out. I'm left alone with Sister Homunculus. I go into the utility closet to get the mop and bucket. There is a little spigot that runs hot water. There is a bottle of ammonia on the shelf. I dump a little too much ammonia in the water, and I breathe a little too deeply in the small space, taking a full hit of the acrid fumes deep into my lungs. I see stars and can't stop coughing, except for the coughing, it feels pretty good, actually. I store this for future reference, cheap high: ammonia.

I drag the bucket out to the yellow puddle in the center of the front of the room. The urine smell is quite strong. I decide I want to do as good a job as I possibly can. If I do a poor job (which is my first inclination) and the class smells like the underpass at Park Street Station tomorrow, Ariel will be humiliated all over again. I don't want that to happen.

I don't really know where to start, I have never cleaned a puddle of pee before. Should I start at the edges, or go right to the center? The puddle is about eight feet in diameter; I estimate it is about a quarter of an inch deep, held at that depth and diameter by surface tension. Were it not for the phenomenon of surface tension, theoretically the puddle could have spread across the floor until it was a monomolecular layer perhaps a mile in diameter. I do some quick figuring and come up with a volume of 75 cubic inches, which is roughly one liter. Owen had been correct; she really did have to go. I conclude that Ariel had made an absolutely heroic effort to hold back more than twice, maybe as much as three times the normal greatest volume of her bladder, well beyond the point where she would have felt the urgent need to go. You have to admire that. I'd heard when girls go they can't stop the stream like boys can. This had been a raging river. I will never forget the hissing sound as the torrent escaped her body, the only explanation for which is that the pressure was so great it forced the liquid through her tiny aperture at near supersonic speed! She must have really been in agony. The volume of whatever was in her shoes, and saturating her knee socks adds an even more heroic dimension to her struggle, but at least I won't have to clean that up.

"Sister, did you know there's about a liter of urine on the floor here by my estimation."

"Mr. Maxwell, do you think that's funny?"

"No, Sister I was just saying. We're learning about volumes and unit conversion in math. I just did the math and mention it as a curiosity, no offense meant."

"Alright, just clean it up."

"How was this my fault?"

"Just clean it up, Mr. Maxwell."

I proceed to wipe the puddle, soaking up as much as I can in the mop by dragging it slowly through the puddle, feeling a sharp twinge in my back every time I turned at the end of a stroke. When I judge the mop saturated, I wring it in the wringer, trying hard, but failing always, not to get any on my hands. I have made a mistake by filling the bucket with water first. I should have left it dry while I soak up the puddle.

"Mr. Maxwell, why do you act the way you do?" Oh-Oh, a loaded question.

"I'm not sure I know what you mean."

"Why did you eat that piece of paper? That was the most bizarre thing I've ever seen a child do in my class." She is checking out some new ear wax. Eating a piece of paper is more bizarre than peeing a full liter?

"I can't help the way I feel."

"What do you feel, Mr. Maxwell? You don't seem to have normal feelings as far as I can see."

This conversation is taking a turn I don't like. I'm making headway on the puddle; I will soon finish, and be able to leave.

"Answer my question!"

"I don't know. I don't know what you mean."

"I asked you why you ate the piece of paper, and you say, 'I can't help what I feel,' not really an answer. I know you can answer questions, you're not totally stupid like your brother." My brother had made it to sixth grade where I'm now. He was kicked out after flunking a number of the courses (he flunked all the courses). He wound up going to the Edison right near Ariel's house. In fact, the Edison schoolyard borders her backyard.

"My brother isn't stupid, don't say that."

"We are talking about your brother."

"Just don't say he's stupid." I defend him even though I know better than anyone how stupid he can be. I keep wiping and wringing, dying to leave.

"You can't help the way you feel, why not? Why can't you help the way you feel? I have to help the way I feel."

"What do you mean?"

"I have to come in here, and teach filthy ragamuffins who wear the same dirty ripped shirts and hand me down pants I taught their stupid brothers in, and shoes with holes in them. Kids who think they're smart, but are just smart asses, kids with slutty pregnant sisters. I teach kids who say the least funny things and laugh like donkeys about them, kids who don't have the decency to leave the size of their private parts out of their conversation. Hopeless kids with drunken fathers, and sad empty mothers, kids who don't belong here."

"Anybody I know? Why are you telling me this? My father's not a drunk. Leave me alone."

"You think that girl returns the feelings you have for her."

"Which girl do you mean?" I definitely don't want to talk about how I feel about Ariel with the Homunculus.

"You know exactly which girl I mean; from where I sit I can see you mooning over her when you should be paying attention."

"I try to pay attention, but..."

"But what, Mr. Maxwell, go ahead and say what you were going to say."

"You're so boring." She hadn't expected that and looks surprised.

"Be that as it may, how could she return your feelings? Look at you. Have you ever taken a good look at yourself?" At this point, she waddles over to the utility closet and opens the door. There is a full-length mirror and she beckons me over to it. I feel as Scrooge must have felt when the third spirit beckoned him to look at his name on the grave. Like Scrooge, I don't want to do it.

"Come over here and take a look, see what I see, don't be a coward." I place the mop in the bucket and walk over to the mirror.

"I'm no coward."

"Well, maybe, maybe not, we'll see. A coward runs away from the truth." She indicates me in the mirror. "Look at this shirt, all threadbare, worn completely through at the elbows. The collar is completely black and you putting on a superior air. Look at these pants, two inches too short, and too tight, even for a bag of bones like you. Your socks don't quite match, did you even know that? Look at your hair, do you own a comb? I can see that you're dirty and you smell." She scrunches her face in disgust. "When is bath night at your house? I hope for all our sakes it's soon. How often do you bathe, once a month? What are we going to do when the weather gets hot? Maybe I should make you wear perfume. I bet your underwear is black and full of holes."

I feel the hot sting of shame. My body is engulfed in flames. I try to respond. "You make fun of me because I'm poor, Jesus was poor."

"Jesus was poor, but he wasn't a filthy ragamuffin."

"By making fun of me, aren't you violating Jesus stricture 'As you do to the least among us so you do unto me?'"

"You're so arrogant, stupid and arrogant, as well as dirty, you parade around here like a filthy peacock, a filthy eleven-year-old peacock and then claim to be the least among us, just filthy peacock arrogance."

"There's more to me than is in that mirror."

"I haven't seen this more of you that you speak of, maybe he's hidden under the dirt, should I try to scrub the dirt away.

"My parents have to make sacrifices to send me here, so I don't have all the fancy clothes."

"Yeah, and they sometimes fall behind, but I bet your father never falls behind on his bar tab. We have let it slide a bit, but if you're going to act the way you did today, then no more, you go the way of your stupid brother."

"My brother is not stupid."

"Son, don't defend the indefensible."

I was shocked, and afraid, afraid that what she said was true. I have to defend my parents. I didn't know what to say, she has a harsh answer for all my glib retorts. I don't even know what I'm saying.

"You say a coward runs from the truth, but you don't know the truth. My father lost everyone he loved, all his friends when

57

he crossed that beach. They didn't make it across. He did, so he tries to fill the hole in his heart by drinking gin. He tries to fill the emptiness of having been such a pussy as to have lived. I hear him talking in his nightmares. He living while Ricky, Freddie, Tyrus and Uncle Ray all get shot to shit and blown to bits. He somehow made it and they didn't, but they won't stay dead. They taunt him cause he's alive, especially Uncle Ray who died in his arms, so you could read in your monotone, and dig for gold. I'm proud of my father, he's the best father in the world.

When I go home tonight, he'll ask me where I've been, and I'll tell him I was cleaning up piss. He'll hit me on the chin, and ask me again where I've been. I'll say I've been cleaning up piss, and he'll hit me again. I'll stick my chin out and say go ahead, hit me again you can't hurt me. He hates it when I say that. I pretend to be tough, 'cause he wants me to be tough. He will, he'll hit me again, only harder this time, but I won't cry, 'cause I'm tough, and I'm funny. I'd rather be dead than let him see me cry. I would never let him see me cry. You think you know why too, 'cause you think you're so smart. You think it's because I hate him, but you're wrong I can't let my father see me cry because I love him. I won't be a disappointment to him by crying like a baby. It's not what you think; he's the best father in the world. So go ahead and call me a dirty ragamuffin, that's what my mother calls me, my mother who was made for better things. She calls me a dirty ragamuffin, then she laughs and then she cries. You think you can hurt me more than my mother can. You think there's anything you can say to me that can hurt me. I've seen my mother cry. Go ahead take your best shot you ....you ....”

I become aware of a sort of high-pitched, desperate animal whine coming from somewhere in the room, I look around, and realize finally it's coming from where I'm standing.

I can't make out what she is trying to do; she is trying to throw her arms around me. I think she is going to throw me to the ground. I try to push her away, but her strength, like her pitching arm, is surprising. She pulls me to her ample bosom, and for a minute, I confess I give in. It feels good to give in. It would be so easy. Instead, I gather my strength and extricate myself. I step away from her. I wipe my eyes on the backs of my threadbare and blackened cuffs.

"You can't take back what you said, can I please go home. I'd rather get hit by my father if you don't mind." She looks at what remains of the puddle and says, "as soon as you're done."

I clean the floor as good as I can. I wash it three times, with fresh hot water and Spic-n-Span each time. As badly as I want to leave, I don't want the classroom to stink. Finally, it is clean.

I leave the room without a word and slam the heavy oaken door. It makes a sonic boom in the empty building. I listen, expecting to hear her heavy footfalls coming after me, nothing. I peek through the keyhole. She is sitting at the desk in what I take is a dejected posture. She has no intention of coming after me. 'Good, I hope you're sad.' I step away from the door and look for my coat on the coat rack.

There are thirty-eight hooks in two rows. The top row contains twenty hooks, the bottom eighteen, staggered to bisect perfectly the distance between the upper hooks. The upper hooks are about five feet, nine inches off the floor, while the lower hooks are maybe four and one-half feet. Generally, the boys, being taller take the upper hooks. (Not a misogynistic viewpoint, just a fact) Sometimes, I find both my coat and book bag have been dumped on the floor, displaced on the hook by the coat and bag of one of my enemies. This happens even though there are only thirty-five kids in the class, and there is always an empty upper hook. They are so relentlessly spiteful and small-minded. The hooks are first come first serve. Each hook is two-pronged. The upper prong protrudes further than the lower from the two by four on which the hooks are mounted. The lower prong extends out from the wall roughly half the distance of the upper prong. The upper prong is straight like a ramrod. The bottom prong is elegantly curved creating a sort of well in which to catch the drawstring of my book bag. The two prongs resemble the skull of an ancient predator that hunted in the teeming waters of an ancient lake, dying there and falling to the bottom to be encased in mud that hardens into stone. Thrown up from the lake bed into the mountains by the vagaries of violent geology, dug up and brought down by a diligent paleontologist, classified in their own phyla because of their strange and vicious physiognomy, then hung on this wall for my coat, finally making themselves useful after so many unfathomable millions of years. Each prong is balled at the end. The theory behind this, I conclude, is that no one should accidentally take their eye out on a pointed prong. While great in theory, it seems to me still well within the realm of probability to lose an eye to a balled prong. When the school year began, I was in the practice of piercing my brown lunch bag on the lower part of the hook so as to store it until lunch. When my lunch went missing two days in a row, it caused me to change my lunch storage strategy. Now, I carry it with me throughout the morning.

When I'm very hungry, I sneak bites of my sandwich behind my open desktop. This happens on most days, because I usually run late for school, and have no time for breakfast. It is the rare day my sandwich survives intact all the way to lunchtime.

I pick up my coat and book bag from the floor where they were dumped by Lothar, Gorgon et.al. I dust them off as best I can. I brush the boot print from the book bag. That was definitely Lothar, I have learned to distinguish the tracks of the various predatory fauna roaming wild through the halls. I put my coat on and stuff the truncated footballs that pass for buttons through the buttonholes, two are somewhat loose. I hope I don't lose them because it is cold outside. I'm still stifling sobs and very angry.

There is one other coat still hanging on a lower hook. It is a red coat, the color of poinsettias. Christmas isn't far off and the altar at church is lined with poinsettias. I know whose coat it is; she wore it at lunchtime. I put my hand on it. It is made from a material I'm unfamiliar with; it is so soft. I pick it off the hook and hold it to me like a tailor might at a fitting. For such a tiny person she looms so large to me. The label reads: Cashmere. I have never heard of it. It feels really nice, unlike my own coat, which has a texture closer to burlap than to this Cashmere. Whoever bought her this coat really loves her. I can almost feel the love.

Holding her coat is an emotional experience for me. I feel connected to her through this talisman. I cement the link between us. I wipe the last of my tears in the middle of the back of the coat and say a little prayer.

"I give these tears to you. They will be the last I ever cry."

I reach into her pockets. There is a piece of paper in one of them. It has a number of hearts with arrows in them and two sets of initials within the boundary of the heart written in her hand. The initials are J.M. + A.L. My heart stops. It couldn't be true, she loves me. It doesn't seem possible. My mood lifts through the ceiling. Who else could it be? It could be Jimmy

McNeill. That's a possibility I can't discount. No, it has to be me. How can it be anybody else? No one loves her like I do; she must see it, and this is her way of returning that love, it has to be true. Perhaps there is a god, and he smiles down at me.

The Homunculus steps into the hall.

"Are you still here Mr. Maxwell? Why don't you go home?"

I skip past her even with the heavy load of the two book bags and the sharp pain in my shoulder blade, waving the paper with the hearts and my initials in the air with a big smile on my face.

"Goodnight, Sister Demetrius." She is flummoxed by my transformation.

It has turned cold outside. The wind bites through my "inexpensive" coat. The air temperature is well below freezing. The wind makes it painful and her house is far away.

It probably wasn't much warmer when Ariel had run out of the building. It had been dark even then. She must have run all the way home in just her uniform. I hope she didn't get frostbite on her little bum. Although I thought it would be nice to rub her bum, you know, just to get the circulation back. I think about her bum, touching it, it is nice to think about.

My thoughts turn to rubbing her bum and how good that would feel. I form a picture in my head of what her bum must look like and I can almost feel the softness of her skin on my rapidly numbing fingertips. I see her standing naked before me, her back to me, her face turned to me looking back over her shoulder. Her voice in my head says; touch my bum. The sight of her naked before me pulls me on through the cold night. My hand extends to touch her bum. She moves away before me at a slow and tantalizing pace. Her voice inside my head says, 'Come get me.' I wonder what vision propelled Scott across the ice, projected from his mind into the night. Did he die before his vision did or did the death of his vision kill him?

This is the first time I have thought about Ariel in such a directly sexual way. It doesn't feel wrong. My penis awakens with these thoughts and almost gets fully erect. However, my clothes are too thin for this weather. My penis feels the undiminished bite of the frigid wind through my thin clothing. The wind sinks its steel teeth into my spine. My penis shrinks back and then some, survival mode in the heart of the city. The frigid wind denies me the pleasurable companionship of a nice tingling erection on this long and miserably cold walk. I wish I had worn my long-johns. I turn my thoughts to other things.

I think about her voice. It is the voice that carries one's spirit into the world. She has such a beautiful speaking voice; she must perforce have a beautiful spirit. Ariel's voice, from the first day I'd ever heard it, had the rare effect of soothing and stirring me all at once. It wasn't just the sound of her voice either. It was how she used it. She answers so many questions in class, that often when I hear her voice it is easing the stress of being called on, and not knowing the answer.

"Name the four Galilean moons? Miss Lirilinghi."

"Io, Calisto, Ganymede and Europa."

"Thank you, Miss Lirilinghi."

"Who was the Incan king who tried to buy his freedom with a roomful of gold? Miss Lirilinghi."

"Atahualpa, Sister."

"Very good Miss Lirilinghi."

What's the fourth root of sixteen.... Miss Lirilinghi."

"Two, Sister."

"Nice job, Miss Lirilinghi."

"What punctuation mark delineates a series......Mr. Maxwell?"

"Uh, I don't know."

"I didn't think so, Miss Lirilinghi."

"The comma, Sister"

"Correct again, Miss Lirilinghi."

I could go on and on. Much of what I've learned comes from remembering the answers she has said out loud in class. I couldn't remember any of what the Homunculus had read in her blathering monotone today, even though I love history. Relaxing at the sound of Ariel's voice has become as reflexive as salivating did for Pavlov's dogs. That her voice could relax me on the one hand, yet make me so nervous when directed to me on the other, is such a confounding paradox.

I can't stop thoughts of what had been said to me earlier from creeping in between the pleasant thoughts. I look at my reflection in the plate-glass windows of the darkened businesses along Washington Street. My reflection does not inspire confidence. I think of what Sister had said; 'You think that girl returns your feelings,' in her most dripping with sarcasm voice. I try to return to the pleasant thoughts, but my mind is in a turmoil. I decide to ask Ariel outright if she does return my feelings.

Thinking of the things that Sister said makes me think about my brother. Just a few weeks ago, we had decided to walk down to Harvard stadium to sneak into the Patriots game. This year they are playing their home games there. It had been a gold and blue late fall day. We took a meandering route down Market to Soldiers Field road by the river. It was just after Thanksgiving. The leaves were all off the trees, as were the acorns off the oaks and the seedpods off the maples.

My brother was bored by the walk. He started to pick up acorns. First, he threw them at me, and I at him. Then he stuck one up one of his nostrils. He pinched the other closed and shot the acorn out of his nose at high velocity in my general direction.

While truly annoying, it was also truly hilarious. He pushes it too far, though, as he always does. He shoves two up his nose, then three. He says he wants to see the spray pattern and study the ballistic behavior of acorn nose rockets. He tries to stuff four acorns, which is one too many, he shoves the first acorn into his sinuses. He is home in bed now with a very severe, painful sinus infection, and facing surgery to remove the acorn. Apparently, acorns don't dissolve all that quickly (if at all) in the human head. My father sums it up succinctly.

"Well, at least now you have something in your stupid head."

It can't be that Sister is right that Donny is stupid. I stop and look at myself again. If she isn't lying about that, maybe she isn't lying about anything. I decide I will just return the coat and go home, that is the best course of action. To ask her outright invites the worst of all possible answers, that I'm just a filthy ragamuffin! Even thinking about her bum doesn't cheer me up.

After the longest of Antarctic T-R-U-D-G-E-S, I make it to her house, the last outpost of Saint Col's parish. Her mother answers the door. She is very obviously distraught as any mother would be after their daughter has run home from school in her urine-soaked uniform. Nonetheless, she politely asks if she can help me.

67

"No, not really." I extend the coat. "Ariel's coat," she takes it from my hands.

"Thank you, would you like to come in?" I'm freezing; I have no hat, gloves, or boots. My ears, hands, and feet are stinging cold.

"Yes please."

I enter the front hall, which is split in two by the staircase at the right. Down the hall, I can see the kitchen. The living room is to my left, it is empty. Mrs. Lirilinghi invites me down the hall to the kitchen. I hear the strains of Stone Soul Picnic coming from a record player upstairs. That's cool, I think. I put Ariel's and my book bags on a little chair in the front hall.

"You look frozen, would you like some hot chocolate?"

"Yes please." Mrs. Lirilinghi opens a cabinet to get the container of instant hot chocolate mix. After opening the cabinet, she stands frozen like a statue, one hand on the box of Swiss Miss. She's forgotten what she'd opened the cabinet for. "Mrs. Lirilinghi, I can make it."

She rouses, "No, please let me. You're a nice boy. My David was a very nice boy too, you know."

"I know," I say, I didn't want to disagree with her even though I don't know David at all or why she feels it's necessary I should know he is a good boy. She heads out to the hall and calls Ariel down from upstairs. I hear her little footsteps on the stairs, and my heart starts pounding. She enters the kitchen. She has showered since she'd come home and is dressed simply in jeans and a sweater shirt.

"Hi," she says. From the way she says hi I conclude that it must be my initials in the hearts.

"Hi, are you alright?"

"No, are you are you alright?" She catches her mother by surprise with this burst of anger.

"ARIEL!" Her mother yells spilling a little hot chocolate on my pants as she does. "Oh I'm so sorry," she says in her Irish lilt. I get up to wash it out at the sink, with a paper towel soaked with cold water.

"Ariel, be nice, this boy came all the way here to return your coat, when he didn't have to."

Ariel somewhat chastened says more mildly, "Yes, but I don't want to have to report how I'm to everyone who asks. I don't want to talk about how I am, it's boring." Something is very wrong, but I don't know what it could be and Ariel has succeeded in making me feel like I've disappeared.

While I finish wiping the hot chocolate off my pants, Mrs. Lirilinghi drags herself upstairs to lie down. This is the perfect, maybe the only opportunity I'll ever get to tell Ariel how I feel

69

about her. All the things I want to say crowd into my head, some quite eloquent and romantic, yet as always I get nervous in her presence. In an effort to be humorous, instead of saying something nice or romantic, I say the stupidest thing I could have.

"Now it looks like I've pissed my pants." She thinks I'm making fun of her. She isn't amused.

"Listen, I think you should go."

"Can I just have a little of the hot chocolate, I'm so cold." I was going to launch into a litany of what I had done, or at least tried to do for her that day. Who else had tried at all, certainly not Jimmy McNeil, or for that matter Coleman Curran? It is pointless; her face tells the story. When she looks at me she sees a filthy ragamuffin. What a crushing disappointment. It isn't my brother who is the stupid one. I feel like crying but remember my promise. I get up without saying a word; grab my book bag and leave.

Outside her door, I ball up the paper with the hearts and Jimmy McNeil's initials and whip it at her door. A stabbing pain shoots through my back; it drives me to my knees. I run home as fast as I can to stay warm, and so my father can still get his licks in, he might as well. I can't hurt any worse.

With a few minor exceptions, Ariel and I have little to do with each other, for a long time. Even so, my feelings for her remain strong. I bottle them up, building the pressure.

During this long interval, I try to improve myself, and I watch and pine from afar, as she grows into the flowering of young womanhood.

The genie of my desire escapes his captivity just once. We are freshmen. I chase her up the back stairs singing a love song. She runs ahead of me as fast as she can, squealing for me to stop. The hem of her skirt bounces as she runs, revealing her bright white underpants with each step. We reach the top, there is no place to run. She turns to face me holding her books out in front of her as a last line of defense. I want to kiss her so hard. Overwhelmed with this desire I push myself into her, her arms collapse and the books are pressed against her chest. I brush my lips against hers. The concrete stairs turn to sand, my head turns into a balloon, full of nothing but air. The roof lifts off the building, there is nothing between us and the sky as we float away.

"Please let me go." She says when I pull my lips away from hers.

I have no intent to harm her, only to love her, so I step aside uncertain of my next step in this dance. I follow her progress down the stairs, trembling with the yearning. Too much in love for her or me to deal with. She looks back up at me from a safe distance and smiles, flattered and terrified in equal measure by my mad, unbridled attention. I never see her alone again.

5. The Dancer and the Dance

I sit in the shadows, dark filaments woven between the eastern-facing windows that line the gym wall. Gary the janitor has spent the last twenty minutes buffing the floor to a brilliant sheen. He was half-finished when I entered and sat down. His steady, determined progress across the floor coupled with the sonorous whir of the buffing machine calms me. Brilliant light streams in through the high windows, intensified by its reflection off the newly polished floor, ensuring the opacity of my shadowy cloak. Gary can't see me. I waved to him earlier and he didn't wave back. Gary is always friendly. He would have waved back if he had seen me. There is no acknowledgment of my presence in his face. I'm a shadow in the shadows. Gary leaves. I return to my history textbook, which is open on my lap. Cromwell and his New Model Army are driving the Irish into the sea.

The heavy glass-paneled, polished-oak doors mounted on their massive hinges with their tarnished-brass push and kick plates swing open. As if the room were not bright enough, Ariel

Lirilinghi enters. She pauses at the opening, one hand on each of the doors, her breasts thrust forward like the delicately carved twin prows of a sleek, fast ship. My heart races from the surprise of seeing her. The truth is, while it may have looked like I was studying Cromwell's campaign against the Irish, I was thinking of her. I was thinking of the time I chased her up the stairs. My thoughts of her are a powerful undercurrent, always there, rising now and again to sweep other less securely anchored thoughts downstream like so much flotsam.

She has become beautiful. While my heart beats like the drums of desire, my mind shrinks back into the shadows. I run through my litany of reasons not to approach her: you're too skinny, you're too tall, you're a filthy ragamuffin (that old gem) and of course, why would someone so smart and so beautiful want to be with me? That's the point that clinches the argument between my brain and heart.

She enters tentatively, carefully guiding the doors closed so they won't make their customary banging sound when closing and alert the authorities (in the person of Sister Mary) that she is here. We are forbidden to enter the gym during our free periods for some reason lost in the mists of time. This is how the nuns are, rules exist for their own sake. She looks around to ascertain that she is alone. She looks right at me. I reflexively raise my hand, but her face remains blank, my presence undetected. Just like Gary, she can't see me. I decide not to reveal myself. She is up to something and I want to see what it is. Perhaps she is no longer the goody-two-shoes of her reputation.

This year, we are in only one class together, Mr. Murphy's English class. When I see her in the hallways, I do my best to pretend that she is no more meaningful to me than my other classmates. Sometimes when she is within earshot, I will talk or laugh a little louder, gesticulate in a more animated way, or by other means show a joie-de-vivre I do not feel. I ache all the time, and she is the cause of my aching. I haven't yet been courageous enough to approach her with my idea that perhaps we might spend some time together, get to know each other, rub our hands all over each other, you know, the normal things. I fear it would feel like death should she reject my proposal, so I stew in silence. A coward dies a thousand deaths; a brave man dies but once. I know it's true because I die every time my mind races through my litany of excuses. I comfort myself with the thought that I live to fight another day and continue to dream my life-sustaining dreams.

She is wearing her school uniform, the dull green skirt and white blouse, with the red and black checkered farmer-going-to-church clip-on bow tie. Ariel makes this gloomy and ridiculous outfit attractive.

She pulls a plastic bag and what I take to be a pair of shoes from her standard-issue drawstring-actuated book bag. She pulls off the clip-on tie and begins to unbutton the blouse.

For a heart-stopping moment I believe I have hit the lottery and she is going to strip naked! She is, however, wearing a white t-shirt under the blouse and a costume underneath that. She unzips the little side zipper and undoes the single button that holds up the skirt. She pulls it down over the gentle curve of her lithe hips and lets it fall to the floor to gather at her feet. The skirt has been replaced by the skirt of the costume she is wearing underneath. She pulls the T-shirt rapidly over her head. Her hair flies away into a gauzy black halo and I hear the crackle of static electricity. The flimsy skirt floats in the electric air, bouncing in the unseen currents as though she were suspended in water. She pulls the dark green knee socks off toes-first so as not to invert them. The socks generate an even louder crackle of electricity. She places the uniform and t-shirt neatly folded and the socks neatly rolled into the plastic bag. She then places that bag and her regular shoes into the book bag and pulls the drawstring. Sitting down on the floor, she puts on the dancing shoes, and ritualistically laces the ribbons, crossing one ribbon over the other as she had done so many times before. She tightly weaves the narrow silken ribbons into a latticework around her calves. I remain quiet.

She is very quiet as well. She stands and paces in a small circle, head down, hands on her hips. She is envisioning what she will do. The cavernous gym amplifies the shuffle of her shoes like a cough in church. She rolls her head forward and back, side to side to loosen the muscles of her neck. She vigorously shakes each leg like Olympic runners and swimmers do to get the blood pumping. She comes to attention facing me. Awash in her solar spotlight, she raises her hands stretching toward the ceiling. She lets out a long slow sigh that she draws up from her hidden depths, an invocation welcoming this accidental worshiper.

She lowers herself to the floor. She stretches her legs out to the side as far as she can by rotating her hips and bending her upper body toward the floor. She leans on her elbows. Her hair settles back out of the air and pools on the floor. She rests in this position, enjoying the strain and tension in her muscles. Again she sighs, this sigh more a groan of pleasure. She closes her eyes and counts her breathes until the strain and tension pass and she knows the muscles are fully stretched. She raises her torso and gathers her thick dark hair firmly into a ponytail, securing it with an elastic band she had around her wrist. All the girls wear an elastic around their wrists. They are supposed to pull it tightly and let it go on the theory that this little reminder of the pain of hell will chase away naughty thoughts. The boys are not required to wear the elastics because the nuns believe the nature of a boy's thoughts place him beyond the possibility of redemption such a minor punishment might offer. Ariel rises from the floor like a wraith from the mist into a graceful beginning position.

She stands as still as a statue—a statue carved from the purest, most translucent marble. Had Michelangelo found this pure rock and released from its captivity the statue bound within, the statue released would be Ariel frozen as she is, frozen in that fateful moment like a duelists finger on the trigger, caught forever in this moment, freighted with possibility. I hang on her every breath. The brilliantly flashing dust motes flow around and through her like a river of stardust. During this lull, while tension builds in me, her face gains a beautiful serenity, a beatific glow. She whispers a word, a solemn prayer of devotion. "David" is the word. David is her brother who was killed in the war. My perverse nature, my wicked self, urges me to throw my voice and say, what do you want this time? Won't you just leave me alone? I wish I had an elastic band, because such a wicked thought sends me hell-bound at a trot I'm sure. If I made a joke out of her devotion to her brother, she would rightly never speak to me. Feeling a little dirty, I will myself deeper into the shadows.

The costume that was hidden under her uniform is a flimsy multicolored chemise. The hem is very short, coming down just below the curve of her backside. On her legs, iridescent silver tights shatter the light. Fleeting subtle rainbows pulse across her legs with her slightest movement. This imparts to her a somewhat insubstantial, other worldly quality. The chemise conforms to the lines of her body and is so sheer I can see the waistband of her tights. I can't, however, see her nipples no matter how hard I look due to extra layers of fabric sewn underneath in that strategic spot. I can however clearly she the shape of her breasts due to the conforming nature of the chemise. Two spaghetti straps traverse her otherwise naked shoulders, front to back. The outline of her small clavicle is clearly visible because she is slender. Her slenderness is rounded and softened in all the places where mine is angular and sharp. She is a beguiling alchemy of strength and fragility. Where I'm hard bone and sinew, she is clouds and light. She is the butterfly fully emerged from her schoolgirl cocoon, so different from the girl who entered the gym. She is sensuous and ethereal, earth and sky at once. She is such a revelation, so enticing that I could not, if I wanted to, stem the rush of blood to my loins.

The bright colors of the chemise run together in a dizzying psychedelic swirl. Pink, turquoise, crimson and streaks of royal blue bombard my visual cortex like a distant fireworks display. I once saw a tropical bird when I was a child. The bird had been blown thousands of miles from its home by a relentless wind. Finally, the exhausted creature was deposited here in this alien land amidst a flock of pigeons. That bird's colors are now altered in my memory to match the brilliant colors I see before me today. Then, as now, the colors were made more brilliant by the contrast with the drab surroundings. The contrast was so striking that at first the bird seemed to have solidified from a dream. I remember its pathetic effort to escape as I bend to pick it up. Frightened, alone, not understanding what has happened, left with only the instinct, but not the strength to struggle, my avian Pheidippides with no victory to announce died in my hands. This was my first experience with death so close-up. I race home thinking that my father could do something. Ignoring my teary-eyed and panicked pleas he threw the poor bird into the fire raging in our building's incinerator[1]. He told me, "Never bring home a dead bird. Stop crying; be a man." I was six years old.

I return my attention to Ariel. She is not a dream either, she is here, more striking, more alien than that errant bird of my childhood. Unlike that bird, she is not exhausted. Her journey is at its beginning. She is ready to fly, ready to ride the wind to wherever it and fortune take her. She is so alive. I feel life radiate from her in waves so strong it almost makes me sad. She has a power I would wish for but know I don't possess. Like that bird of my youth, a hurricane has blown her here. It is the hurricane of her own exuberance. Standing still, she waits, and while she waits I hear music playing.

[1]

A large square chimney flue with a chute opening on every floor, where a raging column of fire incinerates the trash accumulated (sometimes two stories high) therein.

She begins to dance. She begins with her hands fluttering, then her arms join in, dancing a sinuous counterpoint to her fluttering hands. In a flash, she becomes a swirl of color, a human gyroscope un-gimbaled. She is the heart of an inertial guidance system that takes me to a place where reality merges with and becomes indistinguishable from memories and dreams.

She steps rapidly on tiptoe in time with her invisible orchestra, turning ever faster. She whirls about the gym, spiraling ever outwards while spinning on the principal axis that runs through her, a motion analogous to (I can't help but think) a heavenly body in its orbit. In this orbit, she passes through her own zodiac. She changes from a tigress springing from its crouch, into the butterfly fluttering in the breeze. In her seventh house, she is a shooting star. The colors of the chemise trail behind her, fading slowly into the ether. Finally, she is the swan. As the swan, she comes to rest before me. She folds her arms under her small but lovely and eminently kissable breasts, pushing them upwards, presenting them to me as a gift. The swan you see is willful and wanton. The swan is free. My wicked self proposes silently an opening conversational gambit: May I suckle? I suppress a chuckle, for I find the word "suckle" quite humorous. My humorous internal commentary is a thin restraint against my almost overwhelming urge to caress her breasts with my fingers, my tongue, my lips, my breath. I cannot help but look. If she could see me, I would blatantly stare. The fair skin above the chemise is rosy, smudged with the vermillion, the cerise, the scarlet of sexual excitement. It is the color of her beautiful fecundity. I quake in the swan's presence.

I have never seen anything. I have never used my eyes before today. I'm unceremoniously unchained and roughly dragged from the depths of my dark salt mine into this brightest midday sun. I cower in fear as the brilliant light stabs at my eyes. Now I know color and contrast. Now I see the world unfolded in all its three-dimensional splendor. I cannot return to my gray two-dimensional world and be happy there.

She continues dancing in her ecstatic way about the gym, oblivious to the pain in my eyes. The dance culminates with a leap that defies gravity, an athletic move that to look at Ariel, you would not believe she could accomplish. She runs and jumps forward into the air like she was hurtling across a chasm. The earth has no hold on her and releases her to that other realm from whither she has come. Her legs remain straight as they inscribe a pair of arcs in the air, drawn outwards from the bottom, one front one back. Her toes point away from her body; her legs extend the angle between themselves going past parallel with the floor while she continues her ascent. The chemise billows like the smoke from those distant fireworks. Her torso points to the sky, perpendicular to a line formed by her legs and is as still as though she were sitting in a chair at home. Her hands stretch heavenward, fingers splayed, reaching for the catcher in her celestial trapeze act. Her face retains its ecstatic expression, revealing none of the strain that such a grand leap must require.

She remains suspended at the apex of this leap for a breathless moment. Will she come back down or will she float away? She lets he earth enfold her in its gravitational embrace. She allows herself to be silently placed. She goes down on one knee. She extends her arms backwards as though she were the swan folding its wings, coming to rest on the water, a perfect landing after a daring flight. She holds her head high and cranes her neck to complete the impression. I'm certain she hears my heart, but still she gives no sign.

She is done and turns to leave. I'm struck by a premonition. If I don't leave the shadows now and stand with her in the light, I consign myself to them forever. She is almost to the door; time is almost up. If I let her leave, I will never know what love is. I will patrol the less exotic precincts of hell for all eternity where love is passionless and tepid, a shadow of the real love I can know if I try. I will remain a shadow in the shadows. In my hell, she doesn't see me.

I hastily get up, dropping my history book with a bang as loud as cannon-fire. "Please, don't go." I hear my voice echo off the walls the desperation in it startles me. The bang and my desperate plea startle her and she stops. "Wait, wait a second, will you?" I plead.

She turns to face me. As I approach her, I notice one of the straps that hold up her chemise has fallen. I reach up and with my shaking hand replace it on her shoulder. She watches my hand. I let it linger there brushing against her soft skin. She looks into my face, her expression made inscrutable by my inability to think. We stand in silence; I'm transfixed by my nearness to her. Her face is aglow. She waits expectantly for me to say whatever I had needed with such urgency to say. Every fiber of my being is screaming that I must say something and not stand there like a dummy.

"Well, thanks for adjusting my strap," she says, breaking the silence with good humor in her eyes. She looks down at my hand and suggests lightly that perhaps I could let her go now and I do. My mind is a raging ocean. Thoughts rise, struggle to live, but get pulled under where they die. I begin to panic. I've stopped her and have nothing to say. I must look like such a fool, because I sure do feel like one. I find myself wishing for the shadows. I blurt out the one and only thought I can push past my lips.

"I love you."

This too echoes off the walls, cascading in waves of progressively diminishing volume, sounding in my ears like the receding plaintive wail of the demons who'd come to claim me, retreating back to hell where they await, ever watchful, another chance.

83

However, I had imagined this moment, this was not it. I had imagined myself as charming as James Bond, as poetic as Romeo, as seductive as Valentino, as suave as Gatsby. I had imagined myself whispering these words to her as we embrace. I had imagined her in my arms looking up at me with much the same expression as I'd just seen, waiting for me to say these words, longing to hear them, and to say them back to me.

My love for her and this effect she has on me are the two sides of a coin. I hope the spell is broken. I have said, however badly, the magic words. The sky has not fallen. The earth has not opened to swallow me. I have not been struck by lightning. She is however, taken completely by surprise and takes a step back. A step that, to me, seems gigantic as the distance between us telescopes with vertiginous speed.

She regains her composure and rather than punish me for being the inappropriate rube that I am, with a laugh, tells me, "Well then, you must bring me the golden hind." She laughs her singsong lilting laugh, her comic opera aria of a laugh. She turns and runs from the gym, crashing through the swinging doors, singing her laughing aria as she goes. Her laughter and her perfume linger in her wake. The doors swing, groaning their agonized groan, hissing their passive pneumatic hiss, as though commenting unfavorably on my ridiculous performance. Silence descends. This is not a direct rejection; indeed, I have such hope! Where can I get my hands on a golden hind? Whatever the fuck that is? She's forgotten her book bag. I reach into my pants to adjust my penis into a more comfortable position.

"Hey there Joanne, why are you sticking your fingers up your cunt?"

It is Gorgon. He, too, had been hiding in the shadows. I pull my hand out of my pants. My erection has disappeared, which is good, because otherwise I would have had to hide here who knows how long, while it subsided on its own.

"She sucks ass as a dancer, doesn't she?"

He is always able to find the exact worst thing to say and the most vulgar way to say it. My first thought is how good it would feel to beat him to death. My second thought is not to show him he has gotten to me. I know he must have been as spellbound as I by her dance. If he hadn't been, he would have stepped from the shadows to levy his tasteless and ungallant judgment against her. That's the way he is. Had he done so, I would have fought him. I would have defended her honor with every ounce of energy in my body. So much has changed since I was the little pushover in the sixth grade, afraid to strike back because I was outnumbered by him and his so-called friends. He is the lone horseman left from that quartet, the others having either moved away or fallen by the wayside, unable to meet the school's academic standards, just like my brother. That isn't to say the standards are very high—Gorgon remains, after all. If he wants to tangle, he will find out to his dismay that I'm not the pushover I was.

I will not let him ruin this life-changing experience. "I know you can't mean that. Why you would say such a horrible thing? Why don't you instead tell me what you really think? Tell me how beautiful she is and how she moved you too."

He is perplexed when he doesn't get the angry reaction he'd hoped for. He tries to regain the initiative; to regain what I know he sees as the upper hand. "I notice she didn't tell you that she loves you back and uuuh, good luck with that 'golden hind' thing, douche bag." Words lose their power when repeated too often. To be called a douche bag by Gorgon is the same as someone else saying hello. I didn't even hear it. However, I hated that he'd heard me say that I loved her. It felt like a sin, but I kept my cool.

"You would love her too if you were capable of love, but even if you were capable you could never expect someone like her to love someone like you." He just rolls his eyes. The bell summoning us to our next class sounds. I grab my history textbook and her book bag. I push my way past Gorgon, through the swinging doors. I leave the field to him, but take (I am certain) the victory with me.

I make it to class just as Mr. Murphy is closing the door. Gorgon pushes his way in behind me. If Mr. Murphy had closed the door a few seconds earlier, Gorgon and I would have been banished to the hallways. Ariel is standing in the front of the room in her brilliant costume. She stands against the blackboard, her hands spread out beside her, casually placed in the chalk tray waist high. This serves to balance her, as she stands on one foot. Her other foot is turned and placed atop the instep of the foot on the floor. The knee of the non-supporting leg is bent outwards along the wall. The dress, now not back lit, is less transparent. She's turned her head and looks out the window, exposing her neck to be kissed, at least all I want to do is kiss her there. I want to kiss her so badly I'm gasping in some sort of faux-asthma attack. I don't have asthma.

"Maxwell, are you alright?" Mr. Murphy asks.

"He's alright Mr. Murphy, he's just retarded." Gorgon says and the class laughs.

Ariel languorously turns her head in my direction. She is as unselfconscious as I've ever seen her. She smiles almost imperceptibly.

"I'm fine Mr. Murphy."

The boys are abuzz about her costume. While perhaps because she had not intended that her costume be overtly sexy its effect on many of the them is even more powerful. Indeed, until this very moment Coleman Curran had never given her the kind of thoughts he was thinking. She had always been to him a mopey, bookworm, Brainiac sort who talked about things he couldn't understand and didn't want to. He'd already dispensed with phase one. He could barely wait to implement phase two of his plan. Coleman didn't particularly like the feelings he was feeling. He didn't like the idea of anyone exerting any control of his feelings, it made him angry. Besides she had laughed at him while he struggled to read out loud in seventh or eighth grade. He swears he remembers her calling him a Cro-Magnon under her breath. He couldn't have people calling him names even under their breath and especially if he didn't know what it was. He had sworn to get even with her somehow. An opportunity had never arisen and it had passed from his mind. Now the thoughts he's thinking rekindle the flame of his anger toward her. He has to remember to smile at her though and so he does when she looks in his direction. He sees that she flusters when he does and makes a feeble effort to return his smile. There was a way to get even with her. He knew what he wanted to do, it was clear in his mind now and he swore he was going to do it. He would make his opportunity, that's what coach always said you had to do. Pete always said that too.

Today is Ariel's day to reveal her talent to the class. That's what she'd been doing in the gym. She'd had a free period and used it to get herself ready. I sit in my seat, the front seat in the first row closest to the door. I hold up her book bag and say, "I've found the golden hind!" Her smile brightens by a degree so slight as to be indiscernible to those less familiar with her face. She shakes her head, again almost imperceptibly. I should have known that finding the "golden hind" wouldn't be so easy.

This talent show is our new English teacher Mr. Murphy's brainchild. I liked Mr. Murphy right away. He looks like me. He is a tall, thin, blond, soft-spoken, earnest graduate of the University of Wisconsin and an opponent of the war. He is the first teacher I can remember who uses encouragement as a tool to try to get us to produce work. He never raises his voice. When one of us acts up, he approaches the transgressor's desk, and leans on it, bringing his face close to the student's. He then tells the student quietly but sternly to leave the class. He calls this "casting the fallen angels into exile." I have been cast into exile, it means the fallen angel to leave the class and wander the halls, ducking the Vice Principal until the bell for the next class sounds. If you get caught in the halls without a hall pass, it means detention, sometimes Saturday detention at the whim of the Vice Principal.

The Vice Principal is a piece of work named Sister Mary. Sister Mary is world-famous as the one who put the "battle-ax" in "battle-ax". Yes, she's responsible for all of it. Saturday detentions included an informative lecture about what a waste of space I'm and how Jesus will judge me harshly when he returns, no doubt barring my way into heaven. Sister Mary doesn't understand what an ineffective spokesperson for Jesus she is. Single-handed she's driven many of us away from the church.

Supposedly Frank Tempesta once said to her during a Saturday detention "Fuck Jesus!" I knew Frank Tempesta; he wasn't a bad kid. He never showed up at school again. The joke was that his body would never be found.

The talent show isn't a single talent show, but a series of displays of "talent" that run throughout the year. We were each supposed to choose a date, fill in our name and our chosen "talent" on the calendar and be ready on that day to display that talent. The calendar is a large-format sort of pamphlet open on an easel at the back of the class. The front cover is emblazoned: "Let Your Freak Flag Fly" in a font I associate with the artist Peter Max. The letters, very similar to those on the Beatles album Yellow Submarine except the letters are multicolored, not just yellow.

As the calendar miraculously filled itself out (I never actually saw anyone write in it) we were able to see when and what each of our classmates would do on their day. Mr. Murphy said he would grade us on our performance. The criteria for getting good marks were clearly laid out: we had to either actually be very talented or make a real effort. Both of these criteria would be judged entirely at his discretion. He also said that he was going to give A's very reluctantly. He claimed he would give out only three, but that he would give out no less than three. "So you better bring your A game," he said. We groaned at his corny attempt at humor as well as the horrifying prospect of having to "let our freak flags fly."

For me, the strategy seemed simple. I decided to delay until the last possible moment. If I were to go early, there would be no way I could get an A unless I could sell Mr. Murphy on the idea that standing still is a talent and I'm the best in the world at it. He is from the Midwest and very earnest indeed, but he is neither gullible nor stupid. I opted for delay, and my only hope was that he really meant he would give out three A's no matter what, so if there is one left when I finally take my turn, perhaps I can claim it. I admit it is a long shot, but it is all I have.

Ariel was anxious about the grading. She worried that her unbroken string of A's that stretched all the way back to the first day of first grade, when she'd got a gold star for knowing what Dick did, which was run, of course (you filthy perverts), might be broken at the whimsy of this eccentric hippie from Wisconsin. I had no such worry. If I got a C, I would count it a great success being neither the possessor of great talent nor one inclined to make a great effort just to prove that point. Right now, as she stands at the front of the class, perhaps her relaxed aura can be attributed to confidence found during her practice dance in the gym.

Many of the girls had put either singing or dancing next to their names. The boys' choices included playing guitar, feats of strength, acting, one magician, one origami master, one singer, one artist, and one dancer of the old "soft shoe."

There were no A's given to the first few girls, whose parents must have told them how great they were from the day they were born. How else would one get the nerve to lip-sync in front of one's peers and call it talent? I thanked god for my father who was always there to stomp on my ego should I believe anything good about myself. The first few girls who had put singing next to their names lip-synced to the Supremes' song, "Love Child." Mr. Murphy finally had enough after Darlene Constantine became the fifth "Love Child" lip-syncer. By this time, it was obvious that these girls were conspiring to ruin the whole idea. I happen to know that some of them, Darlene herself, have good, if not great voices.

Mr. Murphy fights back. He banned lip syncing, telling us that lip syncing is to talent as pooping is to biological functions. He swore that the song "Love Child" was ruined for him forever. Being the earnest man he is, he was too kind to just outright flunk the girls. He allowed them to try again. They all opted for their next choice, which was dancing, except for Nancy Turner, who retained singing next to her name. Oh this will be good, I thought. I had forgotten that Nancy had been the soloist in the cantata back in eighth grade. She had sung an emotional version of "Oh Little Town of Bethlehem."

The lip syncing had been terrible, but the dancing, on the other hand, was great. I looked forward to the days when one of the girls danced. Some of them were really quite sexy. They danced their own variations on the popular dances of the day— the swim, the pony, the boogaloo, the shimmy shake, and the twist, combining all these moves into one dance, turning their school uniforms into naughty Catholic schoolgirl costumes in the process. I noticed Mr. Murphy averted his eyes during these performances, which seemed unfair to the poor girls who worked their little bums off. After all, how could he judge them if he didn't see them dance?

Rosemond Dawson took the idea of "displaying her talent" to an extreme when she repeatedly lifted her skirt, revealing her bright red panties while dancing to "Do The Hippie Hippie Shake," prompting more than one emergency package rearrangement when she finished. I think even Mr. Murphy needed to do so. Her dance earned her the nickname "Red Rosie," which she seemed to like. While none of the girls who had danced so far was particularly talented, they all, as best I could tell, deserved A's for effort. None of them got an A, however.

Nancy Turner sang Summertime in a sweet, strong, clear-as-a-bell mezzo-soprano, accented by a fast natural vibrato, giving the song as melancholy a feeling as the very popular version currently playing on the radio. In fact, and this is hard for me to admit, because I don't really like Nancy Turner, she sang it better. We were stunned. Even Mr. Murphy was stunned. Nancy was given the first A, setting a very high benchmark indeed, and spreading a mild panic among those who had to follow that act, especially Ariel.

Nancy and Ariel had had a falling out shortly after I ate that note back in sixth grade. I don't know what happened between them, but I witnessed the pain it caused Ariel. Between then and now, they have had a number of these fallings-out. Ariel always makes attempts at reconciliation. Most of these are severely rebuffed. Nancy possesses that quality of nastiness specific to teenage girls, and considering the degree of nastiness Nancy displays during these rebuffs, I wonder why her friendship has remained important to Ariel.

It was plain to see, however, that each rebuff renewed Ariel's pain. She persisted, trying again whenever she gathered enough courage to withstand another painful rejection, or if she thought for any reason the time was right. Ariel genuinely misses her friend, and these little scenes between them have a poignancy that moves me, but it seems I'm the only one to notice.

One day, Ariel ran up behind Nancy. She grabbed Nancy's hand and brought it to her face. She nuzzled Nancy's hand against her softly rounded cheek. I wish I could touch her cheek, I bet it feels nice, it looks like it does. Nancy let's her nuzzle her hand smug and self-satisfied having won another bout in their endless dance of rebuff and reconciliation. I know what it means to let someone touch your face. It is such an intimate thing, such a submission. I never willingly let anyone touch mine. Before I could say "Bob's your uncle" the two girls are conjoined in as tight an embrace as two lovers ever were. They embraced for many minutes. In the wind, their long tresses, Ariel's raven-black and Nancy's coppery-orange, coiled together into the black and orange stripes of a tiger. This gave their teary-eyed oaths of lifelong friendship a certain weight, like a sign that their friendship was meant to be. I can be forgiven for imagining their embrace becoming something other than just friendly or sisterly. I burned to touch Ariel in the way Nancy was touching her. That I should do so mustn't make you doubt that I was also moved to see their deep emotion for each other so unabashedly displayed.

Gorgon, whose real name is Larry Sullivan, did some magic tricks. His act was pretty good and I found myself enjoying it against my will. He pissed me off, however, when he pulled a quarter out of my ear and said "That's a really big ear you've got there; I bet I could get more than a quarter out of it." A jackpot of quarters tumbled from his sleeve and down my shoulder. The class laughed uproariously at my embarrassment. I would have said that you could park a truck in the crack of his fat ass if I had thought of it then instead of hours later. I was very sensitive about my ears, even if I tried not to show it. I was glad when he didn't get an A, although to my surprise, Mr. Murphy said he was the closest so far.

There were some other interesting acts.

My friend Owen told jokes, most of which I'd heard more than once, but he had a certain style that was undeniable. Not everyone can tell a joke, but Owen is very good at it. Nevertheless, he didn't get an A.

Coleman, captain of the football team, quarterback, and reputed basement boxer, did one-hundred push-ups. He did the first fifty on his fingertips, the next forty on his knuckles and for the last ten, he pushed himself away from the floor and clapped his hands between each push-up. The girls, even Ariel, were agog, and his sycophantic teammates chanted "Nice job Cole!" when he finished.

Jimmy Conn, who is also on the football team, bent a steel bar, then challenged anybody else in the class to straighten it out if they could. No one could, including Coleman, who struggled mightily in the attempt. When everyone finally gave up, Jimmy straightened it back most of the way. Mr.

Murphy, flummoxed about how these two considered what they did as "talent," gave them C's. What they did was impressive, and the effort expended great, but feats of strength were not something he considered talent.

I left myself off the calendar in the hope that Mr. Murphy would forget I was in the class, or perhaps tire of the idea, thus relieving me of the burden of again making a fool of myself. If that didn't happen, perhaps during the course of the year I would find some inspiration. Also, if I did find some worthwhile inspiration, I wanted to ensure I would be the last. Ariel also delayed, perhaps trying to put off the inevitable.

When Ariel finally put her name on the calendar, there were, excepting myself, only two people left to perform. They were Julius and Lance Boyle. Nancy had set the benchmark very high and the last two A's had not been bestowed. Julius wrote on the calendar that he would play the guitar. Lance would act in a play he claimed to have written. It was laughable, as Lance is a terrible stutterer—how could he act when he could barely speak? Even if Julius played better than Hendrix and got one of the remaining A's, Ariel was confident she would get the other. Why shouldn't she be—she had that unbroken string of A's behind her, and she knew she was a good dancer. Also, I had confessed to her that I wasn't even sure at that late date what I would do, which she naturally took as my confession of a lack of talent (which it was).

97

Julius did extraordinarily well. He played a very difficult song called "Classical Gas." He lost his place just once for a few seconds, recovering nicely. If you didn't know the song, you would not have noticed. It was hard for me to believe that Mr. Murphy would withhold the A for that slight slip, but if he did, then I was a shoo-in for the last A. I didn't consider that Lance could be any good. My crazy gamble was going to pay off!

Lance entered the room dressed as a woman. I assumed that he was wearing his mother's clothes, but he looked very comfortable dressed as he was. He was fully made-up with lipstick, mascara, and eyeliner. Perfume wafted through the air as he buzzed by me. He wore a form-fitting, jade green silk dress that came to his knees and was slit up the side to his hip. Under the dress he wore garters, black silk stockings, and matching black satin panties. I know this because he unabashedly showed the class the garters and the underwear by doing the can-can as he entered. He did this in high heels, in which he was obviously well-practiced, kicking very high. We all clapped in rhythm with the can-can music playing on the phonograph. This pushed him to kick higher. He finally collapsed in Mr. Murphy's chair, fanning himself with his hands.

"Oh you are such a beautiful audience, thank you so much for welcoming me so warmly," he said in a sibilant, feminine voice without stuttering once.

Larry was playing a famous actress, and Kathy Carey, who had previously lip-synced to "Love Child," was the interviewer. I was laughing so hard that I missed much of it, but I remember Kathy's first question.

"Gwendolyn, you are one of the world's most beautiful women..."

Lance replies, "Please, Deary, don't dwell on the obvious."

"Yes, well sorry. How do you keep the men away?"

"Why, do you need advice? No, just kidding, I can see that you don't need any help keeping the men away. Deary, I don't try to keep the men away. Especially if they're rrrrrrich. If they're rich, it's HELLO SAILOR!" And in a flash, he was up and dancing the can-can again with the same exaggerated vigor. This time, he kicked the high heels off. They flew through the air. My friend Owen caught one, and Carlo Cence caught the other. I laughed my ass off.

The interview went on in this vein for about fifteen minutes, interrupted by bursts of dancing and show tunes. Lance finally left the room pretending to sign autographs. He blew kisses and sang "Somewhere Over the Rainbow" in an exaggerated imitation of Judy Garland's voice. Since I was closest to the door, he raked his velvet-gloved hand across my face and told me I was a "dreamboat." I flushed at the humiliation.

Mr. Murphy announced that he would withhold the marks from Julius and Lance until Ariel and I finish. He wanted to make sure he dispensed the A's to the right people. Lance and Julius voiced their disappointment, Julius doing so in the vituperative manner of the entitled.

"Watch it, Mister, or you'll be excluded from one of the last A's," Mr. Murphy said. Julius was a well-known pain in the ass.

Judging by Ariel's confident demeanor today, she must feel that one of the remaining A's is within her grasp. For me, there is nothing left but to look foolish and get an F. I suddenly don't like Mr. Murphy all that much.

I found out later why Ariel took so long to put her name on the calendar. It had nothing to do with jockeying to get one of those three A's. It was the furthest thing from her mind. She didn't really know she was going to dance in this talent show until the very moment she'd written "dance" next to her name on the calendar. For Ariel, dancing was a secret. She had turned it into a sort of private devotion to her dead brother. I saw this during her practice, when she had prayed his name. Ariel had discovered that dancing eased her pain. She, being who she was, took this as far as she could, and I had the privilege of being the first to see how far that was. She's decided for reasons she could never have said, that it is time to break free of her self-imposed constraint and dance for joy.

The dance in the classroom does not go quite as well as the dance in the gym. Things go wrong from the very beginning. Rather than rely on the music within herself, she brings a recording to play on the broken-down old class phonograph, which is placed on a small table near the corner where I sit, but crowded into the area where she will dance. She bends over the record player, trying to place the needle on the track she wants. She is suddenly nervous and full of doubt. She places the needle on the record and backs away, resuming the same elegant beginning pose I'd seen in the gym, back leg bent slightly, her front foot crossing her back foot, while the toes of her front foot point towards me. She holds her hands in front of her as though she were cradling a baby. Her fingers are delicately articulated, she turns her beautiful face aside and she looks up. A cloud of doubt replaces the ecstatic serenity I'd seen on her face in the gym. This makes me love her more. She stands still, waiting for the correct music to start, as she apparently had a very difficult time placing the needle. The class is getting restless. Since I'm the closest to both her and the phonograph, she implores me with her eyes to please place the needle correctly. I get up and lean over the small table, worried I could knock it over easily. I throw my necktie over my shoulder and put my left hand behind my back to eliminate this possibility. In a husky voice I ask, "Which track?"

"Track four, please."

I deftly place the needle between tracks three and four and sit back down before the music starts. She bestows another of her imperceptible smiles on me.

What happened next was difficult to watch. She tries, but the small space defeats her. The constant need to amend the dance to fit into the space makes her movements less fluid, more mechanical. Even so, she attempts her grand leap as a finale. She once again soars up into the air as she had before. A breathless silence descends as she rises to the apex. The ballistic computer in my brain sees her trajectory, but there is nothing I can do. Her leap ends in a loud crash, made louder by the preceding silence, when she lands right on top of the phonograph. Many in the class roar with laughter. Ariel, humiliated, laboriously extricates herself from the wreckage and limps from the classroom, oblivious to my solicitously extended hand.

7. The Hard Truth of Parting Words

Kathleen was leaving Enzo. He'd driven her to South Station and now walked beside her down the platform to the waiting train, believing every second he spent with her was a chance she'd change her mind. He had no rational reason for believing she would for she was exhibiting that special attribute of her tribe more than once. Once she'd made up her mind she became like the mule, no argument or evidence to the contrary could sway her. Ariel didn't know her mother was leaving; Kathleen had left this onerous chore to Enzo. Enzo, resented this as bitterly as he resented Kathleen's leaving. He hadn't been able to fathom what he'd done to precipitate this parting. That's the way Enzo was; inclined to blame himself.

Kathleen wasn't looking forward to this journey, she wasn't sure of what lay at the other end. She wasn't running toward something she was running away. She hated to travel alone but you can't run into the future if you drag the past with you. She should have known that she couldn't outrun her past. It is the thing that makes us all for better or worse. The train ride to New York wasn't much of a journey. She expected it would be somewhat less arduous than the first journey she'd taken alone.

As a girl of five, she'd made the Atlantic crossing with a note pinned to her coat, explaining who she was and where she was going. She'd worn the coat for the entire voyage fearful of losing the note, despite the excessive heat and humidity below decks. The heat, the motion of the ship, and the foul and cloying stench of her equally hot and sweaty fellow travelers made her nauseous. She could not see the sky or smell the sea in the wind against her face down here as she'd dreamed she might when her mother had first told her she was going to cross the ocean on an ocean liner. She'd wondered why the gangway on which she'd entered the ship was so far below the gangway on which the fancy ladies promenaded to their staterooms up above. Perhaps the fancy world up above was and always would be closed off to her. Perhaps she deserved to dwell here below in this place analogous to hell with four other girls making the same journey, all with similar notes pinned to similar coats, all equally sick and afraid of what awaited them in the new world. They were all desperate economic refugees displaced by the horseman of famine. The word was never spoken for fear that if one said the word then one would make it real. Call it what you will it was there and it too was hungry. This horseman rampaged through Ireland, north and south awakened by the worldwide financial cataclysm that brought with it other plagues; a rain of stockbrokers off high ledges, dirt scratching Okies in broken down jalopies who invaded California. Kathleen herself, a small droplet in yet another wave of tired huddled entirely unwanted masses, if not exactly yearning to breathe free at least in want of regular nourishment, swept ashore on the streets New York City by the currents on events and history. Kathleen could not see the big picture, she could only feel her loneliness and suffering.

Her sister had made her go to work as soon as she was physically able. At fourteen, she got a job as a cleaning maid at a fancy New York hotel. She worked so close to the very rich, she could reach out and touch them, but she was nearly invisible to them. *That's the way it better stay if you want to keep your job*, the nasty groping floor manager had warned. He'd also warned her not to tell anyone of his slimy advances, with the same loss of employment hanging over her head. He was the first man to ever lay hands on her. He would trap her in a room she was cleaning by entering behind her. He'd laid his hands and placed his slimy mouth where and when he'd wanted, stripping her of her clothes and threatening reprisals for resistance. He pawed and licked her until he satisfied his perverted fantasies. One day he demanded she return the "favor". She'd been fourteen and very frightened, she did what she was told, gagging and crying all the way to the disgusting conclusion. This was her life. A bright future in America was an illusion, a deviant fable designed to lure her into bonded servitude to a sister who she didn't know, and to suffer the horror of a kind of sexual enslavement all for want of a few dollars, a grimy bed, and the appearance of respectability. She saw no light at the end of a very dark tunnel. Now Rose had married a disagreeable fellow who enjoyed the poteen a wee bit too much. Her position in the household was untenable. She had no money though because it had all gone to Rose in an agreement she hadn't been a party to. Rose had told her she'd spent the money to support her. She didn't believe Rose and they argued bitterly. She married the first man (the first person) who was nice to her, that was Enzo. She didn't care that he was Italian, as near as she could tell the Irish were no great shakes.

For Enzo, there was never a moments doubt. He was placing the trash cans behind the hotel onto a cart to drag them to the waiting truck at the head of the alley. Kathleen stepped out to empty her bin, which was filled with the collected trash from the rooms she'd cleaned. She'd smiled a sad smile at him and said a sad hello. He was smitten immediately, her beauty and what he took to be her Irish melancholy were to him irresistible. He told her she was the most beautiful maid whoever set foot in this ally. He'd said it with a great smile and his Italian accent which to her sounded like she'd imagined Valentino did. Enzo was at least as handsome as Valentino, if somewhat more ragged. Soon, if not soon enough for Kathleen, they ran away to Massachusetts where the age of consent was sixteen. They were married by the Justice of the Peace in the small town of Holden, made famous by the joke: do you know Dick Hertz from Holden?

If it ever occurred to Enzo, he never mentioned it to Kathleen. He knew she didn't have to come out into the alley to dump her trash. She could have sent it tumbling down the chute from any floor like all the other maids did. She wasn't just the most beautiful girl he'd ever seen in the alley; she was the only one. So he wasn't lying. Enzo could never have guessed that Kathleen took every opportunity she could think of to get away from the slimy floor manager. That kind of thing was remote to him, the kind of thing that happened in a penny-dreadful, not to the girl who was his wife. Kathleen would never have told him anyway.

They set themselves up in a one-bedroom apartment in little Italy. Being a married woman was no deterrent to the manager he still groped her when the mood struck him. Indeed, he objected to her marriage like a jealous lover. She dreamed of one day sticking a sharpened broom handle in his eye. Kathleen did everything in her power to get pregnant so she could leave her job. At the same time, she was trying hard to fool herself into believing she loved Enzo. She never really did love him; he was a ticket out. That he was handsome and nice to her were pluses in his favor. Sometimes she believed she loved him, maybe she did, maybe this was as close to love as she would ever get, the aerie elusive realm of real love as closed off to her as securely as any fancy stateroom. What did she know of love? She was an unwanted child sold to her oldest sister to work, put upon and hounded by a horrid man who should have protected and mentored her. A man who deserved to die, and now Enzo. What did Enzo really want from her except to parade her down Mulberry street on Sunday to show off his prized possession? She'd catch him beaming at the men passersby who with their eyes undressed her, and with those same eyes said to Enzo 'You've captured yourself a fine pretty bird for a guinea garbage man.' She'd bite her lip when she realized that perhaps this was not the passersby but her who thought this.

Enzo, on the other hand, thought he had died and gone to heaven. David was born, then eight years later Ariel, six years after that they'd moved when the company opened its office and transfer station in Boston. They settled first in a two Bedroom apartment on Washington Street and went all in on the little house on Anselm Terrace a couple of years later. You know the rest.

The truth about Enzo was that he was a genius, only he didn't know it. You may say that someone who is a genius and doesn't realize it can't be much of a genius. You may be right, nonetheless, Enzo had a genius IQ, and was too humble for his own good. His genius IQ manifested itself in his need to write and the periodic appearance of a non-specific malaise of the spirit that he struggled hard against.

The things he did have, the things that stood out and identified him clearly to everyone, were a relatively swarthy complexion, brilliantine in his wavy black hair, an organ grinder's accent, and an Italian name front and back. In America in the period after World War II these attributes were not advantages that inspired the powers that be to point at you and say genius (Enrico Fermi excepted). They might inspire someone to point and say of him; Mafioso (although in little Italy that wasn't the issue it might have been elsewhere) but not a genius. Unfair as that was it was especially true in the years immediately after the war, because Americans had died in large numbers in places named Anzio and Monte Casino. That it had been the Germans who did most of the killing even in those places was largely lost on the average American. Enzo could be happy knowing that at least he wasn't a Jap or nigger.

Because Enzo had left war-ravaged Italy as a nineteen-year-old, any record of his genius was lost in the rubble. After the extreme deprivations of the war he felt lucky to land his trash collecting job. Being Italian was a decided advantage vis-a-vis obtaining such employment in New York City. Enzo started earning money, what to him felt like real money, the kind of money with which a man could marry and raise a family if he wasn't profligate and waste it on sharkskin suits and snakeskin shoes like some of those who were no better off than he did. He met Kathleen who was an angel straight from heaven in his eyes and he married her. Enzo lacked two things. He lacked ambition, which is different from being lazy because he was not lazy. He also didn't have a devious bone in his body. He really was something of an innocent abroad, which again isn't something that would identify him as a genius, because geniuses are lots of things but seldom are they as naive as Enzo looked from the outside.

He could, however, conceptualize the complex truth from very little evidence once that evidence presented itself. A power that few people possess. It was a power Kathleen didn't have and couldn't understand. Enzo had realized the truth and conceptualized the entire story of his and Kathleen's "romance" as I've told it here in the few minute's it took for Kathleen to board the train and the train to begin pulling away.

Ariel's absence from this Norman Rockwell tableau spoke volumes to him. Would a woman abandon her beloved daughter to the care of a man she despises? He saw their marriage in a new light. The truth revealed itself like the pattern of a tapestry seen from the mezzanine.

This is where his lack of deviousness figured. He'd trusted his wife that she indeed had a headache and that not tonight meant it would be better tomorrow. Now he knew to a certainty that 'we'll wake the children' had nothing to do with concern for the children. He realized fully the only possible real implication of these and the thousand other excuses she'd employed over the years to forestall and divert his amorous advances that he took at face value, all had a hidden meaning which he knew right down to his bones was the undeniable truth. Kathleen never loved him. She had used him for her own purposes, which she'd never shared, but at which he now made a fairly accurate guess. Poor Enzo, who had so much love to give. Poor Kathleen who more than anything needed love and didn't know it.

There were times when he'd experienced doubts about Kathleen's love. She was quick with the offhand verbal assurance, but deeper assurances were as hard to extract as diamonds. At those times when he doubted her, he struggled against himself believing only an ogre forces himself on his wife. Although he kept his domestic relations to himself, this was an unfashionable view among the macho trash collectors expressed simply as You take what's yours, that's what a real man does. Maybe if he had acted on his base impulses things would have been different, maybe being a gentleman to your wife is the big lie. Where had it landed him, here with a mountain of sadness in his heart?

He stood on the platform and the hard horrible truth of his meaningless fucking life washed over him like lava.

"You never really loved me, Kathleen?"

"Enzo, all I can say is I didn't hate you."

"Ariel was an accident, wasn't she?"

"Only in as much as it was all an accident."

The porter closed the door and the train pulled away. Enzo walked beside the train picking up speed as the train did.

He followed the train down to the end of the platform and watched it disappear into the gloaming, her silhouette in the rear window. Kathleen, in turn, watched him with hooded eyes from the rear of the car. He stood under the stark light at the end of the platform, He receded ever more rapidly as the train gained speed, then he was gone as though he never were. She shivered at the thought and wondered how she could hate such a nice man so much. She concluded as she took her seat that it wasn't him she hated, it was herself.

Enzo stood at the end of the platform like the tin man, frozen in place. He was like the tin man in another respect, He had no heart. It would have been better if like the tin man he'd never had a heart instead of having it ripped out and stepped on.

The end of the platform extended beyond the roof, wind-driven heavy snow lashed his face and settled on his head and shoulders.

Ariel awoke early that fateful morning, overnight a severe late-winter storm dropped a foot of heavy snow on Brighton. Her mother had taken the train to visit her sister in New York for the weekend. Previously, Ariel had always gone with her, but this time, they had argued. She had no idea her mother was gone.

Ariel had not wanted to go. Her only tie to her cousins was the familial one, which she valued now less than she ever had or ever would. Why her mother felt the need to visit at all was a mystery, it seemed her mother hated her Aunt.

Her cousins were alien to her. They had been big supporters of the war and had remained so after David's death and even as the last helicopter lifted off the roof of the US Embassy. She couldn't reconcile their politics with her tragedy. She'd grown away from them in the six years since David died. None of her cousins would admit the US had lost the war. They heatedly argue the point in the most illogical but passionately angry fashion. This had become impossible to endure. On top of that, they were still staunch Nixon supporters who believed he had somehow been railroaded. She saw this as a form of insanity.

Aside from their extreme political differences, her cousins had grown up streetwise in Queens. Those who still lived at home were more interested in running with their friends than having to entertain an odd provincial girl from Boston.

Ariel raises the shade on the western facing window in her bedroom. The world has changed overnight. The bright rising sun casts the spindly shadows of the bare trees across the white world. Ariel throws open the window and leans out to feel the cold. She watches the skeletal shadows record the passage of time across the tabula-rasa of her backyard. Suddenly the fear of death beats its way over her exposed skin like the wings of a thousand birds frightened into flight by an exuberant and wicked toddler.

"Hey Ariel, close the window, sweetheart." She cringes— she can't stand being called "sweetheart" by Enzo "the liar," as she's thought of him since the day she learned he was just a trash man. Sometimes she thought she should give him a break. After all, He'd made her life comfortable by his hard work. Randy Hugh had retired and Enzo had moved into his job. That he no longer rode on the back of the truck granted him no absolution.

She couldn't forgive him the humiliation, when, one day her friend Jeralyn had said, "Hey Ariel, what's your dad doing on the back of a trash truck?" As he waved and called to her enthusiastically, what an embarrassment.

She was getting cold, so she willingly closed the window. She did it as quietly as possible so he wouldn't hear. She knew he was listening at the bottom of the stairs and would doubt she'd closed it. This would force him to come upstairs later and check to make sure, despite her assurances. She got a perverse kick these days from pushing his buttons, unmindful of the pain she caused him. She didn't know anything of what had transpired between her parents. While this was a small jab, after yesterday, every one of these relentless little jabs stabbed him right in the heart. She had the power to hurt him. He had given it to her the day she was born. She had learned how to use it and today he was as vulnerable as a child.

She entered the hallway expecting to see him at the bottom of the stairs with the question in his eyes; did you close the window? He wasn't there. She went downstairs to eat some breakfast. She had planned to go to the library that morning.

She has to write another ten-page research paper. She is the best researcher and possibly the best writer in the class. However, she is such a perfectionist, sets such a high standard for herself that she has a difficult time finishing because she feels it can always be better even though she knows she will get an A+ as she always has on every paper she's ever written.

She threw herself into her last paper with an intellectual fury. She did a lot of research, much more than necessary and much more than anyone else would ever dream of doing. She wrote a careful outline, which could have stood as the paper in its own right and been better than most of the work handed in by her peers for this assignment. She fleshed out the outline with beautiful writing, beautiful in its elegant concision. This paper is about the role racism played in the prosecution and execution of Sacco and Vanzetti.

She built her thesis with citation after citation and concludes.

'The judge, in his decision disallowing the introduction of new exculpatory eyewitness testimony said; 'The defendants were not convicted on the basis of eyewitness testimony, more of such testimony would have had no effect on the outcome, ***especially considering that the preponderance of such testimony favored the defendants.*** [bold italics are Ariel's] *Rather they were convicted on the basis of their behavior, which clearly demonstrated a consciousness of guilt.'*

Would English-speaking men of White Angle-Saxon Protestant descent have been sentenced to die on the basis of such a flimsy argument. I don't believe so. The police, prosecutors and the judge himself painted the defendants as foreign radicals. To the staid protestant jurors, this is what they became. That they were hard-working family men mattered not at all. What mattered, and it was all that mattered was that they were Italian immigrants, WOPs, Guineas, not worth a moment's consideration or an iota of compassion. That she was writing about her own harsh and unjust judgment against her father never crossed her mind. It's strange how the subconscious reveals us to ourselves if we just had eyes to see.

The teacher, Mr. Delaney wrote in red on the first page; 'Good as usual, but YOU can do better,' he gave her an A-. To her it feels like a punch in the face, there has to be some mistake.

An A- was almost a B+! She decides to go to Mr. Delaney's office for an explanation. She finds his response to her inquiry abrupt, positively churlish. He offered no explanation beyond saying that she should accept that her paper wasn't the best paper this time, especially when compared with Mr. Maxwell's lucid treatise on the reasons for and the historical ramifications of the perversion of genius, what he calls the dogmatizing or de-conceptualizing of ideas. "Mr. Maxwell is very smart Miss Lirilinghi, no shame in losing out to him, deal with it, nobody's perfect, not even you, I'm not changing your grade, so if that's why you came you can forget it."

"But why are you comparing my paper against his? He's not even in this class."

"I curve both classes against each other." He said, as though she were a complete idiot for not knowing that.

She knew he wanted something from her. The A-, the churlish attitude were all somehow part of it, a power play, a ham-handed sort of seduction. *He didn't care about the integrity of his marking system.* She hated that she'd been so predictable that he knew he could lure her down here to his lair to petition him to change the mark. She noticed he couldn't keep his eyes from wandering up and down her body in an appraising way. As

117

his eyes made their slow traverse upwards he stopped at the hem of her skirt and at her breasts for just an extra second, but there was no mistaking it. *Should I do a slow spin so you can get a really good look at my ass too*? To her surprise the idea of doing a slow turn for him turned her on. She wondered if she should play along with his ridiculous seduction fantasy. She wouldn't, however, know where to begin, and once she'd begun she wouldn't know how to extricate herself should his desire become persistent. What if he rejected her advance? That would be even worse. She realized that might be what he would do, so as to put her in the horrifying predicament of having to extricate herself from an extremely embarrassing situation. She detested him and his flimsy plan and his transparency.

She was mildly sickened that the thought of his black-hairy-knuckled, simian hands groping clumsily into her underpants excited her. The truth is she was excited. She wanted him to rip away her underpants like they were tissue paper. She'd wanted to have his hairy hands encircle her slender hips, his iron fingers dig into the soft flesh of her buttocks, restraining her from flight in his iron grasp.

This was her sexual awakening. Her thoughts on this day were of such a different character from the non-specific gooey romantic desire she'd felt for the TV actor Bobby Sherman right up to that morning. This wanting struck her with the surprise and blinding fury of Paul's vision on the road to Damascus. Her thoughts were specific, naughty, even filthy, the antithesis of gooey romance. They set her heart ablaze and engendered a fierce desire for irresistibly strong hands to force themselves between her legs against her weakening will. A wet spot appeared on her underpants, tracing the cleft betwixt her now puffy labia-majora. Fortunately, Mr. Delaney couldn't see through her skirt.

She ran from Mr. Delaney's office as soon as possible, glad for the A-, flustered and red-faced. She was determined to track down Jackson Maxwell to read his paper and prove to herself what she already knew, that her paper was better. First she had to go to the girls. She closed and locked the stall door, pulled her underpants down and lifted her skirt. She sat on the bowl, her vulva tingled. She jumped onto a Moebius wheel of her own constructing. She had to clean herself up but the pleasure of rubbing herself with the rough tissue on her sensitized naughty bits overpowered restraint. Images of Mr. Delaney restraining her with his strong hands got mixed up with Coleman Curran throwing a football while wearing nothing but shoulder pads and Jackson Maxwell chasing her naked up flights of stairs and catching her because she wanted him to. He kisses her and kisses her and kisses her and runs his hands all over her. Before she knew it the combination of the rubbing tissue paper and her thoughts brought her close to climax. She was in such an unfamiliar heightened state she let out a low soft moan.

Sister Mary was on masturbation patrol. She saw it as her duty to protect young ladies from the wantonness of their desires. She'd been a girl once and the devil of temptation had visited her, even after taking vows, but through strength and prayer she had resisted. She'd seen Ariel Lirilinghi enter the girls room and had thought nothing of it, Ariel was a good girl. She was however spending an inordinately long time doing her business. Sister Mary went quietly into the girls' room, just as quietly locking the door behind her. She heard Ariel's soft moans. She peered through the crack between the door and the wall of the stall. Sister Mary could see that Ariel was lost in her slutty little fantasy. So she's not such a good girl after all. She watched and waited.

She enjoyed watching the girls play with themselves and this girl was a pretty little one. The moment came. The girl started to spasm and shake in the throes of unbridled, sinful ecstasy. Using her secret spanner wrench designed for just this purpose, Sister Mary quickly turned the pin-lock and pushed the door open. The stalls were deep so the door swung past Ariel's legs and slammed against the inside wall with a loud bang. She stood in the doorway with her arms crossed and her legs spread. "Miss Lirilinghi are you masturbating in here?" It always amused her when the lust filled shaking and spasms turned into unbridled panic as the girl tried to pull her underpants up and get herself in order while under her scrutiny and drill sergeant-like berating. Some girls she'd caught in this same compromising position had fallen over in their absolute keystone cops panic to pull their underpants back up. While engaging in their filthy carnal sin they had let their underpants fall to the floor. In trying to put them back on they would step on them and lose their balance. Over they would go, slamming their empty heads off the floor. One girl, caught the hem of the leg opening on the heel of her shoe. She'd been unable to comprehend what was happening in the full-blown panic induced by Sister Mary's surprise attack. Over she went still desperately trying to pull on her underpants as her head banged off the floor. Out like a light, flagrant genitalia exposed. Sister Mary had been unable to resist her own secret desires; the girl was so painfully beautiful. After she asked god and Saint Joseph for forgiveness and to help her be strong. She did however keep this particular trespass between herself, God, Saint Joseph, and maybe Jesus. She excluded the Blessed Virgin, her confessor and the Mother Superior from her list of those with a "need to know". She also tortured herself with her cilice of rough rope for a month after as an appropriate penance.

"You'll find no holy water down there, Miss Lirilinghi, so there's no sense in profaning your finger in that foul font." Ariel's entire body turned red from the arrogant effrontery of such an outrageous insult. She said nothing though. She pulled up her underpants, which she had let down only to her knees. She straightened herself as quickly and gracefully as her quickness and grace would allow in such a situation. She exited the stall, squeezing by Sister Mary who ruefully pondered the unfortunate circumstance that Miss Lirilinghi hadn't knocked herself out.

"You go to confession and confess your sin to Father Gavin on Saturday, young Lady. You must tell him the specific details of what you've done and what you were thinking while you were doing it. The sin is as much in the thinking as in the doing. I'm going to check with him to make sure you do." Ariel was positively ablaze with embarrassment, crying. She hoarsely whispered "Yes Sister Mary." Sister Mary with some reluctance let Ariel leave. She ran to her hiding place, behind the stage in the gym.

She thought she was alone.

"Are you alright?" She almost jumped out of her skin. "I'm sorry, I didn't mean to startle you, but you gave me a start yourself. You see, you've invaded my private hiding place."

"Your private hiding place, I thought it was mine." It was weird to be talking to one of the boys who had just been featured in her masturbation fantasy. The thought brought the color to her cheeks again. "Sorry," she says. She holds her face in her hands. "I come here when I don't feel like seeing or talking to anybody."

"Me too," he says. "I leave you to it then." He gathers up his stuff to leave, smiles and walks away. He leaves her there with her heart pounding anew. He didn't seem like the crude Cro-Magnon she'd always thought he was.

She'd just been subjected to phase one of Coleman's plan. He'd waited for her in her "private" hiding place every day for two weeks now, for the opportunity to set his plan in motion. Finally, she showed, just as he was about to give up again. Leaving was as much a part of the plan as the "accidental" nature of the meeting. Pete had devised the plan. He instructed him to be nice to her because if she's come to her private place it's probably because she's under duress of some kind. Just a little niceness will go a long way. Pete had also instructed him not to say too much, to let her do the talking. "Trust me Cole, you're a great fighter, but not much of a talker."

Pete also instructed him to leave as soon as he could, better to leave her wanting more than to have her wishing you would leave or worse leaving herself. It couldn't have gone better. Pete had been right about it all. Now he had to wait for his next chance and remember to smile at her in the hallways.

Later that day she saw Jackson Maxwell, she asked him nicely if she could read his paper. He shyly dug it out of his book bag and handed it to her. She'd watched him closely as he dug through his poorly organized book-bag. He was handsome enough, but he seemed to lack the spirit of the boy who'd chased her up the stairs and kissed her.

She had to admit his paper was very good. His fable of Christ returned getting crucified by the "New Romans" was brilliant. Within the context of their Catholic universe it was revolutionary and heretical. He had taken a chance at getting expelled by handing in such a paper. She could never look at Jackson Maxwell quite the same again. Perhaps there was something more under his shy exterior. She handed it back and said it was pretty good. "Thanks," He said. This was just a week before she danced in front of him and he declared his love.

She chose as the topic for her new paper, in an effort to be as revolutionary and heretical as Maxwell the fairly recent court case legalizing abortion. There were so many avenues to explore on the moral, philosophical and religious fronts, as well as how Hollywood treated illegal abortion and its effect on the zeitgeist that ultimately lead to legalized abortion. She could feel this paper already writing itself. She would, however, research and write the hell out of it. She'd show Mr. Maxwell what an A+ paper really looks like.

Ariel comes down the stairs and opens the front door and steps out into the knee-deep snow, stumbling as the weight of the snow grabs at her feet. She lets herself fall, sitting in the snow. She feels the cold snow suck at her vitality. She lays back into the snow. The snow begins to drain her life away as snow will do.

Enzo, in his fragile, half-drunken state, upon seeing his daughter, gets the idea of playing in the snow with her. He hasn't slept and has been spiking coffee with whiskey all night. He looks awful.

He runs down the hallway from the kitchen out the door and jumps over her as though he were Superman. Flying through the air, he lands at the bottom of the steps. It turns out that the heavy snow isn't as much of a cushion as he'd expected. He tastes blood and steel when his head impacts the ground and is dizzy for a few moments.

Ariel gets up from her seated position and goes back inside, closing and locking the door. She knows this will bug the shit out of Enzo. Sure enough, moments later, he bangs on the door for her to open it.

"What's the password?" she asks, expertly getting under his skin.

"Sweetheart, please open the door." She feels guilty, but not guilty enough to open the door.

"No, sorry, 'Sweetheart' is not the password." She waits for another guess, but none is forthcoming. She looks out the little window beside the door. She can see him shivering in his pajamas. She isn't done with the game, however.

"What's the password, please?" She waits, still no answer. Well, this is no fun, she thinks. She unlocks the door and walks down the hall to the kitchen. Enzo comes in a minute later; his bare feet purple from the cold.

He crosses the distance between them quickly and rocks her with a hard slap. The shock of it travels up his arm and the sharp crack reaches his boozy consciousness. He has never hit her before. His first inclination is to beg her forgiveness in a slurred drunken frenzy, He stops himself, he is sorry, but he's not. If a hard slap is what it takes to reach her, then so be it. She recovers from the first hard shock, she tells him to shut the fuck up and leave her alone.

"What a dumb fucking idea to try to be your friend," he says simply. He sits down and starts sipping at his coffee/whiskey.

She begins to berate him for slapping her

"I don't want to hear it, tell someone who gives a fuck. That you could disrespect me so thoroughly, so…. easily" It wasn't the word he was looking for, but it was the word he found and it would do. He waves his hand at her dismissively. "Like mother, like daughter," he says delivering what she couldn't have known was the sharpest insult he'd ever delivered.

Something is desperately wrong, but she didn't deserve to be assaulted for it. Whatever it was it wasn't her fault. She stung from the injustice of it. "I'm going to the library this morning." She says tersely. He doesn't acknowledge that she has spoken. They sit in stony, tense silence. She eats a bowl of Cheerios with a banana sliced into it.

"You like that cereal?" He asks. She doesn't answer. "You like that banana?" He asks.

"Yeah" she says.

"That's my fucking banana, you're eating my fucking banana! That's my bowl and this is my table and this is my fucking house don't forget it."

He's crazy, the smell of trash has driven him crazy. He frightens her, disheveled and brightly crazy in the eyes. She eats her cereal as quickly as possible, puts the bowl in the sink, and goes upstairs to take a hot shower. When she comes back downstairs, she is all dressed and ready to go. Enzo is sitting at the kitchen table, writing. She assumes he is writing one of his stupid stories. He still harbors this ridiculous dream of being a writer! He looks up from what he is writing and down the hallway towards her.

"Am I supposed to wash that bowl?" he asks her, pointing to the sink, which is out of her sight. Her cheek is still pins and needles from the force of his slap. She decides to dig him one last time by saying the worst thing she can think of.

"It's not going to happen, Enzo." She knows he hates being called "Enzo" by her.

"What's not going to happen, dear, you're not going to wash the bowl?" He seems contrite and confused, the crazy glaze is gone from his eyes, displaced by sadness. This gives her a moment's pause, but she feels compelled to slap him as hard as he slapped her. She can't let him get away with it.

"I'm not going to wash the bowl and you are never going to be a writer—you never were and you never will be. You're pathetic, you're a loser for god's sake, a trash-man. Even worse, you're a trash heap, look at you. Goodbye trash man." She slams the door on her way out.

She freezes at the end of the path, unsure of what to do, shocked by her own cruelty. She wants to run back and beg his forgiveness for this and everything else she has said or done that's hurt him. She knows she had worked very hard to earn that slap. She is afraid she has gone too far and she is not even sure why she wanted to hurt him so. This isn't her, she's a nice person! The revelation hits her with force and it's twofold. First is the hard truth that she really hasn't been the nicest person in the world to her father, who obviously desperately needs her to be nice to him. Secondly, she blames her father for David's death. David wasn't there to blame. She knows that her father would trade places with David, and she knows that she has always known that. She turns to go back inside, she wants to say she's sorry and share her grief with him and have him share his grief with her. but she stops, afraid that he will say he didn't want to hear it. She really should have known that he would have forgiven her anything if she just asked, all she had to do was ask. She decides it will be better later when each has had some time to cool off.

She walks to the library in the cold sunshine. The temperature has dropped about fifteen degrees since the storm moved out, making it unusually cold. She walks past Daniel's Bakery and thinks about crossing the street to get some coffee, but doesn't.

I see her pass by from my perch at the counter that lines the plate-glass window at the front of the bakery. Where could she be going on such a day if not right here? She pushes her hat down a little further on her forehead. Her hat is a wool knit that ties around her chin. She never ties it, however, preferring to let the ties, which each have a fuzzy gray ball on the end, dangle. These ties attach to ear flaps and hang down well below to her shoulders. The balls bounce and jiggle with each step she takes. The hat is woven red and gray checks, with a red band that runs around the edge. There is a fuzzy red ball at the peak. Her black hair sticks out, forming an arc just above her eyes. A prodigal tress catches in her long eyelashes, moving when she blinks.

I'm not alone in observing Ariel walk by. Everyone who lines the window follows her, turning their heads in sync with her tortured progress across the wintry tableau. She is such a striking figure, reminiscent to me of that tragic Russian heroine played by Greta Garbo. Ariel is by no means a tragic figure in my mind, just the opposite. It must be the oppressiveness of the snow, or the way her collar is turned up against the cold that triggers this connection.

To observe her now through the window has the feel of watching a movie. She is, like an actress on screen, oblivious to her admiring audience. All the patrons of the bakery seated on the stools that line the counter facing the street watch eagerly. As in a movie theater, all conversation has been suspended. And as in a movie, there is drama and suspense. A couple of times, she slips on a slippery patch in the snow and comes close to falling. Those of us on stools jump up as one, ready to race across the street to help her to her feet should she actually fall. As one, we resume our seats with a collective sigh when she gracefully regains her balance. I watch her from one side of the store, while Coleman Curran watches from the other. Neither aware of the other.

I feel the world fall away, in a way I hadn't in a very long while. I fall into an intense daydream. The bakery disappears; replaced by the darkness of a movie theater. The plate-glass window becomes a screen, no longer transparent. Summer replaces Winter. The air is balmy. The leaves on the trees are the deep green of high summer. The trees line a paved path in a park. The trees are spaced evenly along the path. I'm sitting on one of the benches that alternate with the trees. On the opposite side of the path, sits a middle-aged man. I don't recognize him at first because he is a distance away and in soft focus. The focus becomes progressively sharper, slowly zooming in, until the man on the bench is recognizable. The man on the bench is me.

"Are you waiting for me?" says a sensuous woman's voice off-screen. I know this voice so well and love so much to hear it. The smile on my movie self's face widens to its widest.

"Yes, I'm waiting for you."

"Do you want me?"

"Yes, where are you?"

"I'm right behind you." He stands and turn to see her coming out of the sun, the fabric of her dress made transparent by the light behind her. Never has the sun been so beautifully eclipsed nor the shadow cast by the eclipsing body so suffused with warmth, the eclipsing body itself being radiant. She saunters down the small hill toward him, coming from a direction he had not expected.

The sight of her moves him the way it always has, the way it always will, no matter the length of the interval between their meetings.

"You see me?"

" Yes, you are so beautiful."

"You know you've never told me that before." she says jokingly.

"I've been grossly negligent—will you forgive me?"

"Do you love me?"

"Yes." By this time, they are standing inches apart, the bench between them. She comes around the bench and pushes him down on it. She straddles his legs, hiking up her skirt, grabs his face and kisses him/me.

In her kiss, I taste hot chocolate. She shimmers and disappears. Summer fades with the taste of chocolate, winter returns with the window's sudden transparency as I'm pulled back to harsh reality. I gently kiss the lip of the cup from which I drink.

It is obvious to me that she is going to the library. That is the only other place she could be going. I decide I will bring her a cup of hot chocolate. She will like that. Coleman beats me to the punch. After Ariel turns the corner on Chestnut Hill Ave, he bursts out the door and across the street, in pursuit, holding a large Styrofoam cup full of hot chocolate in each hand. He's also figured out where she is going, which is a feat of deductive reasoning I would have thought well beyond his limited intellectual capabilities.

I overhear the talk. "Looks like Coleman is after that girl."

"She better watch out."

"She's a pretty girl."

"Does anybody know who she is?"

I keep my mouth shut and kiss my hot chocolate. It bothers me that they all know Coleman's name while I'm as invisible as the invisible man.

While Ariel study's at the library, sipping on phase two of Coleman's plan, Enzo stands in his kitchen, looking at the phone's receiver in his hand, the cord stretches away out of his field of vision to the wall unit. The edges of his vision are ill-defined and seem to boil. He isn't sure what to do with the phone, why he holds it, or where he is. His head explodes in pain. He thinks he turns to exit the room. He feels like he is running but inexplicably the floor is rushing up to meet him. He hears, as clear as a bell, Ariel's last words to him: "Goodbye trash man."

8. Adjusting to Darkness

Standing at the head of the little path, she knows something is terribly wrong. The driveway is still mostly covered, the shovel stuck blade first aslant into the snow bank. A trail of distorted footsteps leads across the front yard from the place where her father stopped working to the front door, which is wide open—all ominous signs. She has never known her father to not finish shoveling the driveway once he starts. It really isn't a very big driveway. If everything were just fine the door would be closed, instead it is wide open. Leaving the door open on a cold day is like setting fire to your money he would say, notwithstanding his daredevil dive over her head this morning.

She stands in the doorway apprehensive about entering. The hallway that runs from the front door to the kitchen is shrouded in that temporary but impenetrable darkness caused by the extreme contraction of her pupils and the relative darkness of the hallway when compared with the intense brightness of sunlight reflected off new snow.

It takes longer to adjust to the darkness. She turns on the hall light but it does nothing to cut the darkness. She can't make out the walnut hope chest in the front hall or even the bottom of the stairwell. The fear of stumbling over his body grips her.

She waits. It's all she can do.

There is an eerie gray glow coming from the top of the stairs. The light from the kitchen is very much like the light at the end of a tunnel, marking the destination but not very illuminating for the journey. Her eyes begin adjusting; she steps into the front hall and closes the door. She removes her boots and proceeds down the short hallway towards the kitchen, taking short steps, the bottoms of her socks get wet from the snow melt her father had trailed in with his own boots. If things were okay, he never would have walked through the house with snow-covered boots.

She pauses midway to the kitchen, frightened, certain of what she will find. Her socks soak up the water and ground her in reality, it is the only thing that seems real. The short hallway telescopes away before her yet closes in around her. The longer she stands, the harder it is to move, she feels like the floor is absorbing her as much as her socks are absorbing the water.

"Dad?" she says tentatively, almost to herself.

No answer.

"Dad," Louder now, if he is in the kitchen, there is no way he couldn't have heard her. Her eyes, fully adjusted now, confirm what she feared. She can see the top of her father's head through the opening at the end of the hallway that leads into the kitchen. "Dad!" she shouts. He doesn't move. Terror grips her heart. She leans to her left to see his entire head, face down on the floor. She stands up straight, sucking in air. Confronted with this stark reality, she is seized by a dreadful indecisiveness, afraid to move forward and even more afraid to leave. She tries to be optimistic, grasping for any straw. She tells herself this is just a joke, a way to get her back for locking him out this morning. She fights the impulse to run away.

Be courageous, if he isn't dead, by doing nothing, I kill him.

With that thought, she charges into the kitchen, and kneels next to his body on his left side, determined that she must turn him over. She has to make certain this is her father. The man on the floor might be someone who wandered in and put her father's winter clothes on and then died. She grabs the sleeve of his left arm and lifts and pushes with all her might, but succeeds in only twisting the arm behind his back. She becomes afraid she will rip his arm off. She hadn't moved his body at all. He is too heavy for her. She is hysterical about turning him over, as the germ of the idea that this isn't her father has taken hold.

She could take off the woolen cap, which tightly conforms to his head. She would know immediately it was him because his head of thick, black hair always gives him away, but she can't bring herself to touch his head. It doesn't occur to her to call an ambulance. The phone's hand unit gripped tightly in the man's gloved fingers. It wouldn't have done Enzo any good at this point, but it would have been a better solution than wrestling Greco-Roman style with his corpse.

She talks to him.

"Okay, you got me back good for this morning. Very funny, now if you just help me…." She draws a quick breath.

"If you help me, we can turn you over, on the count of three….one two…three." She gives a mighty heave, trying to lift his left side and then roll him like a logger might roll a log. She isn't strong enough to roll him or strong enough to resist the thought that he is dead weight. She sits back on her heels and closes her eyes, resembling a karate-ka meditating before a difficult match.

Why do I have to be alone? Won't somebody come and help me?

She feels the first wave of an overwhelming sorrow, not as a feeling within, but as a weight—a real weight that's so heavy, it is driving her to the floor. It's the weight of a thousand black birds. The very birds whose wings she'd felt flutter across her skin that morning. They have come back to land on her, to use her as a perch, to roost.

The ravens of despair.

That they should be black with lifeless eyes seems right to her. That they should be the scavengers that pick the carcasses on the road clean seemed so right, as well, have they not come to pick her clean, to scavenge—not her body, but her mind and soul.

They speak to her all at once. A cacophony of voices in which she hears; we have come. You have called us. You will know us. We are your solace. We are you.

No" she yells and shakes herself, flailing her arms and violently tousling her hair. The weight lifts with a loud flutter and cackling like laughter that diminishes slowly then disappears.

"Jesus!" she whispers, frightened. "Was that real?"

She focuses on the task at hand. His right arm is stretched out to his side, opposite from where she kneels, parallel to the line of his shoulders. This caused resistance to his being turned. She reaches over and pulls his wrist down toward his hip. His arm is very heavy or her strength is deserting her, because even this proves difficult.

She stops again to rest.

She then goes down to his feet. Straddling his legs, she lifts his left boot over his right one, laying the toe of the left boot on the heel of the right, reasoning that he would roll more easily if he was started in that direction. She then tries to push him over at his hips instead of at his shoulders. She succeeds only in sliding him an inch or two, unbearably grinding his face into the floor.

Her hysteria increases, she lets out an animal wail.

She sits back again keeping her eyes open while she stares at the ceiling to warn off the ravens. She thinks about how to get leverage.

This is not the time to cry, I will cry when the time comes.

She reaches under him with both hands, working her hands as far as she can, palms up. She grabs the right front of his coat. She brings her knees in close to his body pulling with all her might while pushing in the other direction with her body. She closes her eyes and lets out a scream, pulling and pushing with all her might. She feels him reach the tipping point, just before her strength gives out.

Enzo falls heavily onto his back, his right arm underneath and his left draped over his stomach. Ariel reaches under and pulls his right arm out from underneath him. Just because he's dead, doesn't mean he should be made uncomfortable. She closes her eyes. Now that she has turned him, she can't bring herself to look into his face fearful of the last expression etched upon his face.

You killed me his eternal stare will say.

She can't turn her face to his and keep her eyes open at the same time. Her head works like one of those dolls young girls play with, their eyes weighted so that they closed in mock sleep when the doll is laid on its back. Her eyes close every time she turns her head to look into his face weighted with the guilt of her responsibility in his death. She tackles the problem by dividing it into two smaller problems. With her eyes closed she turns her face in the direction of his. Then she tries to open her eyes. She manages to get one eye opened slightly. She sees a face, twisted in the pain of death, nose smashed, almost flattened, the upper lip retracted in his death grimace of pain, teeth missing and broken, shattered, the pieces strewn across the floor. His eyes are open and unfocused, they point in different directions, the white part of his left eye a flaming red. His jaw is slack, his mouth agape, which she finds alarming. There is no accusatory stare, there is nothing. He is gone

Her next conscious moment she finds herself knocking on her neighbor's door. They are a couple in their late twenties. Karen answers the door, Rick, her husband, stands in the hall behind her drinking a cup of coffee. They are a happy-go-lucky, somewhat roly-poly pair. Roly poly, roly poly, roly poly pazan... the lyrics to the song run unbidden through her head. She is pretty sure the word pazan isn't really in the song but she likes the word preferring it to whatever word is really there.

It is her word and it is oddly comforting.

"What's the matter dear?" Karen says, quite alarmed. Ariel bears the look of someone who's had their lives turned upside down. As a nurse it was a look Karen had seen many times before.

Ariel, out of breath, whispers "Could help me?"

"Of course dear, please come in?" Karen says. Ariel had run from her house to here, through her father's footsteps and across Rick and Karen's lawn cracking the hard crust that formed when the temperature dropped with every step and sinking in spots up to mid-thigh where the snow had drifted. Her socks and jeans were soaked through by the Time she'd completed her short but arduous journey.

"Yes, help me please."

"Come in honey," Karen says kindly and leads Ariel down the hall to the kitchen. "I'll make you some hot chocolate. Rick will you go see what's going on over there,and bring her boots back, they're probably right in the front hall, please?"

Rick first reaction is that he doesn't want to. He was relaxing after shoveling his own driveway. His back is a little stiff, but he does what he has to. He dons his coat and pulls his boots on and head across to Ariel's house.

Karen makes hot chocolate, one for her and one for Ariel, Rick returns. He is somber. He reports to Karen what he's seen, including Ariel's attempt to tape her father's mouth closed, which lent a truly macabre element to an already macabre scene and which she did not remember doing. Rick, who was a gentle soul would carry the image of the excess of tape over the dead man's mouth to his own grave in the not too distant future.

Karen gently extracts what information she can from Ariel. She calls down to New York and speaks directly with Kathleen who is terribly upset. They dispense with practical business as Karen volunteers to call McNamara's Funeral Home to come and get the body. Kathleen makes a dark joke about them not being swindlers or so she'd heard. Kathleen and Ariel speak for a moment. Karen could only hear Ariel's side; she pleads movingly with her mother to hurry home. Ariel hands the phone back to Karen. Kathleen asks her to "watch over" Ariel until she can make it back, which will be tomorrow at the earliest. It is snowing hard again New York and this new storm was headed to Boston, train service was suspended.

Ariel watches the mortician come and carry the body away in a body bag, under a blanket, on a gurney. She watches as he roughly shoves her father's shrouded body into the back of the hearse, he is only cargo now. The mortician perhaps feeling her eyes on him looks around in a pantomime of a guilty conscience. The world to her has become a surreal nightmare. He looks right at her but cannot see, even as she weakly raises her hand to wave at him. The hearse fishtails in the deep snow of the as yet unplowed street, but manages to make it back to the funeral home.

"Sweetheart, do you want to stay here tonight? You're welcome to," Karen asks, thinking Ariel wouldn't want to spend the night alone in the house her father had just died in.

"No, that's alright, thanks."

She accepts a hug from Karen, who assures her that she can call at any time if she needs help of any kind.

"Thanks," is all Ariel says.

She reenters the house, struck by the fact that this house is no longer the house she grew up in. This house is no longer the safe, happy place of her childhood, but a mausoleum—or at least, it had been a mausoleum that afternoon. The thought doesn't frighten her but fills her with a pervasive debilitating melancholy bordering on madness.

She wanders into the kitchen. There is a tiny trickle of blood where Enzo's face had lay. His heart had already stopped beating by the time his face hit the floor like a sledgehammer. Ariel cleans it up by boiling the tea kettle until it whistles, then pouring the hot water over the blood. The stain dissolves from the linoleum, leaving a pink puddle on the floor, which she mops up with a rag mop. She repeats the process until she is satisfied there is no more pinkish hue to the puddle. This proves difficult because there is red in the linoleum, so she reenacts Lady Macbeth's 'out, out damn spot' soliloquy and 'what will this floor never be clean' with equal fervor, if silently.

She rambles around the house like a ghost revisiting the past, like those literary ghosts, doomed to observe—if only in her mind—those things she might have changed but could not. The world, unaffected by her presence or what had happened. The world already grinding on. This grinding represented by the relentless turning of the hands on the electric clock that hangs above the windows over the kitchen sink.

She wanders aimlessly about, and each time she makes a circuit of the downstairs rooms, she glances at that clock with its kitschy, smiling Mr. Sunshine face. That face had made her smile as a child but now it mocks her. Each time she passes the clock, she is surprised to see how much or how little time had passed since her last check. Time passes in random, irregular chunks. Her ability to measure time internally is lost. She stares at the smoothly moving second-hand to reassure herself that time still passes at a regular pace.

She picks up the picture of her taking first holy communion, longing for that simpler time when her faith was unquestioned and the world was bright. She picks up a picture of her and her father at the beach, squinting against the sun—at first, not even recognizing herself in the picture, then remembering the day vividly. David had chased her, dangling a crab by its claw, and she ran away until he convinced her that the crab couldn't hurt her. Her mother took this picture of her holding the crab, one claw in each hand like those photos of fishermen holding up the big fish, her father squatting down beside her, with one big hand on either side of her waist, and smiling. She smiles now, back at him in the photograph, and replaces it on the table, full of regret.

She meanders—no place worth standing in for too long, one place as good as another. Now she is in front of the fridge, opening the fridge. She looks out the front window into the darkness. She sits on the sofa watching Charles Boyer torture poor Ingrid Bergman in Gaslight.

Charles Boyer, you are a horrid monster.

She does this for hours. She is tired to the bone, so she turns out the lights. She is not a frightened child. She will sleep.

Upstairs, she pulls the covers down on the neatly made bed—the bed she had made herself. She climbs in, still dressed as she had been all day, except for the jacket, hat, gloves and boots that she had shed at some point. Where and when she can't remember and doesn't care. She lies on her back and pulls the covers up to her chin, eyes open, staring at the shadows on her ceiling.

The shadows are of the bare tree in her backyard. The upper branches, which shade her room in summer from the setting sun, offer no such protection now from the glaring floodlight in the schoolyard. The branches sway rhythmically in the winter wind, the biting, cold, merciless, winter wind. Their movements are amplified by the distance between the light, the tree and the ceiling. She gets up and pulls the shade, transferring the shadows there.

She closes her eyes and tries to breathe calmly, counting her breaths to try to lull herself to sleep. Still awake, she suffers another vision of despair. The bed has become the surface of the ocean on which she floats. What ocean or where in the world she is, she doesn't know. She only knows she is afloat on a vast ocean. She is immersed in, and saturated by, total blackness. The sky and the water are indistinguishable from each other, and she—indistinguishable from either. The boundary between herself and the universe has dissolved. The blackness flows down into her. The blackness outside and the blackness inside are as indistinguishable as the black ocean from the black sky. She finds not just the barrier between herself and the universe dissolved but feels herself dissolving. The blackness soaking into the fabric of her being.

Am I empty? She asks.

It feels too real and is too scary a sensation to tolerate calmly, so she opens her eyes, hoping the vision will depart and the question will remain unanswered.

She becomes aware of the skeletal shadows of the branches wavering across the window shade, striping the illuminated rhomboids of the windowpanes there.

The branches dance, sometimes together and sometimes counter to each other in a pattern that repeats itself exactly every few minutes. A bird lands on a branch, casting its shadow, a noble bird blacker than its own shadow—the eyeless shadow-stoic and accusing.

"No," she says to the shadow.

More shadowy birds land on the dancing branches. Finally, there are so many that their individual shapes are lost in the merged, blacker than the blackest black shadow. They weigh the branches to the breaking point, yet they keep coming, landing on top of each other, clawing each other for purchase, their flapping wings; maddening. Her heart is beating so fast. She jumps out of the bed and raises the shade. There is the bare tree, unburdened.

She wraps herself up in a blanket and turns the heat up. The house is cold. She turns on all the lights to ward off the ravens and the accusing spirit of her father. She tumbles into her surreal dream of the world. She welcomes this sleep. If there is a prince's kiss that can reach into her depths and awaken what is now still and silent, he had better come soon. Her forest of thorns grows mighty and silence beckons.

9. Acquiring the Golden Hind

Everybody I know from the projects is a shoplifter to one degree or another. Poverty will do this to a person. We tell ourselves we are Robin Hoods, stealing from the rich to give to the poor. That I happen to be the poor for whom I steal perhaps makes me less of a hero, but it's a philosophical debate for which my circumstances don't allow. That doesn't mean I feel no guilt because I do. To ease that guilt I normally stole only small things that I stuff easily into a pocket or down the front of my pants, which I cover with a too baggy t-shirt worn just for that purpose. As I got older, I became enamored of the grab-and-run technique because I can run fast. No store manager could chase me down—they are always either too fat, too old, or just plain slow.

I get a thrill from the chaos I create with my rush to the exit. This method lets me steal larger items. I'm also a practitioner of the buy-one-thing-steal-three technique, which is the technique I use when violating the first rule of thumb. The first rule of thumb is not to shoplift where you or your family shop on a regular basis. This rule led me from a young age into Boston proper and Cambridge to shoplift. Today, I'm on my way to Cambridge. It isn't exactly a shoplifting mission it is more or less a major heist. I have found the golden hind and I must have it.

Cambridge is a short bus ride from my apartment. The number 54 bus leaves me at the Central Square red line station, right in front of a small radio station, WCAS 740 on the AM dial. This was back in the day when AM radio still played music and many American cars offered FM radios only as an option. WCAS played an arcane brand of music they called progressive. For example, you will never hear The Rolling Stones there, but you might, if you're lucky, hear King Crimson.

I notice that despite the anti-litter campaign of the crying Indian, the gutters of Central Square are rich with the detritus of modern civilization. It will take a few more years for the consciousness raising begun by that campaign to take hold. Meanwhile, my father still freely throws trash from our car. I duck into the Dunkin Donuts next door to the radio station and sit down at the counter, craving a cup of coffee before I descend into the train station.

I slowly sip the coffee. I take it with cream and sugar, a lot of sugar. People tell me I use too much sugar because I really don't like coffee. That say I like sugar. My father tells me I drink my coffee like a woman while giving me a disgusted look. I laugh (to myself, to avoid a smack) at him and at these other people. They don't realize that the cream, the sugar, and the coffee complement each other, and form a flavor that is so much greater than the sum of its parts. As I taste the sweet, earthy goodness, I feel a wave of pity for these sorry souls who dare not break out of their rigid thinking and really live, like I'm really living just now.

149

While thinking these thoughts, I finish the last drops regretfully. All that is left in the cup are the viscous sugary dregs. To drain these requires that I hold the cup to my lips and tilt my head back until the thick, sweet liquid finally makes it to my mouth. The sugary dregs are the best part. Dunkin Donuts coffee is so good, the flavor is reminiscent to me at that moment of burning leaves, cotton candy and the earth. I want another right then.

I reach into my pocket to check my meager financial reserves. Even though I know I don't have enough, I'm always hopeful that maybe my loose change will miraculously multiply. I have only enough for the train to and from Harvard Square, and the bus back home. I decide I don't feel like hoofing it so I will have to do without, unless I can figure out a way to shoplift a cup of coffee. The waitress, observing my forlorn expression as I hold the cup halfway between the counter and my lips, hoping there were a few more dregs at the bottom, asks, "would you like another?"

I hesitate for a moment, thinking I could take a cup and quickly drink it then dash out, but not wanting to burn my lips or miss out on the dregs, I smile at her and lie.

"No thanks."

I said it as brightly as I could, which apparently wasn't brightly enough for she, being a particularly observant and insightful waitress, says,

"Are you sure, honey?"

"If you're giving it away...." I hold out the cup hopeful. "More please," quoting what I knew of Oliver Twist in my best English accent.

She gives me a severe look as though I had just asked her to disrobe, a thing very far from my mind considering her obvious inability to stay away from the donuts. She puts the pot down and hastily walks to the other end of the counter. I see no point in staying if the coffee isn't free, so I put the cup down. I walk out past the small cluster (in number not in volume) of waitresses who, standing behind the glass case where the bismarcks, éclairs and other higher-quality pastries are displayed like expensive jewels, are having a chuckle at my expense.

I was always doing that kind of thing, suddenly switching into an English accent and quoting what little I knew of Shakespeare or Dickens, or even mixing them with random, nonsensical associations that spring into my head and leap out of my mouth. It is one of the things about me that people took as strange. The fact that I would laugh out loud at my cleverness enamored me to no one and forced me to resume my place behind my wall of taciturnity.

I can't help myself, really. I'm in a constant battle with boredom. I find so many people boring, like that waitress. She had no idea that I was quoting the famous scene when little Oliver, holding his bowl in a supplicating attitude as I had held my cup, courageously asks for more gruel. I could tell by the glaze that came over her eyes. I didn't want to explain myself or the reference to her. She would just think I was accusing her of being stupid, which I would have been.

I couldn't believe, though, that she didn't know I was referring to that scene. I would have thought that it was common knowledge. We could have shared a laugh and (more importantly) I might have triggered her very latent magnanimity, obtaining more of that delicious coffee. I should know by now, however, that knowledge—any knowledge—isn't common in this world.

I walk out into the brisk Cambridge winter, cross the street and dive headlong down the stairs into the outbound Central Square red line T station, a dingy, nondescript underground of gray concrete tinged black by years of dirt and equal doses of poor maintenance and poor lighting. The walls are tiled in a mosaic of white and maroon. The name of the station—Central—is spelled out at regular intervals along the wall opposite the track using the little maroon tiles. I pause

152

momentarily, thinking I will jump the turnstile after the train arrives, I still want more coffee, but the man in the booth is already eying me suspiciously. I put my quarter in the slot and push my way through. I assume my wait-for-the-train stance close to the edge of the platform, near the booth occupied by the rightfully suspicious T employee. I make a quick study of my fellow commuters for signs of madness. I determined that while those in close proximity indeed all seem somewhat mad, none seems mad enough to push me in front of an oncoming train.

I relax my guard. Even so, there are a number of interesting characters on the platform. There is jiggly girl, dressed in a short denim jacket and a short skirt. She is inappropriately dressed for the cold. She is cold and jiggles to keep warm.

There is World War I man. A skinny fellow dressed in a soldier's greatcoat, with a couple of medals pinned to his chest. He rocks back and forth, heel to toe. His lips move like a bad ventriloquist's. He is mouthing artillery coordinates. He has fear in his eyes. He is shell-shocked. That's what they called it back in World War I. They also called it battlefield psychosis, as though being afraid of the very real possibility of being torn apart by a five-hundred-pound artillery shell was delusional, and anyone so afraid was psychotic.

It's so interesting, the names they choose. I like what they called it back in the Civil War—they called it nostalgia. There was

153

nobody left alive who had fought in the Civil War. No one living had ever heard the rebel yell given full throat in a real charge. I thought that when the train came into the station, I would let out a yell—my own rebel yell. A yell that has been building up inside me all my life.

Anyway, World War I man wasn't going to push me from the platform. Truth be told, he probably couldn't push a broom, judging from the sickly look of him.

There were some other characters—there was suit and tie man, briefcase man and security guard man. Security guard man was a sorry sight, slight of build, with greasy hair. He was engaged presently in setting the world record for depth of finger in nostril. I was going to tell him he should wait until the world record people arrive to acknowledge his feat, but it seems pointless. I turn away before he finds what he is looking for.

I had become nervous about being pushed in front of a train when I read an article in The Globe recounting how that very thing happened right here in Central Square. There was a picture that accompanied the article. The picture showed rescue workers jacking the train away from the platform so the hapless victim could be extracted from that tiny space. His waist had been pinched between the train and the platform. How he had wound up in that position, I couldn't imagine. He wasn't dead when the rescue workers arrived but died shortly after being extricated. The picture was truly horrific, much more so than if he had been run over by the train. If he were under the train, no one would have been able to take his picture and I wouldn't be trying to measure the murderous capacity of my fellow travelers.

I feel the breeze of the oncoming train and hear the distant squeal of the metal wheels grinding on the metal track. I lean forward and glance down the tunnel in time to see the headlight peek around the bend. I consider how unnecessary the headlight really is. The breeze intensifies as the train nears. The distant rumble becomes a roar as it bursts into the station, pushing, just as Mohammed did, a tornado in front of it. I and those daring, fellow travelers who stand relatively close to the edge of the platform sway as the train blows past. We look like unwilling dominoes fighting to stay upright.

The women hold down their dresses and skirts as best they can against the blast. Jiggly girl, caught unprepared, shows her pretty pink undies to the appreciative crowd when the transient hurricane lifts her skirt way up high before she can react. Suit and tie man looks at me with a "hey did you see that" leer. I shoot him back the "yeah I saw that" leer, without wanting to but unable to stop my face from mimicking his expression as though I were a chimp at the zoo. I turn away, disgusted, not with him but with myself for enjoying the show too much. This is not the way of a gentleman thief, I tell myself. It is important that if I'm going to be a thief, I be a gentleman thief.

155

The train comes to a stop, one of the four-per-car, pneumatically operated doors swooshes open right in front of where I stand. I step into the train and turn to face the man in the booth, bracing myself against the onslaught of my fellow passengers who wish to go further into the car and grab a seat. They express their annoyance by battering me. I lock eyes with the man in the booth, bravely shooting him the finger just as the door closes. The train picks up speed.

Amused by his angry expression, I turn and face into the train with a grin on my face. An old lady glares at me, having seen my gesture. I fidget uncomfortably for the three minutes it takes the train to reach Harvard Square. She glares but says nothing. She doesn't have to, as my conscience assails me for both the ungentlemanly and cowardly nature of the gesture. I almost apologize to her. I'm on the verge of saying it when the train pulls into Harvard Square station. I'm relieved of the compulsion to apologize when the doors swoosh open. I race up the stairs. She looked in no mood to accept an apology anyway. I move so fast; I'm on the street before that old lady even hits the stairs.

I am on my way to Harvard's Widener library. My plan is to steal a particular book. It is a rather valuable book, worth who knows how much. Harvard had so much money, I reason, they won't miss one little book. The coat I'm wearing has been altered for just this purpose. I have slit the lining in the back, forming a sort of kangaroo's pouch between the lining and the shell, into which I plan to place the book. Then, I will walk nonchalantly out past the front desk when they are relatively busy—a thing I had done innumerable times with groceries, calmly paying for a box of spaghetti while secreting steaks in my coat.

The book isn't one of their exceptionally valuable books, like the Book of Hours. Access to the real valuable books is restricted to faculty and then only under the most strictly guarded conditions. This book is a book that is just on the shelves, free to be checked out by anyone with a Harvard student ID who wished to do so. I had come across this book by accident. It would never be found missing, I was sure. I had done some research on both this author and this book. It was not a famous book at all and would likely never appear on any syllabus. It is, however, as close to the golden hind as I'm likely to get in this lifetime.

Some might say that it is reprehensible to steal and doubly reprehensible to foist that stolen article on someone unsuspecting. I say, you are right, but I was able then to rationalize away the whole thing by telling myself I was taking a big risk for the sake of love. Love conquers all, right? I would also be giving this book a home, where it would be read and greatly appreciated. The recipient would never have to know I stole it. I had concocted a cover story in case she asked where I got it, knowing that with her curious mind, she may not accept that she shouldn't look a gift horse in the mouth. Here, it would just gather dust–that is, if the books were allowed to gather dust.

Harvard Square is its usual three-ring circus, full of characters and crazies and students, too. My favorite was the crazy who stood by the station kiosk singing over and over again a song she had written. Neither the song nor her voice were worthy of being heard in public– the real entertainment was her ranting against the Harvard students who would come down and take notes for their psychology courses. She, being a paranoid schizophrenic, thought they were copying down her fantastic lyrics so they could record her song and make the fortune that would be denied her. To my knowledge, her song remains unobtainable.

I walk the five hundred feet eastward along Mass Ave to the entrance of Harvard yard, just in front of the imposing facade of the library. I walk past the front desk, which is manned today by two people. Neither of them seems very concerned about my very unexpected appearance in their oh-so-humble library.

Anything but humble, Harvard's Widener library is a palace–no–a fortress of books, a modern monastery of quiet and sometimes not-so-quiet study. It is a magnificent building, a Renaissance temple, that when I go there, I'm forced to give some thought to my mother's dream for my career as an architect, although I have a hard time imagining summoning the arrogance and presumption the design of such a building must require. The well-lit and vast gallery with the arched paneled ceiling is reminiscent of the ceiling in the pantheon (I'd seen pictures), only the library's ceiling is cylindrical and not spherical. It is the most impressive internal space I know of—really breathtaking. There are six levels plus a number of secret sub levels that I have not, as yet, explored.

Stealing a book from this place seems like it should be easy, considering the steady flow of human traffic coupled with the inability and disinclination of the library staff to keep such a careful watch. For most of the library staff, the idea of a book being stolen from under their noses is inconceivable. The sheer grandeur of the place presses down to impose the moral imperative—thou shalt not steal—on most of the people who enter here. However, despite its temple/fortress appearance, the place IS designed to lend books (not to me but to Harvard students). I'm just planning to borrow a book for a very extended period and avoid the inconvenience of returning it.

Today, I didn't take the time to go into the main gallery as I usually would, just to take it in and be awed by it. I'm on a mission. I take the nearest elevator to the fifth floor, where the French literature collection is located. It is the largest French literature collection in the Unites States—or so the sign proclaims, if you can believe signs. Harvard is big on this kind of thing: the largest endowment, the most expensive, the oldest university in America, stuff like that. They want everyone to know how great they are and they aren't shy about telling, which was one of the things I hate about the place. That and Love Story takes place there.

The book I'm there to steal is entitled Horace and the author was a woman named George Sand. It is bound with a black leather binding, which had been during most of its existence religiously oiled to preserve its pliability. It hasn't been oiled since coming to Harvard, but being crammed amongst the other books preserves it in a relatively pristine state. The pages have been skillfully and elegantly stitched into the binding with gold thread. The spine would never crack, unlike modern day paperbacks, which are glued together. The pages are thick vellum rag, straight cut and gilt edged. They do not stick together, but fan like a new deck of playing cards. The covers, front and back, are blank. The title and author's name are gilded on the spine in script. The bookmark is a silken swatch also sewn into the binding. It is the French flag with a yellow fleur-de-lis in the middle. The text is an easily readable font. The first letter of each chapter is enlarged and illuminated in the way medieval texts are. There are about ten illustrations spaced throughout, sketches done by a then-struggling artist named Claude Monet.

George Sand's real name was Amantine Aurore Lucile Dupin, also known as Baroness Dudevant. No wonder she changed it. No, of course she changed it for the same reason as Charlotte Bronte and Jane Austen, who were published originally under male pen names or anonymously. It was impossible for a woman to get published, especially when the heroine of the story faces her troubles alone and overcomes them without the aid of a man. Although the publisher originally refused to publish a book that was built around such a preposterous premise, Horace was eventually published years later.

The text of the edition I'm stealing is in French. Ariel, being widely known as a lover of all things French, will love it for that alone. It is a book that has been translated into English only once, and that edition Is difficult to get, so there is no way I could read it to see if the story is any good. I have learned all this stuff right here in this very library. I'm not going to take this risk without knowing what I was taking a risk for, that would be just stupid. I did know, without even the benefit of any research that this is the most valuable book I will ever hold in my hands, by far. Stealing it is necessary because these pompous Harvard clowns don't know what they have. It never occurred to me that some student could have placed it where I found it and the library staff has been searching for it. It will be a piece of cake to steal. I tell myself for the thousandth time.

There is no one in the stacks. It takes me some time to locate the shelf on which I believe the book resides. It isn't there, I'm perplexed for a moment. Since it had indeed been placed at random by a student, its placement did not conform to the cataloging system. I should have taken more careful note of exactly where I had seen it. For a while I search in a casual way. I look like a normal library patron out for a browse. My search quickly becomes frantic, like Eli Wallach's search for "Bill Carson's" grave in The Good, the Bad and the Ugly, the grave in which he thinks the money is buried. My search resembles Eli Wallach's in its swirling disoriented nature The difference is I'm much handsomer than the man who was cast to play the titular ugly. Just when I'm about to give up, the gilded script on the binding hits my eyes like a lighthouse beacon.

I take it down. As deftly as a well-practiced magician I make it disappear between the lining and the outer shell of my coat. Now you see it, now you don't. I make sure the coat hangs naturally enough and proceed down to the main gallery, where I can be observed by the staff. I grab a book from the stacks and bring it over to a table and sit down on the tail of my coat and thus on the book itself. I pretend to read the "fascinating" book I had grabbed, some book about medieval foundations in Britain. This was the tough part of my mission. I should have grabbed Pere Goriot by Balzac from the French section, since I'd been promising myself I'd read it. Sitting quietly perusing a book in the

162

gallery was part of my plan. Someone in no apparent hurry would be unlikely to have a valuable book between the lining and the shell of their coat. I struggle to suppress my desire to look around and check to see if anyone is eying me suspiciously, reasoning that to behave suspiciously would bring suspicion down on me. I feign interest in what might be the most boring book I could possibly have chosen, Medieval Foundations across Great Britain. I sit staring blankly at the pages, turning them at regular intervals to give the impression I'm reading. Despite staring at that book for the last half hour, I learn nothing about British medieval foundations.

It is time to walk the gauntlet to the front door. I put the book I'd chosen as a diversion back in the shelves. To anyone observing, I'm a good and considerate library patron.

There is no gauntlet. I'm invisible to the staff and the students, except for the few who eye me with disdain as someone who obviously doesn't belong at daddy's Hahvahd. I stuck my hands into my pants pockets to hold the tail of my coat back and keep the weight of the book from swinging the tail back and forth, thereby revealing its presence to an astute observer. I force myself to keep my pace slow and my eyes front, someone unconcerned. My heart is pounding in a way that it never does when I steal groceries, this is a serious offense for which a vindictive Harvard would insist I do jail time. I make it to the door and can't resist bursting into a full sprint that brings me all the way to the Harvard T station subway entrance and face to face with the paranoid schizoid singer.

She immediately begins to rant about how I've been sent by the CIA to steal the lyrics to her song. Amused about the idea of how the CIA might use her song to torture our supposed enemies, I smile at her, which stops her in her tracks. She wanders a few steps away, eying me confusedly, fidgeting from foot to foot. Perhaps by smiling, I have confirmed her suspicions that I'm indeed from the CIA.

I am exuberant at the success of my mission. The thought of another cup of coffee at the Central Square Dunkin Donuts is front and center in my mind, displacing (if only momentarily) she who is usually front and center. There are three ways I know of to insure I can get another cup of coffee. One is to jump the turnstile, which is risky, and use the money I would have paid for the train. The second is to steal from the tip plate at the Out of Town newsstand, which is even riskier. Get caught, get a broken arm. The third way is by panhandling, which I immediately start.

I am being honest with my fellow travelers as I beg for a quarter to get a cup of coffee. I have great success. My youth and my abnormally pretty face forces normally hard people to reach into their pockets. I also misquote Shakespeare and Dickens to those who give me a coin, like the man with the twisted lip who panhandled in London in a Sherlock Holmes story I had recently read. I also put on my crazy English accent, like I had back in the doughnut shop.

"Neither a borrower nor a lender be, Guvna'," the irony lost on me, but not on the generous, intelligent, and handsome bloke who'd just given me a quarter. He rolls his eyes and smiles.

"A drop in the comprehensive ocean of your kindness, I'm sure, Miss." I say to a pretty co-ed who has handed me a dime.

"What a piece of work is man, kind sir," I exaggerate the tipping of an imaginary hat and bow deeply to those generous enough to help me out in this my desperate coffee craving hour of need. "For this is their finest hour." I commend all who pass unabashedly on their beauty and intelligence, raising smiles on the faces of most, scowls on the faces of some. I commend these all the more.

Some people gather a few feet away to witness my impromptu and eccentric performance. I'm amazed and terrified. Who am I? I feel as though a different person has crawled inside me and taken the controls. I'm attracting a great deal of attention, not a wise thing to do with a valuable stolen commodity hidden in my coat. The crazy song lady rants on from a safe distance about how I'm invading her space and why does someone from the government need to panhandle anyway?

Within ten minutes, I have collected two dollars. I give a quarter to the crazy song lady saying "a grateful nation thanks you," then head down into the subway, exhilarated. I let out my rebel yell scaring the daylights out of my fellow travelers who collectively back away from the edge of the platform just in case.

10. The End of Magic

So now I have my golden hind. All that is left is to give it to Ariel. My visions of this transaction are very pleasing. I get so much pleasure from dreaming of the different ways I will present this gift to her and the different, yet of course, always favorable reactions she would have. So I hold the book and enjoy my daydreams.

The fantasy that most often runs through my mind and is as vivid as any I've ever had, has me making a meal in a large well-lit kitchen. I see myself in silhouette against a large Palladian window, chopping vegetables on a granite counter top. My sleeves are rolled tightly past my elbows and I'm building a Karakorum of vegetables around the spot where I'm cutting. I have a towel thrown over my shoulder. I periodically wipe my hands on the towel. In real life I have no idea how to cook a dish that involves vegetables beyond boiling the shit out of them, leeching any nutritional value from them, which is how my mother cooks vegetables. It never becomes clear to me exactly to what use I plan to put these vegetables.

The phone rings, it is Ariel. That she should call me is very important. I tell her I'm making a special dinner for her. She agrees to come over.

She enters, but she is not alone. She is accompanied by two small people, boys, each of whom is about half her height, miniature people, fully formed if somewhat doll-like. These boys know Ariel well and she quite obviously has a very strong affinity for them. The three of them exhibit a natural ease with each other. I notice this affinity right away and they make no effort to hide it from me. This affinity is old and born from having been through much together. Although perplexed that she might bring along unwanted and uninvited others, I decide it's best not to get upset. To get upset would be like getting upset that he's attached to her arms. I sense that to treat these companions nicely would be a thing that she would greatly appreciate, a sort of test.

I offer the little people a drink and they take it gladly and thank me politely with their squeaky comical voices that would have made me laugh out loud were I not sensitive to the aforementioned affinity. I ask them if they would like to watch the Wizard of Oz on my home movie screen, the house of my dreams being such an opulent place, so different from the dingy dirty tiny apartment in which I lived. Their squeaky little voices

are so reminiscent of the munchkins it brings the Wizard of Oz to mind. The little people go into the next room, from which shortly comes the lilting strains of
"Over the Rainbow."

The book sits on a book pedestal placed just outside the radius of furious vegetable chopping. A small spotlight shines on it. Finally, after many subtle and some not so subtle attempts to direct her attention to the book and away from the direction in which the little people have gone, she takes notice. She removes the book from the pedestal and begins to read. She comments, picking through the various piles of chopped celery, carrots, lettuce, tomatoes mushrooms and broccoli for little snacks that she would like to take the book home and read it. I say in my most magnanimous way that the book, of course, is hers.

She is so pleased with the gift that she comes around the counter and finishes making the meal that would never have been made were it not for her. She, I and her companion little people have a very good time the rest of the evening, except the little people won't eat vegetables, which causes Ariel no small amount of consternation and opens a rift of discord in their previously perfectly harmonious affinity.

The evening ends with the four of us sitting on the sofa aligned with the westward facing window that overlooks the vast expanse of my emerald green lawn that slopes gently down to the ocean. There, the sun sets over the mast of my lightly bobbing sailboat, that lays serenely moored in the center of my small harbor. It is moored, yet it's sleek lines and polished teak give the impression it is speeding away to a distant paradise at the far corner of the world. If such a place exists it can only be if Ariel is there.

The real view from my own kitchen window is not nearly so idyllic. It is of a truck junkyard behind a rusting fence across an oil spotted stretch of asphalt that had served as our "fields of Eton" when I and my contemporary project co-habitués believed touch football was the best game in the world. The rotting hulks of the trucks float on a sea of poisoned, oil impregnated, and impacted dirt. It would take a fearsome wind indeed to speed these halfway disassembled ferric-oxide monsters away to paradise. I have never seen a place like the place I see in my dream, it is constructed wholly from my imagination and from pictures I'd seen in the architectural digests my mother buys on occasion in the hopes of sparking a desire in me to be the architect she wants me to be. I have never seen a real sailboat up close, I've only ever seen sailboats in advertisements for Newport cigarettes. Judging from those ads; sailing and smoking go hand in hand. It's hard to ignore the admiring expression of the sailor's female companion looks at her hero/sailor with as he maintains a firm and steady hand on the till and firmly clenches an as yet un-lit Newport between his

169

smiling white teeth. and I will be the firm handed sailor who takes her.

This dream springs from the same place in my imagination as the happy homes I compulsively drew on the wall over my bed as a child. These pictures form a pastoral mural. These picture were the genesis of my mother's belief that I wanted to be an architect. When really these murals were driven by the primitive urge to create a happy home by the force and will of my imagination. If I could just draw the perfect happy home, perhaps it could live in one. Perhaps my drawings served for me the same purpose as the pictures of food that lined the walls of Egyptian tombs, painted there to nourish the spirits of those who'd passed into the other world.

The wall above my bed is still covered with these tableaux. In it I can't see the happy homes I thought I had drawn as a boy. Instead I see the scribblings of a mad and untalented Picasso who could not realize his work as the home in which I live is as chaotic and unhappy as the pictures on my wall.

As pleasant as my fantasies are, they can be nothing compared to real life, so I set my mind on delivering the book to Ariel personally. I write an inscription at the front, unwittingly committing a terrible act of vandalism and diminishing the books value in the process, although I optimistically believed I was enhancing its value in the eyes of the only person whose opinion on the subject could matter to me. I wrote:

To Ariel Lirilinghi: who dances in my dreams.

I believe this poetically encapsulates her dominance in the kingdom of my psyche. She will see and appreciate this even if it is kind of corny. She does dance (and do other things) in my dreams, and when it comes to her, there is no romantic notion too corny for me to think it isn't beautiful, as well.

There is a fight club in Brighton. This fight club is a vibrant ongoing gambling enterprise run by a person who fancies himself the local crime boss. He goes by the nom-de-guerre of Crazy Pete. By all accounts, Crazy Pete fit the name and the name fit him. Word was that it was Crazy Pete who threw the Molotov cocktail through Jeremy Telford's window, incinerating Jeremy's crippled grandmother and her cat, which was sitting in her lap when the bomb went off. Granny and the cat were instantly welded together for all eternity, what was left of both buried in the same coffin. Through a horrid mistake (or maybe granny wanted it that way), the cat is mentioned above granny on the headstone.

171

Crazy Pete, of course, had an alibi and witnesses to back him up and the case was never solved, and really never even seriously investigated, the local gendarmerie having, if you'll pardon the pun, bigger fish to fry. Jeremy, who couldn't fathom why anyone would want to kill his poor grandma, went way off the deep end, killing himself in a stolen car that became very unstable at very high speed. So unstable that it apparently rolled over many, many times before sliding on the roof for almost one hundred and fifty feet, then catching fire and sending poor, clueless, unconscious (everybody hoped) Jeremy to the same hell as granny. Everyone said Jeremy wasn't a bad kid, just not a very good driver.

In the crazy world and crazy mind of Crazy Pete, it wasn't such a bad thing to be seen as so inexplicably and illogically dangerous. He would neither confirm nor deny the rumors about Jeremy's gran, but let his various interlocutors come to the conclusion to which he would lead them, depending on just how crazy he felt on any particular day and whether said interlocutors were connected in any way to law enforcement.

Crazy Pete ran his criminal empire, such as it was, from the apartment two floors directly above ours. He seemed to like me because I would say good morning to him or ask him how he was doing, and I didn't appear to be afraid of him. Crazy Pete was so crazy that although he spent a large percentage of his waking hours instilling fear into people, he hated to see it reflected back at him, much like any wild animal that senses fear. I wasn't afraid of him because near as I could tell, I had no reason to be. I wasn't even really on his radar and was, in my innocence, largely incapable of comprehending someone as irrationally violent as Crazy Pete. I should understand irrational violence by now, my brother and father could be as violent as Crazy Pete. Either could, with just a touch of ambition, fill Crazy Pete's shoes. I willfully retain my innocence despite their best efforts to knock it out of me.

Anyway, I'd never seen that reputedly dreadful look of acknowledgment—that is, until it was focused on me one day. It is a warm end of March day. March is going out like the proverbial lamb. I'm hitting golf balls in the playground across Faneuil Street, using my trusty Bobby Jones model, hickory-shafted, dimple-faced five iron. I could say it is my favorite club and I wouldn't be lying. That it is the only club I own is also the truth. The fact that it is in my possession is my only claim to ownership because try as I might, I can't remember where it came from, yet I knew it wasn't me who'd stolen it. However, despite the signature of the greatest golfer ever, there was no other provenance, so I claimed the mashie as my own through that marvelous legal concept of adverse possession. Since I had nine-tenths of the law on my side, I felt quite comfortable laying claim to this magic golfing wand. You see, it really is a magic wand.

I knew nothing of golf and had never swung another club, but put that Bobby Jones model, hickory-shafted mallet in my mitts and I was as elegant as Hagen, as accurate as Hogan and as graceful as the man Jones himself.

I am so busy swinging and marveling at the beautiful arc of the white balls as they land—one by one, one hundred fifty yards away within a ten-foot circle—that I'm startled when Crazy Pete comes up behind me unannounced and says more loudly than necessary, "not bad." It shatters my reverie as the last ball I'd hit reaches its apogee and plummets towards the small circle of his brothers.

"Thanks."

Crazy Pete reaches out and grabs the club from my hands. I resist mildly for a moment. I don't know if Crazy Pete even notices my resistance, he wrests the club from me rather easily.

He swings wildly, ball after ball spraying left and right, his shiny, black boots with the pointy toes and the thick heel giving poor footing for his violent swings, the kind of violent swings that are so effective in other aspects of his life and are so ineffective here. Here, he has to conform himself to a set of demands that he'd have difficulty understanding if I tried to explain. Hitting a golf ball requires meditative calmness, and most importantly to me, an inner eye. This inner eye allows me, when I choose, to

174

close my eyes and hit the ball without looking. I see the club head meet the ball in my mind and the next thing I know I see it sailing in that graceful high arc.

I wasn't going to bother to explain this to Pete, so he continues to swing wildly, more wildly as his frustration mounts. Most of the balls would be very difficult to find and some, those that fall among the poison ivy, are irretrievable. All the hours spent hunting these balls going to waste. I know better than to object though, so I hold my tongue. Sweating profusely both from the action and his humiliation, Pete takes a break.

"How am I doing?"

This is it, this is the moment. If I tell him he is doing good, he will get mad, especially since it is obvious he isn't nearly as good as I am. If I say he is doing poorly, he might get mad, I don't know for sure. If I say he is doing okay, he will think it is a cop out and that I'm a pussy.

I choose to go all the way in. I choose wrongly.

"Crazy Pete, you suck."

Crazy Pete gets very angry. I have crossed the line on two counts. First, I have called him crazy. Nobody actually calls Crazy Pete crazy to his face. I'm too naive to realize this. I've also told him he sucks, which has the effect of making me wish I had said almost anything else because he wouldn't have become angry and maybe wouldn't have done what he did next.

You see, I carried the book with me at all times. I did this for the simple reason that I didn't want my brother to see it. My brother isn't the smartest, but there are two things he does well. One of the things he can do is spot things of value. He has an innate sense of the worth of things. There is no doubt he would try to sell the book, he being a great proponent of the legal theory of adverse possession himself. This is a thing he sometimes carries to an extreme.

For example, if you have a Twinkie or a Suzy Q and my brother wants it, he will take it, he holds the firm belief that his desire imparts ownership. I've seen him knock people senseless and take the cake from their hands just as they are about to bite it. This leads me to the other thing my brother is good at—perpetrating violence. I wonder sometimes if we really come from the same family, but the physical resemblance is undeniable and I wish sometimes I was more like him.

Crazy Pete doesn't hit me. He just pushes me around a little. He is trying to provoke me into defending myself. If I did that, all bets were off. He is shorter than me, but very strong, and built like a middleweight fighter. Pete has a broad, flat nose and piggy little eyes. Under his nose, he wears a mustache of sorts, really just the intimation of a mustache. I marvel at tough guy Pete's inability to grow a mustache. While he is pushing me around, the Beatles' song "Piggies" is going through my head. It helps calm me down.

Don't think I'm not afraid, I'm scared to death. I can see how dangerous Pete is right in his beady, little-piggy, scary eyes. He pushes me again, this time so hard I spin around. He grabs me around my neck and starts to choke me with his right arm. He puts a switchblade to my cheek with the other hand, drawing blood. Pete likes to think of himself an ambidextrous killer. It doesn't seem like he is kidding.

"Now what have you got that you can buy your way out of this. I already have your golf club; I'll take it if I want to. Even though golf is obviously a game for pussies."

"I have something," I manage to say.

Pete let me go. He put away the switchblade and retrieved the golf club from the ground at his feet.

"Give it to me or we'll see if I'm any better at hitting your head."

I take the book out of my pants at the small of my back and hand it to Pete.

"A book?" Pete is obviously disappointed. He turns the book over, studying it. I see a dim flash of inspiration in his scary eyes. "Oh my god, this is the book! You stole this book from Harvard didn't you? You fucking little crook. This book has made the news you fucking scrawny little bastard." He eyes me with a new respect. I was shocked, I hadn't been paying any attention to the news. I'd had no idea it was so valuable it would make the news. Now I would have to wait for the hue and cry to die down before I could give it to her, assuming Pete gives it back to me. No such luck.

"I'll tell you what," Pete says, as he throws my golf club over my shoulder as far as he can. I mark where it lands so I can pick it up later. "Come to the fight club Saturday night, I'll give you one chance to win the book back. You're a tough guy, right? You put a kid in a coma once, right?" Pete walks away

"Be there or else. There's no telling what might come through your window," he walks away, waving the book over his head, chuckling to himself.

I am upset with myself for having been such a coward as to have given him the book. I walk over and pick up the golf club, thinking maybe hitting the balls will calm me down. It always does. I address a ball and swing, clang off the toe into the poison Ivy. I try another, a pull hook. I don't remember ever hitting a pull hook before. I line up another, still my turmoil and activate my inner eye, closing my real eyes. I miss completely. Crazy Pete has sucked all the magic out of my magic wand.

I break its hickory shaft over my knee, drop it to the ground and walk away. I have swung a golf club for the last time.

Ariel wanders into the subterranean labyrinth at the bottom of the high school. She is in her school uniform and she carries her normal load of books. Her skirt is short and tight; it must have shrunk in the wash. She couldn't remember putting it through the drier, but she must have. Her mother had always told her to never put the skirt in the drier. The hem has risen so high that her legs exit the skirt just an inch below the V of her crotch. It feels like she's had to wrap herself in a hand towel after a shower because no bath towels are available. Her skirt is insufficient for the job of maintaining her modesty. She is both petrified and excited by the prospect of eyes probing her and watching her with barely contained desire. She flushes at the memory of her skirt riding up past her rump while she sat in class. She noticed all the boys got erections while staring at her naked thighs. She flushes with excitement at the thought of what it might feel like to have one of the boys stick his erection inside her and move it in and out. She ponders which of the boys she would let do this, mentally narrowing her list and surprising herself that the list is as long as it is. These thoughts fill her with a vaporous, queasy excitement that implodes into her nether regions. She observes that perhaps the reason why girls aren't supposed to wear such short skirts isn't just because it gives the boys erections, but to wear such a short skirt also seems to engender as many naughty thoughts and as much excitement in the wearer. She's surprised her mother let her leave the house with the hem of her skirt so high, or that the nuns haven't sent her home because the skirt hugs her bottom so tightly.

She sees Gary the janitor. Gary is always friendly. She says hello to him as she's done a thousand times. She'd expected he would say hello back to her as he had always done each of those thousand times. She takes a few steps before she realizes he's made no response. Things are very different down here. She turns to look at him. He in turn is looking at her. His eyes are hollow, not empty of emotion or intelligence, but empty as in no eyes occupy the space of his eye sockets. His face is set in stone. A wave of fear passes through her, she sees his face is not completely empty. She looks straight through his hollow eyes to see his all-consuming deviant janitorial desires. She sees through him to the things he wants to do to her with a plumbers helper and a drain snake. The worst part is that these things don't produce in her the appropriate revulsion. Instead they excite passion as well as terror. She runs ahead to the next corner uncertain if it's the terror or the passion that is most frightening. She reaches an intersection and turns the corner. She goes back to peek around to make sure he isn't following. He has disappeared, gone away to perform his deviant janitorial duties elsewhere. She leans against the wall, breathing hard in relief. She pushes her heels out and leans her shoulders against the wall so she can relieve some of the weight of the heavy pile of books she carries by leaning them against her stomach and give her weary arms a little rest. It is a burden to be so smart and to have others raise such high expectations for you. A poster hangs on the opposite wall. It's one of those posters that exhorts students onward. It says in large red letters; *You can do better!* I don't know if I can she thinks.

She walks on a little further, directionless, unable to orient herself to those places in the building above. She's never been down here and it seems like the building above was built according to an entirely different set of plans.

She bumps into Melanie Hawthorne at the next intersection. You may remember Melanie as the shy, plump girl who froze with Ariel's note in her hand many years ago. She has since moved well beyond plump.

"I'm sorry, please excuse me," Ariel says politely if somewhat automatically.

"Hey, why don't you watch where you're going-skinny little bitch. You don't own this corridor. I have as much right to be here as you do. Who do you think you are?" Melanie is so damaged she sees everything as an insult, even the most innocent accidental bumping. She stands with fleshy fists pushed into fleshy hips. She thrusts her fleshy elbows outwards,

181

making herself nearly as wide as the narrow hallway, purposefully impeding Ariel's progress. The silly school uniform that Ariel makes look sexy, especially with the shortened skirt does nothing for Melanie. She is a lumpy, earthen mound in a high-school girl's uniform.

Ariel apologizes and asks if she may pass.

"You look like you could use a few cupcakes, you skinny little bitch. I make the world's most delicious cupcakes, you know," Melanie says.

"I'm sure you do," Ariel says, completely confused by this sudden turn.

"Better than you could ever make, you skinny little...I promised myself I wouldn't get mad if I ever saw you again."

"Me, why would you be mad at me?"

"You once told me I was too fat to make cupcakes!"

"I couldn't have said such a thing. Please, you are remembering it wrongly."

"Now you're calling me a liar."

"No, I never would." Melanie is scary and Ariel is frightened that she will fall on top of her and suffocate her. "It's just...I always try to be nice to everyone. Plus, it doesn't make any sense. 'Never accept a cupcake from a skinny person,' I

182

always say." Her little joke crashes against Melanie's humorless, imposing edifice.

"Now you're calling me a fatso!"

"No...I... don't know what to say, you take everything I say the wrong way."

"Now you're calling me stupid, too, you're unbelievable. We've been talking for thirty seconds and you've already called me a fat stupid liar. You're the cruelest person I'll ever meet."

"Melanie, I never called you those things."

"So now, what am I deaf, too? Have you run out of things to call me?" Melanie begins to sob uncontrollably.

Ariel tries to muster some sympathy for Melanie, but Melanie has made herself so unsympathetic, it proves impossible. Ariel decides to go in the direction from whither she's come as fast as she can. She is unwilling to wiggle her way by Melanie, fearful that should she try, Melanie will crush her against the wall and force cupcakes down her throat. Besides, she's so disoriented one way seems as good as another.

She goes past the turning (at least she thinks so) where she'd seen Gary. She doesn't want to risk encountering him again so she continues down the dimly lit corridor, hoping to find a staircase that leads upwards and wishing fervently to avoid his covetous stare and another glimpse into the wasteland of his psycho-sexual landscape.

This corridor seems, however, to slant downwards. There is a figure in the distance, a distance greater than any she would have believed could be encompassed by the building. The figure is a woman standing against the wall. She is wearing bright red stiletto heels, black silk stockings, a green silk dress and a floppy summer sun hat. The dress and the hat are vaguely familiar and this familiarity scares her. The woman has one foot raised against the wall like a streetwalker waiting for a trick. All the pressure on the tiny tip of her other heel is breaking the tile beneath her feet. Maddeningly, her face is entirely in dark shadow.

"Sssssssooooo, Ariel Lirilinghi what bringsssss you down here into my kingdom?" There is no mistaking the sibilance—it is Lance Boyle. She remembers he doesn't stutter when dressed as a woman.

"What do you mean, your kingdom, Lance?"

"I reign down here. I know you know what that meansssssss. You're a sssssmart girl,"

He makes it sound like the worst insult. The pure blackness under the hat is making her skin crawl.

"Lance, you wouldn't know how to get out of here would you?" She asks, trying to look the blackness in the eyes.

"Well, sweetie, there's only one way out of here." Her knees begin to shake as she is gripped by an unreasoning fear "Before you go sweetie, I have a little bone to pick with you."

A whimpered "no" is all she can manage. Lance takes a draw on his cigarette mounted in the end of a long mother-of-pearl inlaid cigarette holder. Ariel feels the heat from the glowing ash on the lit end. A cloud of acrid, cloying smoke emanates from the black void beneath the hat, enshrouding her head and making her cough.

"Yes, you know, you laughed at me every day from fourth grade through eighth grade."

"I would hope you wouldn't hold a grudge for so long."

"How long should I hold a grudge?" He snaps. "Besides, did I say I held a grudge?"

"I'm glad to hear you don't hold a grudge. It was a long time ago."

"Well, I didn't ssssay I didn't hold a grudge, I've been known to hold a grudge FOREVER". She is stunned into fear by his surprisingly fearsome yell. Her arms, legs, lips, knees, nostrils, eyelids, and her little tummy are all a tremble. She trembles so uncontrollably she fears she may fly apart. Lance recovers his previous sinister equanimity. "It may feel like pleasant nostalgia to you, but to me it packs the same sting as if

185

it happened (sssssssigh) today. I never forget." A thick cloud of acrid smoke swirls out of the blackness.

The smoke makes her dizzy. "Please Lance, I try to be nice to everyone. I'm not a mean person."

"So you say. I have a different view. Sometimes, I think you are the cruelest person I'll ever meet. Although I must admit you're very sweet all a quiver like this. Nice ssskirt by the way." He lifts the hem with the mouth end of his cigarette holder. She is helpless to stop him because her hands are filled with the heavy books. He contemplates her helpless near nakedness. She senses his amusement. "Nice undiesssss too; all white and pure just like you huh?"

"Lance, I've changed, I've suffered, I'm really sorry. Please forgive me if I ever hurt you."

"Oh sweetie, that's all you had to sssssay. Now kissssssssssss my hand." Lance holds out his hand, bent downwards at the wrist. Before she can stop herself, Ariel does just that. His hand tastes like cherry lifesavers, her favorite.

"Lance, can you help me get out of here?" She asks in a quavering voice.

"Sssssssure sssssweetie, jussssssst keep going the way you were." Lance points down the hallway and Ariel swears she sees his eyes flash orange, like a furnace door opening and closing very quickly in the depths of the swirling smoke and blackness beneath the hat. Her trembling worsens, has she lost her mind or are Lance Boyle and Satan one and the same?

"Thanks Lance." She heads further down the tilted corridor. The slope steepens with each step until it seems she's walking upside down. She sees a man hunched over. He is moving heavy bags from one pile to another. She comes up behind him.

"Excuse me, sir" she says.

"Tell someone who wants to hear it." He says

"I'm sorry sir, what did you say?" he keeps moving the heavy trash bags from one pile to another. The pile he moves the bags from gets no smaller and the pile he moves them to gets no bigger.

"I said; what's the password sweetheart?" An iron ring tightens around her heart. All of a sudden the man is not moving bags, but shoveling what could be snow from one never shrinking pile into one that never grows, he works diligently. He stands to stretch his back but doesn't turn to face her. "Phew, I think I'll be doing this forever."

All of a sudden she is desperate to see his face. She grabs him, but he resists turning. she has to put her books down. He is too strong for her to turn. She grabs him by the coat and with a mighty heave she turns him. She looks into his face. His eyes look everywhere but at her, his nose is purple and smashed into his face. He speaks; his voice un-muffled by the rough tape that covers his mouth.

"Say goodbye trash man!" He screams, while lifting his shovel overhead to strike her. She turns and races up the steep slope until she is running right side up. The monster swinging the shovel chases her. She runs by Lance who blows a cloud of smoke that gathers around her head and runs with her, making running difficult, but she dares not slow down.

"Leaving sssssssssoooo sssssssssooooon ssssssweetie." Lance yells after her.

She sheds the cloud of smoke and the monster seems to have stopped chasing, but she dares not slow her pace. She runs as fast as she ever has. Her greatly elongated stride causes the snug fitting skirt to ride up her hips with every step. Soon the hem has ridden up past the V of her crotch. She can't hold her skirt down or stop to adjust it because of the heavy load of books is back in her hands. She must use both hands to hold them and is fearful of shortening her stride for fear of slowing her pace and being caught by the monster. She feels the weight of being smarter than everybody else. She keeps running Her skirt has turned itself upside down revealing her pristine white underpants and the swath of skin between the elastic waistband of her underpants and the top, which is now the bottom of her skirt. She feels like her underpants are ever so slowly creeping downwards, and if she doesn't find a way out of this cursed basement soon she will be naked from the waist down. She is being chased by Gary the lecherous janitor who keeps insisting she slow down so he can empty her trash and sweep out her basement. To her surprise Melanie appears beside her; she is perplexed that Melanie can run as fast as she can.

"You think you're so smart because you can carry a bunch of books and give the boys a boner by showing them your slutty little underpants at the same time. You're not so smart, You aren't even smart enough to keep your underwear up and I bet you don't know how to make cupcakes." It's true, her underwear has slipped down over her hips and rolled themselves up below her vagina, fully revealing her rear end to lecherous Gary who seems to be gaining; her stride shortened by the rolled up underpants which seem content at least to fall no further. Gary stretches out his hand to touch her. speed stretching out to try and touch her bum. She exerts herself to try and gain speed. Melanie runs beside her with great thundering ease, commenting desultorily on Ariel's lack of skill when it comes to making cupcakes even though she is a little cupcake eager to get cream-filled by boys with fleshy-rigid protuberant cream injectors. Ariel would never have guessed that Melanie could have used protuberant correctly in a sentence.

The chase is joined by a disembodied pair of simian hands that pull and tug at her underpants. On the edge of despair, she finds herself at the bottom of a steep stairwell. She climbs the stairs at a run. Lance, Melanie, Gary and the Monster stay at the bottom. Melanie throws cupcakes up at her that thankfully fall short. Gary keeps yelling for her to come back down so he can polish her bum. Lance says "Sssssseeee you sssssssoooon Ssssssweetie. A cloud of acrid smoke chases her up the stairs The cloud has a smashed nose, a taped mouth, and eyes that roll around like a vortex of water going down the drain. The books she carries are an onerous burden that she can't shed no matter how many times she drops them. Her feet hurt, for her shoes are not for running. The disembodied hairy knuckled hands and fingers shred her underpants like tissue and invade her private spaces.

There is a door at the top of the stairs. The door is thrown violently open. Sister Mary stands in the doorway and berates her very sternly for using Mr. Delaney's hands to masturbate with. She piles more books onto Ariel's already excessively burdensome load, chiding her as she does to get her mind out of the gutter. Ariel squeezes past Sister Mary and runs down a long corridor to another door. This door is locked. She can't figure out the puzzle of locks and is very tired from her long and heavily burdened running. She lies down and sleeps beneath the unopened door.

Kathleen finds Ariel lying asleep in the little mudroom behind the kitchen. She lay on her left side facing away from Kathleen. Her right leg is draw up toward her chest and the left is straight. She is naked except for the white cotton t-shirt she'd gone to bed in. Kathleen had picked up the pajama bottoms and underpants Ariel shed on her way down here. She takes note of Ariel's near perfect body. To Kathleen, Ariel seems perfectly situated between lithesome girlhood and sultry womanhood, in the most perilous stage of this transition, her beauty perhaps at or near its apex. Her beauty undoubtedly outstripping her ability to deal with the desires both noble and salacious such beauty generates in the hearts of well-meaning gallants and malicious satyrs alike who will accost her at every turning and who will be difficult to tell apart. She is like a fawn caught in the open, alone in iron lion land. Kathleen's heart aches for her, she knows her daughter's mind isn't quite right as evinced by this somnambulist adventure. Ariel's thick, raven-black hair splays out around her head like the train of a demon's bridal gown, like the corona from a dark star, like the crown of a dark princess. Although It was Enzo who most often called Ariel his dark princess it was Kathleen who bestowed the name.

Kathleen sits next to and gently strokes her daughter's head. She sighs, at her naked beauty. There is no denying she's grown into a real beauty, exotic, almost alien. Especially so in this heart-stabbing, vulnerable pose. *If her mind is marked her body surely isn't.* She feels the pain of wounds yet to come. *For one such as you; beauty can only ever be a mixed blessing.*

"Poor thing." She says lovingly, putting her voice to her thoughts, letting the lilt of her girlhood speak. "You've suffered so much. I'm heartily sorry for it all. I know about nightmares and from the looks of things yours must be fierce indeed. It's true you were an accident, but you're the most beautiful accident there ever was. We're in this together, we'll make it through no matter what. You'll see. I know how it is to be frightened and feel alone. We'll get through this." She rouses Ariel enough to get her back up the stairs and into her own bed. She lays down with her until she sleeps.

12. Fight and Aftermath

Some of the concrete floor is covered with a rubber mat that had at one time in its existence been white. Now it has be-come decidedly off-white, turned so by the dust of years being ground into it by the countless steps of the kids who have fought here. The mat is also stained here and there with the blood of those who'd been vanquished. There are congealed puddles of mucus, indelibly marking the spot where the loser had had the snot beat out of him or her, this fight club having no particular regard for the gender of its participants. Until this very moment I had believed the expression 'he got the snot beat out of him' to

192

be just that, a colorful expression. Strange how heightened one's senses become at moments like this, enabling me not only to notice a thing so small, but to realize its meaning in a flash

I suppose some came here willingly to fight and prove themselves, and only when they had left their blood on the mat could they accept their defeat with some measure of equanimity. I, on the other hand, was here unwillingly and would find defeat to be a very bitter pill to swallow.

Tonight, there are three people in this dingy basement room. The room smells of the musty undertones of mold and dead rats, smells so strong they mask the smell of sweat and fear that would have, by themselves been enough to cause a re-action in more sensitive souls. However, the smells of mold and dead rat, sweat and fear are like traces of clove or cinnamon found in a fine wine, things that require swirl time on the soft pal-let to be detected. All these other smells strong as they would otherwise be, add a distinctness to but pale when compared against the overarching, eye-stinging, retch-inducing reek of stale urine that predominates.

In the center of this mat stands Crazy Pete and his fighting champion, my classmate, Coleman Curran. I had, for most of my life, been able to maintain a distance from Coleman. For his part, he seemed mostly disinterested in closing that distance and allowed me to give him the wide berth he required. Coleman is dressed in a baggy gray sweatshirt, fighting shorts and fighting boots. It's hard for me to convey the impression I have when I take in those boots. I know immediately that Coleman hasn't spent however long it would take to lace those boots for no reason. Also, to be completely honest, he appears like a man while I, though as tall or taller, still look like a boy.

He is all business, he is ready.

I, on the other hand, am not ready. If I had a few months' time, perhaps I could be ready, but I'd optimistically wandered into the lion's den and I couldn't feel god on my side. The lions seemed pretty confident. My optimism was rapidly waning.

I was dressed in my trusty Keds, jeans and a t-shirt that said Don't be a Doink!

Pete reads my t-shirt. I bought and wore this t-shirt be-cause the absurdity of it amused me.

"Don't be a doink, good advice. Why can't you take your own advice?" He says. I wish I had worn any other t-shirt. He holds my book in his hand. It seems so incongruous here.

"Is this Ariel your girlfriend motherfucker?" He doesn't even attempt her last name, gone is his new found respect for my daring. I don't answer but I learn what it means to hear a name taken in vain. "Coleman has promised me that he may not dance in your dreams, but he will gladly dance on your head." They both find this uproarious. "Then he is going to give your

194

book to this Ariel chick and do what Coleman? What did you say you were going to do to her?"

"I'm going to fuck the shit out of her." They both laugh at this, too.

"Coleman, you're a hopeless romantic," I say. This only makes them angrier. They know I'm funnier than they are and if we were here to trade witticisms, I'd have a puncher's chance.

Coleman's gaze returns to a fixed murderous stare. An array of sweat beads stands out on his forehead, which is an-other portent. He had been warming up for this encounter. I should have been flattered, I suppose, that he deigned to, and wasn't taking me completely for granted. He shakes his head and sends the beads of sweat outward, like a large dog after a swim—or more appropriately, like the great bull, el libertador de la muerte (the bringer of death) before his deadly charge. I play the part of the not-so-great toreador El scared witless.

"I'm surprised you came. I'll give you that much," says Pete. "I figured for sure you'd pussy out." Coleman smiles a mocking, condescending half smile. He conveys without words that I'm moments from my demise and my demise will be pretty funny.

"I want my book back." I shout.

"No need to shout all you have to do is beat Coleman and you can have it back."

Coleman's rolls his eyes and shakes his head, his hands and feet as Ariel had done before she danced. I find myself hoping he's not as good a fighter as she is a dancer, despite his reputation.

If there were a time to beg for mercy, now was it. I knew there would be none, Pete and Coleman were deadly serious and I was in a lot of trouble, much more than I bargained for. In-stead I asked "What are the rules?"

Pete and Coleman laugh their mirthless, sinister laughs. Excluded from their private joke now, I do feel like a doink, which I know now means a hapless fellow who runs headlong where angels fear to tread.

"There is only one rule. The winner wins! That's it, so be sure to follow the rules," says Pete, his voice again dripping with sarcasm. "Now fight!"

Coleman is a trained mastiff let off the leash. I have no chance to voice an objection. I was going to say 'wait' but Cole-man is used to this and has no qualms. I get off one hard punch right to his nose, a much harder punch than the punch that had supposedly put Devlin Flynn in a coma.

It had no deterrent affect at all. Coleman is on me. Before I know it, I have lost contact with the floor. He lifts me up and slams me down on the mat like a rag doll while simultaneously landing full force on top of me. The last sound I hear is the explosion of pain in my head (yes, it made a sound) as the large bone in my upper arm snaps in half. Then my lights go out.

I come to, very much in pain and soaked in urine. My first thought is fuck; I can't believe I pissed myself. I could feel the flame of humiliation begin to burn. Then I realize, to my horror, that I haven't pissed myself at all. The flame of humiliation becomes a fireball of rage, disgust, and shame. Now I know whose urine accounts for the stench; at least I'm not the only one who's been subjected to this humiliation. This offers no consolation. I remember the gross lunger he'd spit at Devlin Flynn. He's graduated to more sophisticated methods of signifying his victory.

I wonder if I should stay in this dank smelly room and never leave. Me and my friends, the dead rats. I would have, except I can't stand it, it stings and it burns. Whether it's physical or psychological doesn't matter, it burns like acid. I have to wash it off and hope the shame will wash off with it. I struggle to my feet, woozy from the concussion and wondering what month it is. Why would anyone want to do this to me? Everybody loves me.

It wasn't true, not everybody loves me, especially the girl for whom I've, at least in my mind, undergone this ordeal. I wanted to believe I was lovable even if I knew there were things that mitigated against me; not the least of which were being defeated, humiliated, broken and urine soaked in a dingy project basement.

I assess my situation as best I can, considering the concussion induced confusion in my thinking. If my arm hadn't taken most of the force of Coleman's body slam the injury to my head would have been much worse than just a concussion. My senses begin their recovery from the shock. I have a funny taste in my mouth. I realize the import of this funny "taste". The vomit inducing reek of the room coupled with the funny taste do just that, I go back down on my knees and suffer an episode of violent uncontrollable retching. Pain explodes in my head and arm with each violent retch.

"Fucking barbarians," I whisper as I cry. I cry myself out, I can't help it, boyhood resolutions to be tough are meaningless here. Coleman has taken my book and my pride. I will get him back somehow. I just don't know how yet and no inspiration is arising. I feel as impotent as I've ever felt. It takes all my strength to stand and leave that room.

The basement in which the 'fight' occurred is no more than a few hundred feet from my apartment, the building I live in being part of the same building where the fight club is, distinguishable as separate because they have separate entrances, though not separate structures. I have to go outside to get to my building.

I stagger up the mold-encrusted stairwell and along the wall of the building. If there is anything fortunate that has come of this, it is that my right arm is broken. Since the building is on my left, I'm able to put my weight on it. I'm having some trouble standing. The pain is so intense, it's sapping my strength and my will. I have broken bones before but this is a magnitude of pain I have never experienced.

Nobody came to help me. I had to make this traverse alone. Anyone who saw me must have been scared off from helping by the urine soaking me. I had become an untouchable. I wasn't conscious of anyone attempting to help me, maybe someone did, maybe they didn't, my memory of that short but arduous journey is hazy. All I was aware of was the next step I needed to take. I make it to my apartment door, which is locked. My mother is in the habit of locking us out when she needs some peace and quiet. This is one of those times. This means that she is in the apartment and would have to answer the door. I have no explanation ready as to why I'm covered in urine from head to knees.

I don't care.

She relents and opens the door after long minutes of my knocking as the only response to her repeated jibes of "go away, little girl." She must have thought I was my sister, Mary, who she taunts relentlessly and quite gleefully over not belonging here. I push past her to the bathroom, dragging my 'Don't be a Doink' tee shirt over my head, with my left hand, I put it in the clothes hamper. My mother, meanwhile, had followed me into the bathroom, naturally curious about why her son was in obvious, urine-soaked pain and firing a series of questions in an effort to ascertain the cause. I am incapable of carrying on a conversation. I am consumed by the need to clean myself. I strip my jeans away by undoing the buckle and unzipping, then while supporting myself on the sink, dragging one leg at a time out of the pants by stepping on the hem and then shaking them off when they were low enough on my legs to do so. It was a Herculean task to strip myself out of the pants which seemed to want to cling to me.

I don't remember but I tell my mother what happened in a very confused manner. She is the only one I ever could tell. I strip off my underpants and socks and step into the hot shower so I can go to the hospital without being covered in urine. I wash myself as best I can, including lifting the broken arm to make sure I get under my armpit. This sends a great jolt of pain into my head. I hear the ends of the fractured bone grinding against each other.

My mother drives me to St E's in her little Ford Falcon station wagon, with the fake wood panels on the sides and the shot shock absorbers. It is nearly as painful a journey as my traverse from the basement. Again I violate my old pledge about never shedding another tear as the world becomes an anxious hell, waiting for the inevitable next bump and the accompanying grinding and stabbing—and yes, crying, even though I try not to.

At the hospital, they take a number of x-rays, posing me in the most painful positions possible. I see the fracture, the humerus bone, my humerus bone sheared and displaced. The doc-tor says I was fortunate that it didn't come through the skin.

"I can't begin to tell you how fortunate I feel," I say sarcastically.

"Well, I can see that fracturing your humerus has made you no less humorous." He laughs at his own joke. I look on in total amazement as my doctor literally chortles. I had never seen anyone chortle before and now I know what it looks like.

"Doctor, I can just tell by your uncontrolled chortling that you've been waiting all your life to say that."

"I've spoken with your mother; you've been viciously as-saulted. Retaining your sense of humor speaks well in terms of prognosis. Laughter is the best medicine."

"Doctor, do you see me laughing, if you'll forgive me you're the only one laughing here. You could prescribe some-thing a little stronger, couldn't you? To be honest, I don't feel right. Everything seems......strange."

"You mean, your arm?'"

"Yeah that, but not just that." He took out a prescription pad and wrote a prescription for a narcotic called Darvon for the pain and one for Valium if I feel too...strange. He is actually a real nice guy. Meeting someone nice is a help. He hands the pre-scriptions to my mother. He then cinches me into a canvas sling that wraps around me and pins my arm to my body. I actually feel a little better. "You'll recover." He says firmly.

Three days later, as I walk up the alleyway toward my apartment, floating under the influence of the Darvon, I hear someone from behind say, "Hey toilet mouth."

I cringe. It is Crazy Pete.

"Hey toilet mouth, wait up."

I stop and turn to face him, there is no point in pretending he isn't talking to me.

"Hey toilet mouth," he smiles. He loves his clever new name for me and is going to say it every chance he gets.

I seethe with impotent murderous rage, I have no knife to plunge into his throat, silencing his ability to say anything never mind the obscene (as I find It) comic (as he finds it) nickname he has bestowed upon me. I can't mask that I'm seething.

"Toilet mouth, you look a little upset."

"My name's not toilet mouth," I say between clenched teeth.

"Yes, it is."

He punches me lightly, but not too lightly, right in the spot of the fracture in my upper arm. It hurts almost as much as if he had kicked me in the balls with none of the work.

"Wow, I can see that hurts."

His face, however, betrays no sympathy, only amusement, "Now what's your name."

"It's Jax!"

"You know, toilet mouth, you never should have called me Crazy Pete. That's not my name and Jax is not your name, your name is toilet mouth."

He punches me again in the shoulder, a little harder.   "Now, what's your name?"

I look into his piggy, psycho eyes, knowing that he will punch my arm off unless I succumb. I quickly weigh whether it was to my advantage to have Crazy Pete call me toilet mouth for the rest of my life (or until I can silence him) and retain my arm, or to be without my arm and still have Crazy Pete call me toilet mouth for the rest of my life. I envision myself with no arm and Crazy Pete saying, 'hey toilet mouth, you're missing the flush lever.'

I almost laugh at my own dark humor, but who knows what Pete would have done if I had laughed. He ends my inter-nal amusement by punching me a little harder still.

"Alright, alright stop, please, my name is toilet mouth."

"Good, I'm glad you know your name. That's the name you're going to fight under this coming Friday. I enjoyed the bout between you and Coleman so much I've scheduled a rematch."

"Pete, I can't fight. How can I fight?"

"You can fight this Friday under the proud fighting name of toilet mouth," he says, as though he has invented sarcasm, "or you can fight some other time under the not-so-proud fighting name of the human torch, get it?"

I know right then that it had been Pete who threw the Mol-otov cocktail through Jeremy's grandma's window. It isn't a lie on his resume. I see a flash of evil inspiration pass through his eyes. He is so proud of himself and this new idea.

"No I got it," he snaps his fingers. "Even better, if you don't come Friday, then you will taste the other stuff that comes out of my prick and then you'll fight as the mighty sword swallower. We'll see who sucks then."

The only thing left for him to do is pat himself on the back for his own brilliance.

This conversation is taking place virtually right under my apartment windows. Pete makes no effort to keep his voice down. He operates in this neighborhood with near total impunity. He isn't in the least concerned about who might hear his crazy threats, which I know firsthand are not idle, like so many of the threats that are exchanged in this place every day.

I was so shocked and afraid. He has decided to make my life a living hell. He is going to mercilessly extract every ounce of atonement from me until he is satisfied and he will not be easily satisfied. I surmise that Jeremy Telford had for some reason been subjected to a similar program of atonement extraction. The Molotov cocktail had been meant for Jeremy, Jeremy's gran was unintentional perhaps. Jeremy had decided on his own way out. His accident hadn't been an accident at all.

I rage inwardly with murder in my heart. I wish him dead in a thousand ways. This is not a theoretical exercise. It is I realize him or I or whoever else in my family gets in the way. I am going to have to do something. With all of these myriad inventive, satisfying ways to kill Pete dancing through my head, we stand eye to eye—he with amusement in his piggy eyes, me with my impotent, murderous, consuming rage that is almost blinding me.

Pete's head jerks violently, I hear the snapping and crack-ing of bones. A hard object, a cinder block grazes my forehead leaving an abrasion in its wake. Blood drips into my eye. I am hit in the face by a spritz of liquid. Just a little spritz, a mist. I jerk my head back in surprise, thinking at first Pete has spit at me, it all happens so fast. I can't remember whether the cinder block grazed me or Pete's blood spritzed me first. Pete goes down, his cables snapped and the wicked acceleration of gravity takes him all the way to the basement. I look at him as he lay crumpled at my feet, his head split wide open. The cinder block that had hit him on the head lay broken on the concrete walkway.

I look up to the roof at the spot from where the murderer had thrown his projectile. Blood stings my eye. No one is there. My arm is throbbing despite the Darvon. Serves you right, I say to Pete's motionless body. I feel the urge to spit on him, to exact some small measure of revenge for myself. I can't though, I realize if I can't spit on him now I never would have been able to kill him. It's one thing to wish someone dead another to see it happen and something else entirely to do it.

I go inside. I hear footsteps coming down the stairs from the roof. I wait at my door. The footsteps stop. The cinder-block assassin stands in the hallway above.

I hear his breathing.

"Thanks," I say. "You know you could have hit me just as easily."

"Just be glad for once in your life."

"OK, sorry."

"The cops are gonna come, are you ready?"

"I think so."

"You better know so," he says, somewhat fervently.

"I'm ready," I say with as much conviction as I can muster.

"Good, now go inside." Having been so seriously injured earned me my own key to the apartment. I do as I'm told and go in. I listen at the door as the killer's heavy footsteps run past and out the door at the other end of the hallway. There goes my hero, I know who he is, but I am sworn to secrecy. That's the way life is you can't know everyone's secrets and this one really isn't my secret to tell. The reasons why he killed crazy Pete were his own, they had nothing to do with me. The killer has done the hard part; all I have to do is lie to the police.

No one is home. In the bathroom mirror, I check myself out. I wash the tiny mist of blood off my face and out of my hair, where it has coagulated—I thought appropriately—into fine threads, like a spider web. Pete, the mean old spider, spins his bloody web no more. I clean and bandage the abrasion. I sit on my couch; our cats gather around me. I turn on the Merv Griffin show loudly. Moms Mabley is on, a regular on the show. She's an old black woman with no teeth who tells funny, roundabout stories with her lips flapping all over the place. Merv is such a tight ass, he has no idea what to make of her, or maybe that's just part of the act.

The cops will knock on my door. Whoever was in my apartment when it happened had to have seen or at least heard something. Crazy Pete is lying no more than fifty feet away from where I'm sitting, dead as a doornail. Who gives a shit?

As far as the cops would ever know, I neither saw nor heard anything. 'I was too busy watching Merv Griffin, officer, isn't that Moms Mabley a hoot?" They take one look at me and are certain I couldn't have done it. The cops have seen enough killers to know who isn't one. Also, Owen's father, who is a cop in Southie, vouches for me. As far as the cops would ever know, no one saw anything. The only thing of consequence that came from Pete's murder was that the housing authority locked the doors that led out onto the roofs, at least for a while.

It is now early April. Raw, rainy weather comes upon us for the next few weeks, the coldest rawest April in living memory. I withdraw into my mind to heal. I forget about Pete. Coleman, the book, Ariel and the world for a while.

13. Intermezzo

I finally entered my name on the talent show calendar and next to it I put: 'will read a story I've written.' I don't remember doing it. I go through the motions of living, wanting nothing to do with the world. I don't remember anything from the day after Crazy Pete got his melon smashed until the day I finally awaken from my delirium filled healing slumber.

I can tell you that when I did finally wake up It feels like I have traveled through time and space in what the science fiction writers call suspended animation. I love science fiction writers they are very inventive and imagine the most bizarre things and make the reader believe them. The really good ones are also constantly retelling the great and meaningful stories. Mr. Murphy gave me back the original of my story, so I enter it here.

Moira in Brazil

Moira went to Brazil with her boyfriend Eduardo Goncalves. She didn't know that his father was second in command of the military junta and that Eduardo was above the law and used to getting what he wanted. What he wanted was for Moira to marry him. He would not take no for an answer.

Moira being a highly compassionate person of moral integrity could never marry a man whom she'd overheard saying 'who cares how many peasant children die, Brazil needs the chemical plants.'

Moira who loved all the little children could never accede to what she could now only think of as a hollow pantomime of love. She shudders.

Yet here she was against the best advice of her father, trapped in an elegant suite of rooms with only a thong to wear. Eduardo (not his real name as it turned out) had said "if you won't go to Ipanema with me you will at least dress like it." So, distasteful as it was to wear the thong, it was that or be naked and she wouldn't give him that satisfaction. He had taken her passport and all her money. She was helpless and at his mercy.

She'd been a prisoner there for two months and she could feel herself wavering. She had to get out before she became fully Stockholmed and agreed to marry Eduardo, or whatever his name is. She finds herself sometimes thinking about how handsome he is. She has to make her escape soon, either she would cave in to his demands or he would tire of waiting. She could only imagine what he might do then.

Eduardo had ordered that security remain vigilant so that Moira not even attempt to escape. In the two months she'd been there naturally that excessive vigilance relaxed. One day she climbed out the window in the early morning light and scaled the west wall before the dogs were let out. She let herself down on the other side and ran westward into the poorest warrens of the old city.

She encounters a beggar who is setting up shop for the day. She says in her best Portuguese, "Sir would you please help me."

"You sound nice he said but how can I a poor blind beggar help you"

"Do you have any money, any at all that you can spare me."

"I have none that I can give, maybe you could sell me an article of your clothing. I'm always looking for clothes."

"But sir, all I have is this thong that I was imprisoned in."

"That will do, I can use it as a hat band."

210

Moira felt she had no choice she traded the thong for a token sum that almost made her cry and stood before the blind beggar naked.

The blind beggar lifted the eye patch he had over his right eye, looked her up and down and said, "In the land of the blind the one eyed man is king. I feel like a king, you sure you don't want to sell me something else?"

She is so humiliated she ran into the old city, the blind beggar's laughter echoes in her ears, seemingly chasing her. She wanders for the whole day in the heat of the tropical sun. People snub her. Dogs bark at her and boys throw sticks at "louco menina estrangeira"(the crazy foreign girl). She avoids people as best she can. By sundown she is sunburned, desperate and exhausted. She is at the end of her rope when she enters a seedy barroom to use the last of the blind beggar's money to buy something to drink. The seedy bar is filled with seedy men, all of whom look at her in such a way they she knows she's made a terrible mistake by entering.

She turns to leave but her way is blocked by a well-dressed man of about fifty-five. She whimpers slightly thinking this is it, she will be sliced to ribbons and fed to the dogs, or worse. Instead the man removes the light jacket he was wearing and so as not to hurt her sunburned skin, gently, belying his appearance, covers her. She looks into his rugged scarred face, a face to be feared a face from nightmares.

211

"Cherie, come with me s'il vous plait." She is rocked by the contrast between his face and his kind voice.

She quickly runs through her options, she has none. "Yes, Thank You."

Two men rush them. The Frenchman shoots them both with a Beretta he'd had in his waist band at the small of his back. The second man dies while clutching Moira's ankle. The Frenchman and Moira back out of the saloon and are not pursued, "Just like zee James Bond, No Ma Cherie."

She is too exhausted to walk anymore so he carries her to his rooms like she weighs nothing. When they arrive there he gives her a drink of cold water and runs a cool bath.

"Take zee cool bath cherie it will stop zee burning." She sits in ~~zee~~ the cool water until her fingers prune, her lips turn purple, and she shivers uncontrollably. She steps out, there is no towel and she has no clothes. Naked and Shivering she enters the salon in which the fearsome Frenchman lounges drinking espresso and reading Le Monde. He jumps up and wraps her in the softest towel she's ever felt. He insists that he be allowed to pat her dry, what could she do she feels helpless. She has traded one hellish situation for another. He must feel that because he saved her life he can touch her where and how he wants. It's true, how can she object when she knows she'd be dead or sold into slavery by now were it not for him. She

mentally prepares herself for his rough hands. He does however just gently pat her dry, and avoids touching her where she doesn't want him to.

"You must pat dry when you are so badly burned. Never rub." He explains.

He insists she allow him to massage her with aloe wherever she can't reach. She falls asleep while he gently rubs the soothing aloe into her painfully seared back. her last waking thought is; I wonder how my thong looks as a hatband.

She awakens, dressed in fine silk pajamas to a full breakfast of eggs Benedict, coffee, a champagne cocktail, and dry toast. Enough for four people. She is so hungry she eats it all. After she finishes she looks at him apologetically.

He'd watched her eat with great amusement "Don't worry about me ma cherie rouge, I ate earlier" He laughs

"I appreciate what you've done, but why are you helping me?"

"Don't be so suspicious. Ma Cherie you look so much like my dear sweet Adele" He puts his head in his hands and cries. She goes to him and gently touches him. again rocked by the contrast between his exterior and his depth of feeling.

"We are both escaped prisoners, you and I, I did not escape in time to help my poor Adele and now she is dead

213

because of me. When I saw you, you stabbed my heart and I decided to help you as I could not help poor Adele."

Blah blah blah blah blah blah (is there any end to this story, I'm thinking not really).

Moira makes it back; the junta is overturned. The rebels drag Eduardo's (his real name was Silvio) body through the streets and use his head in an impromptu soccer match. She never hears from the rugged gentle man again, except for a Christmas card postmarked Paris, France that says Bon Noel Ma chérie rouge.

Mr. Murphy wrote a comment at the bottom: *I love it; I don't think in the annals of fiction a writer ever admitted to not having an ending. This may be unique. Imaginative, humorous, not self-conscious like so much contempora+ry writing and not overwritten! What could be worse than being sliced to ribbons and fed to the dogs!? You have a real voice. You are the only one who attempted writing as their talent, as you might expect, since I teach creative writing, a thing close to my heart. You get the third A.*

I don't remember writing or reading the story in front of the class, though some of my classmates have taken to saying "Just like zee James Bond, no ma cherie," when I pass them in the halls. So I must have done it.

When I reread it I have to admit it's an amusing story, I like it, I don't know if that's good or bad because I usually hate what I write. It's also obvious to me that Moira is a thinly disguised Ariel and I'm the rugged scarred Frenchmen. The story is just another expression of my constant wish to be her hero, and to touch her, and be gentle with her, and to love her. I don't know who got the second A. I guess I don't really care, I don't remember any of it.

14. The Shattered World

The day presages a brilliant summer. A warm, sweetly scented breeze caresses my mind. A thousand voices in the breeze speak softly to me about a life I've never lived, and the love I've never known. The breeze stirs in me the ancient urge. I wake from my long dream with my fingers laced through the chain link fence behind Ariel's house.

Ariel is in her back yard. She sits on one of those cheap, omnipresent lounge chairs made of woven green and white flat plastic webbing suspended in a lightweight metal frame. Ariel has adjusted the chair so that she is sitting up.

She is sitting in the sun, but she isn't actively tanning. If she were actively tanning (inasmuch as tanning can be called an activity) she would be reclining, not sitting. The project girls, some of whom are experts in the field, always recline while tanning, exposing the full length of their bodies equally to the light. They follow a strict ritual. They unhook their bikini tops when they lay on their stomachs to eliminate the tan line on their backs. My friends and I often watched to see if we could catch a glimpse of Patti Burrell's tits on tanning days. So far, she has managed to keep those beauties concealed.

The project girls time themselves and rotate like a slow-motion rotisserie so their tans are even. They face the sun directly and move their chairs in unison out of the shadow of the building as the day moves on to get as much tanning time as possible. Were Ariel tanning, she also would not have one knee pulled up to support the book she is reading. I have never seen any of the project girls read while tanning. Ariel's tan is ancillary to her love of reading in the warm sunlight and her desire to not be confined in the house where the worst that could happen, did.

If you've ever read Moby Dick, you know that Melville spends a great deal of time describing whales. He gets very specific and dwells in great detail about the dimensions of the whale, down to the thickness of the flukes at various points progressively distal from the body. Moby Dick is a great book, maybe I should copy Melville and describe Ariel as completely as Melville might. There is nothing I'd rather do to be honest, but I haven't taken Ariel's measurements though, so I can't give a full accounting. There are a couple of measurements of interest that I can approximate with a fair degree of accuracy. She is wearing a cream-colored bikini bathing suit that is no more than a millimeter thick, and that covers no more than five percent of her epidermis. In my opinion, these measurements are far more interesting than the progressively distal thinning of the whale's flukes. Ariel does have two important things in common with Moby Dick. Firstly, she is a force of nature, secondly, she is the object of an obsession.

I have a theory about Moby Dick. My theory is that the book isn't a story about a white whale at all. Moby Dick is a very personal story about Melville's obsessive need to write, his obsessive need to fill the blank page. The white whale is the blank page. The blank page swallows Melville whole; it drags him down to the depths where he can't breathe. He needs to kill the white whale/blank page so he stabs at it with his harpoon/pen. He is obsessed with the idea of killing all the blank pages, which are, much like the whale, white and loom large in his psyche. He personifies his obsession in Ahab. My theory certainly goes a long way to explaining the length of the book. Hey it's a theory, if you don't like it come up with your own

217

theory about anything. Let's see if you can and if you can and let's see how you do.

I climb the fence. Ariel is so absorbed in her book she remains unaware of my presence until I cast my shadow across her eyes. When I do, she looks up. She shades her eyes against the sun, which, judging by my shadow, is eclipsed by my noggin. I have the strange thought that my shadow gets to kiss her, while I stand by and watch.

"Hey," I say.

"Hey," she answers, giving nothing away.

"Are you expecting someone?" I sit down in the empty chair next to her.

"If I were, where would they sit?" she asks sarcastically.

I make an equally sarcastic show of looking around. "I guess they'd have to sit on the ground, or, if you're expecting Jeralyn," I leer in a villainous manner, "she could sit on my lap."

"Lucky for Jeralyn, I'm not expecting her."

I'm pretty sure that trading sarcastic barbs isn't why I've come, so I silently concede. She returns her attention to the book and awaits my next brilliant conversational riposte.

I have always found it maddening that I can't think of anything to say around her. My heart starts pounding and lucid thought evacuates my mind, like panicked theater-goers scrambling to get out of a blazing auditorium. I have a name for this condition—I call it "Ariel's aphasia." I notice, today, that I feel differently. Perhaps what's happened has changed me.

I look around and notice that the yard is uncared-for. The grass is getting long—evidence of her father's passing. He had always taken meticulous care of the yard and the house. The lushness and length of the grass are reminders that he is gone, as if she needed any. This is how it happens isn't it? The grass grows; the paint peels; the brickwork crumbles; the roof falls in.

"The grass is getting a little long," I say, launching my brilliant riposte.

"I am grass; let me work." She says, without looking up.

"I love that poem."

"Yeah. Can you recite it?" Again she doesn't look up, but I can tell she's trying to trip me up. After all, how can you claim to like a poem if you can't recite at least some of it?

I recite the poem, eager to demonstrate how smart I am. It speaks of how the grass grows to hide the tragic consequences of war, healing the scars on the land, eradicating the horror from our collective memory, retrieving pastoral serenity from the cacophony of war until we no longer remember. "What place is this?" We ask. Her face clouds over while I recite. For her, it is too early to forget. Perhaps the grass could never get so long. She neither looks up nor says anything.

"I'll cut your grass for you if you'd like. Do you have a lawn mower?"

She looks up from her book and smiles a real smile. "Yeah, would you? That would be great. The mower is in the shed." I had only been half in earnest, expecting she would say no as likely as yes. I was committed now, though—no backing out. Fortunately, the yard is small, maybe 4,000 square feet, including the house (take that, Melville).

I open the shed door. One of those old-fashioned, rotating-blade, man-powered mowers is right inside. I expected it to be rusty, because I had never seen one that wasn't, but this one is sharp and well oiled. The rotary head is covered with an oily rag. It rolls smoothly and cuts nicely. Her father had maintained it well. Living in the projects, I have never had to cut grass, so it takes me a moment to get the hang of it, but I do. While I work, she goes back to her book. I mow the entire lawn, front, back, sides all around her, passing close to the chair until finally she has to move.

"Miss, please excuse me. I'm cutting the grass. Let me work." She smiles and gets up. I move the chair and mow the last bit of grass. I move the chair back to where it had been and make a sweeping gesture, inviting her to sit back down.

"Milady," I say. She smiles again. I love her smile. I sit back in the other chair after putting the mower, wiped down and re-oiled, back into the shed.

"Thanks for cutting the grass."

"No problem, I wouldn't mind doing it for you when it needs it and when I can do it. When those two things converge." I wave my arms in front of me in a weaving motion.

"That's nice, I really appreciate it."

Wow, it's great that she's so grateful. "There is just one little condition I have, if you don't mind."

"What is it?"

"You have to be here while I cut the grass and you have to talk with me."

"That's actually two conditions, but I agree."

"I mean, I'd feel a little stupid if I was cutting your grass and you were, you know, off somewhere having a blast."

"Wow, that's gonna be tough, because of course I'm always jetting off somewhere to have a blast," she says.

"A touch, a palpable touch," I say, quoting my main man Bill Shakespeare, inappropriately perhaps considering we weren't involved in a sword fight, but I liked to work him in where I could.

221

"I was thinking of getting some iced tea. Would you like some?"

"Yes, please, I'm a little thirsty."

She stands and places the open book pages down on the chair. She walks the twelve steps to the back door. Needless to say I watch her every step of the way. The bathing suit is a little small. It rides up over her buttocks, forming the top half of a hyperbola, the bottom of which is formed by the lines that divide her bum from her upper thighs. Her sensuous gait and small, though beautifully rounded rear end turns me on quite a lot.

I pick up the book when she goes out of sight. When I do, a letter falls from it. I know the book; it is the book I had stolen from Harvard that was in turn stolen from me. The book that made the news, the book that has caused me so much pain. I remember Coleman's threat: "I'm gonna fuck the shit out of her." Now the book is here and she is reading it. I wonder if he succeeded. Coleman doesn't seem like the type to make idle threats.

More curious about the letter than about the book, I put the book back as she had placed it and pick the letter up. It is handwritten on lined paper folded in the traditional way of letters with the writing on the inside. It is addressed on the back of the middle panel of the triptych: "To my Dark Princess." The writer must have placed it in the book, been interrupted, then forgotten it. The impressions made by the ball-point pen are deep. I can feel their depth on my fingertips. *I surmise from this, Watson, that perhaps the writer had been agitated, judging by the depth of the impressions. I deduce it was written by an agitated man with strong fingers. I also deduce it was written after the book passed from my possession. (I say this because I know I didn't write it.) If the letter were written before I took possession (allow me this euphemism, Watson) the impressions would be flattened and the folds razor-sharp. Now the impressions are only slightly flattened and the folds still retain some roundness. See? Look, Watson!* I hold the letter up to my imaginary Watson.

As I recall, the day I took possession, the book was squeezed tightly between the other books on the shelf. We have no reason to believe it had ever been moved from that shelf from the day it had been placed there until the day on which I took it. Since then, it's obvious the book has been stored in a relatively uncompressed state.

I suppose Coleman could be the author. However, I don't believe he has the imagination it takes to coin such an evocative nickname. Also, there is no extant proof that he can actually write.

As you know, Watson, when we exhaust all other possibilities, what remains, however unlikely, is the truth. Therefore, I surmise that this note could only have been written by Ariel's father. Hmmmm, "dark princess"– a curious pet name for a father to call a daughter. The game is afoot, what do you say, Watson?

I say brilliant Holmes! Truly brilliant. My mental Watson intones enthusiastically.

It dawns on me that I'm holding Ariel's dead father's last letter to her. I can be dense at times, but the importance is not lost on me. I feel the responsibility of delivery.

I remember the note I ate back in the sixth grade to protect her little secrets. Perhaps I should eat this letter too. I think I should read it though so I may know better what to do. I don't want her to catch me reading it, so I fold it in half and stuff it in my pocket to give myself time to think.

"Here you go." She hands me the cold sweaty glass, ice cubes gently clinking against the sides. I love that sound; It makes me think of that one nice Christmas when I was a child.

"Thanks so much." I was thirstier than I realized. I throw the tea back before she has a chance to sit down.

"I could make some more, if you want it," she says distractedly, disbelieving the speed with which the liquid leaves the glass.

"Oh no, this was great, thanks." I lie, not wanting to appear greedy or be a nuisance. She picks the book up and sits back in the lounge by straddling it with her skinny pretty legs and slowly lowering herself. I call this sitting "western style" as opposed to the English style of sitting down on one side, legs together. She reopens the book to her place, fully intending to resume reading as though I weren't there.

"What are you reading?" I ask, as if I didn't know.

She holds the book up to show me, turning it over so I can see the text is in French.

"Oh, you're so smart. You might be the smartest person I will ever meet," I marvel, trying my best not to sound sarcastic.

"Thanks, but I know there are smarter people than me. Hopefully I'll get to meet some of them."

"They will have to be very smart indeed."

"Thanks." She blushes, and so do I at how corny I am. "It's a really lovely gift, don't you think? It was given to me by Coleman, Coleman Curran. You know Coleman, you must."

I feel a little queasy. "Well, Coleman and I aren't exactly what you would call the best of friends, but yes, it is a lovely gift. He must have put a lot of thought into it," I say, unable even though I try, to completely mask my rage.

"Yes I suppose he must have. You don't like Coleman very much do you?"

I suppress the urge to rail against Coleman. I would be unfair to take my rage out on her and I don't wish to scare her, I can't assume that because I hate Coleman she does. I must assume just the opposite. "I don't want you to think of me as someone who is full of hate. Really, I'm someone who has love in his heart. I like to think my life is a dream of love. It may be the only thing that keeps me going."

"You speak so strangely; you are so different from the other boys."

"Is that a good thing or a bad thing?"

"I haven't decided yet."

"So there's still hope for me."

"Hope for the hopeless!"

"Oh great, so now I'm hopeless, thanks. Anyway, we've both known Coleman all our lives. I won't say anything about his thoughtfulness, because for all I know he is the most thoughtful person alive." I'm doing my best to keep my tone neutral. "I'm not trying to knock him now, but I never would have thought of him as a bibliophile, would you have?"

"People are full of surprises, aren't they?" It is an ominous sign that she seems to be defending him. I wonder how surprised she'd be if she knew Coleman had slammed me to the ground and knocked me unconscious, then relieved himself on me while I was helpless. Would she be surprised that I feel like a fool and a coward for letting it happen? Would she tell me to get over it? Would she tell me I am a fool and a coward? Would she be surprised to know that Coleman's gift of the book is nothing more than part of a scheme to "Fuck the shit out her" not out of any love for her, but to complete my humiliation? It flashes through my mind that having the shit fucked out of her is something she may desire—why not, I do. I might be surprised to find she is not and never has been who I think she is.

"I like to think that I'm full of surprises too." I say.

"Really, well, surprise me then."

"Alright, how about this: 'Those for whom we have the greatest affection are seldom those we hold in the highest regard'."

"What's that?"

"It's the first sentence of the book you're reading."

She hastily turns back to the first page, reads, then says, "You said 'seldom' when you should have said 'not always'."

"I stand corrected." It seems hardly a point worth debating.

She stares at me intensely for a moment. "Mildly surprised," she says.

"Well, score one for me then." I mark the tally in the air as though I were scoring a game of darts. "Do you like surprises?"

"Depends on the surprise."

"How about this one: 'To Ariel Lirilinghi: who dances in my dreams'."

I can see that quoting the dedication I'd written into the book not only surprises, but distresses her. She doesn't say anything for a minute as she ponders how I could know this. "Very surprised, I admit." She says.

"I thought you might be."

"What I'm surprised about is that you would try to pass off what Coleman has written as your own."

"I'm confused by your thinking. If I didn't write it, how could I know it?"

"You read it while I was inside getting the tea."

"Ah, of course I did," I say contemptuously. "Score one for you then." I mark another tally in the air; she looks annoyed. Things aren't going well. "I have one more surprise, if you're up for it."

"What is it?"

"I can't tell you this one, I have to show you. Do you have a piece of paper and a pen?"

She has a notebook and a pen in her book bag, which is behind her chair. She hands it and a pen to me with a blank sheet exposed. The notebook bears the telltale well used look of a constant companion. I sneak a peek at the previous page and notice it's dated in February. She hasn't written in it since before her father's death. I rewrite the dedication and hand the notebook back to her.

She reads what I'd written and looks up, confused. "Compare it to the one in the book." I say. She finds the dedication in the book and closely compares the two. She hooks the pen into the notebook and shoves it back into the bag. She folds her arms in front of her. Her brilliant inner light goes dim.

"Is it so bad that It was me who wrote it and not Coleman? Am I that terrible?"

"You've proven your point. I can see it was you who wrote it. You should be happy now. You're so much smarter than I am." She looks at me. "Am I supposed to jump into your arms now? For your own sake, you should go."

I had thought in the dim recesses of my mind that she would be grateful to me for warning her about Coleman, if nothing else. It takes a few moments because I'm so willfully blind. Coleman must have made good on his threat. Why else would she be as upset as she appears? Why else would she say 'should I jump into your arms now'?

229

The world and everything in it shatters into a billion tiny fragments. We are remade as we are broken. It happens so quickly I don't perceive the breaking or the remaking, only that it seems that all of a sudden I'm a different person standing in a different place. I have undergone a noticeable transformation.

"Why are you so troubled?" she asks. "I can't really see why you should be."

I reach up to wipe my cheek, and sure enough, there is a tear that formed all of its own in the remaking of the shattered world. I wipe it away. I think of the note folded in my pocket. "Do you remember that day I ate a note you wanted me to pass to Nancy?"

"Yeeeesssss..." she says, waiting for the proverbial other shoe to drop.

"What do you remember about that day?"

"What do I remember about a random day so many years ago? We were children."

"Funny, I remember everything. I remember how cold I was when I brought your coat back home to you. Do you remember that coat? Your little red coat, it was so soft. "Cashmere," it said on the label. I cried into that coat that day. You never knew. I swore it would be the last time I ever cried. You don't remember anything about that day?"

"I remember you eating the note."

"You were glad I did, weren't you? I had a sense you really didn't want that note read out loud."

"No, it's true. I didn't. I guess I was glad you ate it. It took everybody by surprise, speaking of surprises."

"Sister Demetrius whacked me with the pointer. She was like a Japanese stick-fighting master with that pointer. I know you never got whacked, so you might not remember, but that pointer was as thick as a pool cue. With her second whack, after the "warm-up" whack, she chipped a piece off my scapula. Do you know what it feels like to have a piece of your scapula broken off?"

She rolls her eyes. "No, I don't, do you wish I did?"

"No, of course not. She hit me I don't know how many times after that, each whack it seemed exponentially more painful than the one before. It was the time between them though that was the worst, wondering if I could stand it, If I could last longer than she could. I stifled my screams because I'm good at that. I knew something like that would happen when I ate that note. But I did it anyway, because I thought it would help you out. You are the only one in the world I would have done that for. You should know, it took a long time for the bone to heal. It was painful for more than a year. I had to quit baseball because of it. Did you know that? I loved baseball, but I couldn't swing a bat or throw a ball without real, shooting pain."

"It wasn't my fault, was it? I remember I screamed for her to stop."

"That was you, I never knew. Anyway, it doesn't matter, I said I loved baseball. I didn't say I was good at it." I don't know why I tell this lie, because I was very good. When I played baseball I felt so free. "I didn't mind having to quit baseball. Even when I saw you at games cheering for the team and it hurt me all over again because it couldn't be me you were cheering for. I had done what I did for you as I saw it and I never complained. You never heard me say I had to quit baseball because of you, did you?"

"No. It sounds like you're saying it now, though."

"No, I'm just... reminiscing. Does it really sound like I'm complaining?"

"Yes."

"Then I guess I am. What else do you remember?"

"I remember I stopped those boys from hitting you."

"You know why they stopped, don't you?"

"I thought it was because I made a compelling case for why they should stop, and they saw the reason in my argument."

I burst out laughing; she was so sincere. She doesn't think it's very funny.

"You can't reason with animals. No that wasn't it; it was because they all believed that if they didn't stop you would tell Coleman. Everyone thought you were Coleman's girlfriend." She winces visibly. "I know I did. They didn't mind hitting me, but they weren't going to risk having you sic Coleman on them. None of them was brave, just vicious—a pack of hyenas, really. I was grateful at the time, don't get me wrong. I was about to pass out from the pain; I was sure that if I did, they would have laid the boots to me. Even though it was four-on-one, somehow I got stuck with the reputation of letting a girl fight my battles for me. I don't quite follow the logic of it, but there you have it. I've had to fight more than most just to rehabilitate my reputation, such as it is. I'm not afraid to fight—I'll fight anybody. I'll even fight your precious Coleman again if I have to."

"He's not my precious Coleman! I was just trying to help. I can't help what anybody thinks. It was just me. I couldn't stand to see those boys hitting you. If that counts for anything."

"It does, of course it does. It counts for a lot." It was a nice moment and maybe I just should have left it there, but I had things I needed to say. "What else do you remember?"

"If you want me to say I remember wetting my pants, how could I forget that?"

233

"If, by 'wetting your pants,' you mean flooding the classroom, then yeah, that's what happened." She turns red. "I can see you're embarrassed about it even now."

"It was humiliating. I haven't been able to live it down. People still call me "old yellow stain," you know, from the play The Caine Mutiny. You know freshmen come up to me and ask me to tell them tales of the flood of '06. Pushy, annoying boys mainly, whom I don't even know and who sometimes won't let me pass. I try to ignore them, but they get right in my face. I'm not a big person and I find it intimidating when they won't let me pass."

"I can kick their asses if you want me to."

"That's tempting, but no thanks."

"I always wanted to know what was in that note that was so important that you would humiliate yourself before divulging it?"

"The note said," she pauses to gather her strength. "'My brother has been killed.' It's still very difficult to say. Back then I just couldn't, I tried. I wanted to tell Nancy. She was my best friend, but I couldn't even tell her. I couldn't speak the words so I wrote them in a note. That way I could tell her. At least that was my plan, and it would have worked, too, if you had just passed the note.

"The reason why I couldn't say it in front of the class even under that extreme duress, I think you'll understand, is that I was paralyzed by the idea that someone would laugh. I fixated on that idea. I don't know what I would have done if someone laughed. I just sort of mentally dug in my heels and decided Sister Demetrius wasn't going to break me, no matter what. But of course she did, and you saw the result."

"Do you really think someone would have laughed?"

"I don't know, what do you think?" I ran through the cast of characters in my head. Undeniably there were some kids with a naturally cruel bent who might have. It wasn't a totally crazy idea.

"Yeah I suppose there were. Sorry I said it was a stupid note." I was proud of her.

"How could you know? Most of them were stupid, I suppose."

"Have you ever given a thought as to who might have cleaned up the flood of '06?"

"No, I thought it must have been the janitor. Don't tell me it was you."

"It was me, I did it for you. Well actually, I did it because Sister Demetrius made me. However, I did the best job I knew how because I didn't want the classroom to stink. I knew you were humiliated; anybody would have been. I stood in that puddle and washed and rewashed that floor to make sure the room didn't smell of stale urine. I didn't want you to be humiliated all over again the next day. I did that for you; it was all I could do.

"While I cleaned, Sister Demetrius lectured me about what a loser I was and how you didn't know I was alive and how you would never do for me any of what I was apparently willing to do for you. With every stroke of the mop, pain stabbed me in the back, but I kept on mopping for your sake. With every passing minute, I was getting in more and more trouble with my old man for getting home so late. He knew I was at detention and that's all he needed or wanted to know. The first place he will hit me will be on my back; that's where he starts, I thought. Still I took my time to do the best job I could for your sake.

"Then I brought your little red jacket home through the cold. I froze my ass off, 'cause I wasn't dressed for it. I was never dressed for it. I hate the winter. I know each passing minute only served to make my old man madder. The madder he got, the harder he hit. But I didn't care; I could think only of you. I didn't want you to have to come to school the next day without your jacket. I thought you might be cold, as cold as I always was. Stupid me for not realizing that you probably had more than one jacket, because I didn't. Stupid me for not realizing your father would never make you walk through the

236

cold without a jacket, because mine would. Sister Demetrius was right about everything. I'm who she said I was and my father and brother are who she said they were. I stopped defending them a long time ago.

"I never could have believed she was right about you; turns out she was. I have, for the most part, been invisible to you. I was too proud to realize she was trying to help me, too cocksure of myself for no good reason. Now look at me, I'm neither. I haven't been living a dream of love. I've been suffering from a delusion. Like a thirsty desert vagabond who sees the mirage of his salvation dissolve into the sand, I'm thrown into despair. I swore back on that day that you had the last of my tears. But it seems I can't stop giving them to you. I hope that answers your question.

"There are a thousand other little things I did, like following you home to make sure you got there safely. I wonder if you even know that I used to do that. I followed at a distance, hoping for my opportunity to be your hero. I wanted to be your hero, like the time Coleman saved you from Flynn, remember? How awful for me that I've spent my life loving you and you've spent yours loving him. The evidence was right in front of me and I didn't want to see it. I remember the look of love on your face when he walked away.

"Remember when the nuns made us exchange Valentine's cards? I always made a special one for you and you never gave me one, not once, but I always forgave you. Of course you were just fine with or without my forgiveness, oblivious in the first place to the pain you caused me.

"A thousand other little things I did with you in mind, right up to that book you hold in your hands. Right up to cutting your grass and volunteering to do in perpetuity. 'Yessum Miss Scahlett can old Moses do anything else fuh y'all? Eyes luvs bein' yaw slave.' You never saw the little things I did for you because I was invisible to you. Like a servant to a queen, all these little acts of kindness are nothing more than what is due to a dark and haughty princess. Why should you take notice?" Her eyes widen when I call her a "dark princess," but she doesn't comment on it.

"Why are you trying to hurt me? Haven't I suffered enough?" She searches her mind for something. "What about that day in the gym? You weren't invisible to me that day. You must know that. I danced for you, just for you, isn't that something?"

"You didn't even know I was there. Until I ran out in fear that I would always be in the shadows. I showed myself and by some miracle you saw me. How stupid and impulsive I can be. The shadows are where I belong. You know we weren't alone in the gym that day. Someone else lurked in the shadows. I won't tell you who, It's not important. After you left he came out and offered his critique of your dancing. I won't tell you what he said it would be hateful to do so. I'm really not trying to be hateful, just the opposite. Let's just say his critique was highly unfavorable. I told him he was crazy. I told him he could not see and had no love in his heart. I told him that he could never expect that you might love him as though to not have that hope is the worst fate he could suffer, as though your love was within my reach. It was beyond my power to imagine that he could have cared less. Now I think it must be me who is crazy. It is me who sees the world wrongly. I'm so desperate for your love. I made myself believe it exists for me alone, but now I know it doesn't."

"I don't know what to say. No one has ever spoken to me this way. You express yourself very well, maybe too well."

"You say I express myself too well as though that were a bad thing. I don't know why I had always thought that would be something you'd appreciate. There is a higher mode of expression locked away in me. Words that I could only ever speak to you, only for you, words that you can't just hear but have to feel to understand. I feel these things banging around inside me wanting to come out. I thought you might want to hear them. These words that need most of all the right listener. That you prefer men who speak in grunts and drag their knuckles on the ground while walking, I never would have guessed. Just another of those nasty little surprises you say people are so full of."

"I hate having what I say so twisted, You're not being very nice."

"You're wrong, I am nice. I think I've proven that time and time again, like I said, even today. Maybe what I'm finding out is that it's you who isn't so nice. Maybe I've finally awakened from my silly dream of love."

"If I'm so terrible, why did you say you loved me that day in the gym?"

"I thought I knew. I meant what I said, but now that's just another terrible memory. I tell you I love you and you tell me to bring you the golden hind. You laugh in my face then run away laughing at me the whole time. You can have a good laugh at this too, I was actually thinking about what you could mean, what I could bring to you that would serve as an adequate substitute. Where could I get my hands on something of such extreme value that I might exchange it for the smallest hope of your love. Where would such a filthy ragamuffin like me get his hands on such a priceless thing? Does such a thing exist? Little did I know I could have done it with a book that I once held in my possession, that book." I point to the book she's reading. "All I have to do is pretend a few simple, empty, romantic sounding words written in the front are my own and voila, the trick is done.

"I had held in my hands the philosophers stone capable of compelling the beautiful dream of my life to roll over backwards

240

for any Tom, Dick or Coleman who possesses it." I had no way of knowing the power of the phrase 'roll over backwards' and its effect on her. I had hit on it by accident. "Of course the magic resides not in the stone itself. That's why it works for Coleman and it could never do it's magic for me. Now the world and I are shattered. Isn't that a hoot?"

"STOP IT! Please, don't say such hateful things to me I don't deserve it. I'm precious, you know I am. If you have to leave, then leave but no more cutting words. I can't stand to hear them. Your words are not who I am, they could never be." She raises the book as if to throw it, but thinks better of it. "I think you're wrong. For you to think I didn't see you in the gym is just craziness. How could I have missed you. You were right in front of me!" she pauses to let the meaning of this sink in. It is devastating. It turns the shattered world upside down. She continues more softly. "I think you should judge me by what's in your own heart and what you see with your own eyes and not put so much stock in the hateful opinions of your fellow shadow lurkers.

"For you to think that I could be made to roll over as you so tastefully put it, for the price of this book..." She pauses in great distress and it takes a moment before she can continue. When she does continue, she does so very quietly. "...Can only mean that you don't know me. How can you love me if you don't know me!" She pauses again to control the overwhelming emotions torturing her and again proceeds very softly. "If you love me, then tell me. Tell me I'm precious to you, more precious than any book. Tell me I'm the most precious thing in the world and that you love me more than life itself, otherwise.........please......... just leave."

She has tears in her eyes. It costs her to say these things, to hold out to me this reprieve. She is stronger than me. I don't have the strength it takes to get down on my knees and beg her to forgive me, to tell her how precious she is and how I love her more than my miserable life. To say those things I should say rather than my foolish litany of recrimination. I want to, my head is screaming that I should. Be big, have courage, admit you are wrong. Admit you are the king of being wrong. Say that being wrong is what you do best, maybe you can even make her laugh. Accept any penance she might demand. If I ever could be a hero, now is the time. Say something kind, say something. Do it you fool. DO IT!! I float outside myself, and watch as I murder my dream. I have committed the sin of jealousy, now I'm doubling down against my will with the sin of pride, the very thing I had accused her of—the very thing Sister Demetrius tried to cure me of.

I get up heavily from the chair to leave. I'm drained, hungry and near exhaustion. The very air weighs on me. I feel like an ancient mammoth must have when he stumbled into a tar pit. I remember her father's letter in my pocket. Who the fuck do

I think I'm that I should keep it from her? I fish it out and show it to her with the address facing away, not that she could see it, considering the unbridgeable distance between us.

"I should go then, but I think this is yours."

She looks up, "What is it?"

"It's a letter."

"I can see that! How do you know it's mine?"

"It fell from the book while you were inside getting the tea. It's addressed 'To My Dark Princess', that has to be you cause it sure as hell isn't me."

She draws her breath in sharply and visibly tenses. I wait with my hand extended and flutter it a couple of times in her direction. She will not take it, so I drop it in her lap. She doesn't immediately pick it up.

"It's from my father, but you knew that, didn't you? Did you read it?"

"I thought it might be, but no, I didn't read it."

"I've been carrying it with me since...I'm afraid of what it will say."

"How bad can it be?" I didn't know what else to say and didn't have the energy to say it. She picks up the letter. She holds it between her fingers as though it were hot. She turns it over a few times and plays with the folded edge, snapping it like a croupier might do to a new deck of cards. She drops the letter back into her lap.

"Just so you know," she says,

"Yeah, what's that?"

"I see you now." She still offers a reprieve. She is still so strong. Her hands flutter and she wrings them together under her chin in this endearing way I've always seen her do when she is agitated. I'd seen her wring her hands just this way on that very first day. She looks at me intently to emphasize that she sees me. I must be a blur, as her eyes swim in tears.

"I know." I say, by way of offering my flag of truce.

It's funny how things work. A simple phrase, a familiar gesture, a tear, these things speak more eloquently and convey deeper meaning than all my cleverly combined and concatenated word

15. The Sleep of Shattered Crystal

i

Ariel steels herself. She unfolds her father's letter and reads. Emotions race across her face like shadows from high clouds across the ground. She finishes and gets up off her chair. She darts this way and that, but like a mime trapped in an invisible box, she can't escape. She darts in my direction. The emotional tsunami crests and crashes, she turns one last pirouette and falls backwards.

I have never seen anyone faint before. I thought it was a plot device, a thing actresses do to avoid kissing the villain. Ariel falls so quickly I barely have time to react. Luckily, she falls toward me, otherwise she might have pitched over the lounge chair and been hurt badly. I try to catch her, but she is limp and continues to slide through my hands. I can't stop her completely—all I can do is slow her fall and this by not very much. She had fainted while in motion and her fall is violent. It is not the Victorian heroin's gentle back of the hand to the forehead, slow sit onto a damask-covered divan. Trying to catch her is reflexive. In the process I pull off her top. It is still tied around her neck, but her breasts are fully exposed. She must really be unconscious. If she were faking, she would not have tolerated having her clothes ripped away. Her deeply ingrained modesty would have prevailed. The smack her head takes when she hits the ground can't have helped.

I have pierced the looking glass. Ariel lies in the newly cut grass. She lies similar to the way the model was posed in a painting I'd seen on a field trip the class had taken to the Museum of Fine Arts during our Freshman year. The painting is of a nude, reclining woman. Like Ariel, her hands are thrown above her head. Unlike Ariel, her breasts point in opposite directions. Unfamiliar with the effects of gravity on an amply endowed woman I wonder how a great artist could make such an obvious mistake. Ariel's breasts are right in front of me and they resist gravity almost entirely. The woman in the painting has an exaggerated female shape, very narrow at the waist, voluptuous at the hips. A wild profusion of pubic hair blossoms exactly where you would expect it. The painting is shocking to me when I first see it. To see a life-size naked lady floating like a fleshy cloud above the heads of a gallery full of patrons, and most oblivious to her presence, is not something I see every day. However, she is posed with her legs together. It occurs to me if the artist had really wished to shock, to defy convention, he would have parted his model's legs.

The woman's face isn't painted in great detail and the only real color in the painting is two pale red circles on her cheeks. The lack of color and detail creates an illusion. As I stare, her face continually changes in character, oscillating rapidly between angelic and demonic like the quantum leaps a sketched cube makes between jumping off the page and falling into it. The redness in her cheeks fluctuates with the angelic demonic cycle between the blush of a virgin and the war paint of a harlot, with no transitional states between. The artist's greatness and the truly shocking thing about the painting lies in his ingeniously revealing the truth about his mistress while disguising a mirror to my soul in her face.

While I intently stare at the picture a crowd of the girls from my class gathers behind me, Ariel among them. She, ironically enough poses like the woman, mocking my interest in so lurid a picture, eliciting giggles from her girlfriends. I'm only vaguely aware of the commotion behind me, hypnotized by the paintings ever-changing character, and consumed with thoughts of art, nakedness, and the duality of man in general, and myself in particular, as I can sometimes be. The other girls, with the exchange of a few quick glances, decide as a hive mind to play a little joke on Ariel, too. They rapidly and silently move away and are displaced by a group of boys who are attracted by Ariel's posing. I turn around and catch her in mid pose, her hands thrown over her head, her newly budding breasts thrust outwards. She turns beet red and so do I. She turns around in search of moral support and finds her girlfriends displaced by the boys. She turns an even deeper red. She runs away on her skinny pretty legs. She is greeted with gales of laughter when she rejoins the huddle of her girlfriends with whom she pretends to be angry. She laughs and smiles along with them. Her eyes are merry. She is beautiful.

My friend Owen joins me in front of the painting. After a moment of mock serious consideration, he denies being able to see the contest between good and evil in the woman's face. In his confidential way, he says that instead of La Maja Desnuda, he would have—were he the artist—called the painting *Spanish Tart with Winter Bush*. We burst into laughter. Sister Karenina shushes and hustles us away from the painting, which she declares unfit for viewing by Freshman Irish Catholic boys with a smack to the back of our heads.

Back in the here and now, I realize I'm in a serious position. Should someone from one of the adjoining houses look out their window they would see me standing over their neighbor's beautiful, unconscious, almost completely naked daughter? The police would be summoned. Any explanation I might offer would be seen as a lie. Ariel may even believe I had removed her top when she was unconscious to catch a peek and cop a feel. I will be taken away in handcuffs, my life ruined.

This puts a damper on the sexual excitement her naked tits would otherwise engender. I have to act quickly. My first instinct is the first instinct of any good project kid—hit the fence and make a run for it. I master this impulse. I can't leave her naked and helpless, that would be despicable. If she doesn't hate me already, she would have good reason to do so were I to abandon her at the very moment when she needs—if not mine specifically, then someone's help.

248

It takes all my strength to lift her and to keep her from melting through my arms. I curl my right arm under her knees, it, like my psyche, has not completely recovered from the fight with Coleman. The bone aches the way my legs used to from growing pains. My left arm passes under her arms and across her back. It is very awkward. Fortunately, she weighs only about a hundred pounds. As I lift her, my left hand firmly grasps her left breast. It can't be helped. This is my first time ever touching any girl's naked breast, never mind hers. Under the circumstances, it feels strange, but not so strange as to compel me to move my hand away. I could adjust her position to make her easier to carry, but I would have to remove my hand, so I make do.

Moving as fast as I can for fear of dropping her, I turn open the back door with my right hand. I maneuver quickly but carefully through the little maze formed by the back door, foyer/mudroom and kitchen entry way so as not to smash her head on the door jambs. I rush through the kitchen, down the hallway, and make it to the living room in time to lay her gently on the sofa just as I reach the limit of my endurance. Try carrying a one-hundred-pound bag of water some time, and you'll know what I mean. I go out to the backyard and bring in the book and the tea glasses. I close the back door then return to the living room, flexing my arms and fingers all the while to relieve the cramping in my forearms.

She holds the letter limply. I take it and sit down in the chair opposite where she will be able to see me when she awakens. Too curious about what her father could have written that would make her faint so dead away, I read.

Ariel,

After losing David, I became afraid of losing you, too. I don't want to lose you but it feels like I already have. In a way, I find this even sadder because you are right here and I can't reach you. You are no longer the little girl who loved me with all her heart. So I will not write to you as though you are.

I'm supposed to be strong. It turns out I'm not as strong as I thought I was or I might wish to be, so I drink sometimes. I promise I will stop. I want to make you proud of me again if that is still possible if you ever were. It kills me that you're not. I'm sorry you found out what I do the way you did. That was unfair, I should have told you. I always thought I would be something else, but Monday turns to Friday and January turns to September and before you know it you are what you are. If you could love me for being me just a small fraction of how much I love you, I'd be the happiest father in the world.

I know you blame me for David's death. You think I encouraged him to join the Marines. Maybe I did—if I did, I accept the blame. I hope that helps you, although I doubt it does. There is one thing that helps me and maybe it will help you. I know that David died a hero and though I want him back as much as you, this eases my pain a little. I want to believe that the stuff that was in David is the same stuff that's in you. I know you have as big a heart as he did and if you look, you'll find forgiveness there.

Your mother has gone to New York because we have agreed to get divorced. I should say she wants a divorce. It isn't what I want, but she's sick of being married to a trash man who hasn't lived up to the promises he made to her. I guess I promised her she'd be happy. She is not happy. She can never be happy, for reasons I can never fully understand for there are things that she won't share with me. She blames me for her unhappiness. Her heart is hardened against me. I wonder would you have decided to go with her had you known.

What you said to me this morning hurt. I'm sorry I slapped you, but it was all I could think to do. I lashed out at you, such contempt as I heard in your voice I didn't think you were capable of and I wouldn't have believed I could inspire. How sharper than a serpent's tooth it is to have a thankless child. Ain't that the truth. Maybe I will never be a writer but you shouldn't hate me for trying. As for being a trash man, you've wanted for nothing. Look around and tell me where I've fallen short as a provider. It's true, we don't live in a castle by the sea, but many kids right in this town don't live as well as you do. I've sacrificed my own happiness for your sake. Everything for the sake of what was all an accident, ask your mother, don't ask me. Now I have to face the hard truth that in the end, I'm nothing but a trash man in your eyes. That's all I'll ever be. In your world, trash men aren't allowed to dream. If I have to sacrifice my dream, too, then tell me where I should lay down so you can shovel real dirt on me, not just the dirt of your contempt. Real dirt would be so much warmer.

I guess I could say a lot more, but brevity is the soul of wisdom, I have a headache and someone has to shovel the driveway, speaking of shoveling.

Dad

P.S.

Trash men have feelings, too.

He must have been very drunk or very angry when he wrote this letter. Would he have taken it back if he could have? Now she knows that she had hurt him badly on the very day he died. She will blame herself for killing him with her careless and lethal contempt. She can't make amends or show him what a big heart she has, the very big heart she has shown me just today. She can never tell him how proud she is or that she loves him when it's obvious to me she must have loved him very much. Now she knows that she is nothing but an accident, that it was all an accident. Very, very difficult things to live with. It isn't just the words. There is a little stain here and there that I take to have been caused by tears. He cries while his life falls apart. She is too perceptive to miss this. She must have felt these as gunshots to her heart.

Finally penned that tearjerker you've been trying to write all your life, eh, old trash man? I say to myself, whistling past the graveyard if you will.

I wonder if her mother told her she'd decided to leave. If her mother didn't know about this letter then it would make no sense for her to do so. To coin a phrase: let sleeping dogs lie. That she's found out that her mother not only left her father just before he died but that she left her too will she hate her mother for it? Everything can go to hell in a heartbeat, can't it?

I wish now that I had eaten this note, too. No one should be allowed to communicate from beyond the grave. It's no good for the living. I let out the breath I've been holding, refold the letter, and place it on the small table that stands next to the chair. There is a large format art book on the table called The Doors of Dublin.

I stand over her while she sleeps. She lies on her back with her feet flat. Her knees are raised slightly and rest together against the back of the sofa. Her abdomen is concave above the bathing suit, stretched between the crowning crests of her ilia. Her taut, flat abdomen flutters ever so slightly in time with her heartbeat. My gaze wanders to the suggestion of fuzz that runs below her belly button and under the bikini bottom. I remember the fuzz that covered her forearms when she was a little girl and how it had excited me. I had wanted to touch her forearms then, to feel how soft she is. She was like a kitten. Now she is a full-grown tigress, devouring and primal. My urge is to place my hand on her and slide it down over her taut and fluttering stomach; over the soft, downy fuzz and into the bikini bottom, to follow that silky road to the gates of paradise where it leads. I reach down and touch the soft fuzz. Her abdomen reflexively draws away. I feel the same agony of love that I have felt every day since that first day when I was a very little boy, and she was a downy angel.

Her naked breasts rise and fall with every breath. The whiteness of the skin surrounding her brownish-pinkish nipples has an opalescent depth. Her left breast has the angry, pinkish outline of my hand embossed onto the delicate skin like an accusation. I did not think I had been so rough. I want to kiss her and say "I'm sorry, forgive me." I kneel beside her to bring my mouth there. I raise my quivering fingers to touch her, and I do ever so lightly. Her nipple reacts to my touch. I marvel at its spontaneous wrinkling and the little bud that sprouts.

My head is swirling with the intoxicating thought of untying the little bows that hold the front and back of her skimpy bathing suit bottom together. Once the bows are untied, I fold the tiny patch of fabric that barely shields her from my touch downwards to reveal her entirely. *She awakens, her arms reach out to me. She pulls me to her. She embraces me with her arms and legs with a strength driven by passion. She kisses me and pulls me inside her and we begin to move together. No words are spoken, none need be.* I'm shaking with the strength of these desires, yet I dare not untie the bows. What remains of my senses warns me that a different reaction is more likely.

She is fitful in her sleep and she dreams. She languidly places her expressive, gentle hand tenderly over her barely covered vulva. In a throaty, seductive whisper she says, "Please, kind sir, don't touch me." She implies with both her voice and her languid, dreamlike manner that perhaps this kind sir might—if he were bold—do exactly the opposite and be rewarded for his boldness. Her indomitable brio shines in her darkest time. I cover her with the blanket that is neatly folded over the back of the sofa to protect her—not from her assailing, chimerical, kind sir but from me.

I sit back down in the chair opposite. Soon she stirs and opens her eyes.

"Are you alright?" I ask trying to sound casual.

"Yes.... No.... What happened?"

"Well, you read the letter and then passed out." I was going to go into what a hero I'd been for catching her, which in truth I barely did. I stop when she sits up and the blanket falls away. She becomes aware immediately that her breasts are exposed. She crosses her arms in front of her and cups each tit in the opposite hand.

"I hope you got your fucking rocks off?"

She lifts the blanket to make sure her bottoms are in place and throws me a contemptuous glare. I have to agree with her father, it is withering.

I start to sputter my explanation about how it happened when she fainted. What she does next stops me in my tracks. She removes the bikini top by ripping it over her head. She gets up from the sofa and unties one side of the bikini bottom.

"Is this what you want?"

The bikini falls down on that side revealing half the inverted triangle of her pubic area, whose boundary is clearly marked by the gently curving line between her upper leg and her lower abdomen. She doesn't wait for my answer. She spreads her legs slightly and unties the other side and the bikini bottom peels away and falls to the carpet. I follow it down then raise my eyes to her.

I can't take my eyes off the black wing of her pubic hair. Her hands flutter—one minute modestly attempting to obscure that area; the next, pulled away, defiantly revealing it. Her pubic hair is shocking midnight in a coal-mine blackness, against the whiteness of the negative image of the bathing-suit bottom on her skin. The black hair is the legacy of her Mediterranean heritage; its wispiness, a tribute to her Irish side.

The slit of her vagina is easily discerned. The great artist who made Ariel has given her a beautiful vagina. She quivers with the intensity of her emotions, trembles on the verge. Hanging down from her vagina is the white and slightly corkscrewed string from a tampon.

I have no wish to make her seem ridiculous because she is not. She is from where I sit as far from ridiculous as anybody could be. Her physical and emotional nakedness make her not just beautiful, but formidable in my eyes.

"Is this what you want?" She repeats herself. Her voice quavers with raw emotion. Her hands continue wavering between defiance and modesty. If this is an act of naked tough-girl defiance, she isn't very good at it. Not that I really know anything about naked tough-girl defiance, but it does seem to me that in order to pull it off, one must commit to it completely. Tough girls from the projects don't express their anger by getting naked. They bash you in the mouth with a closed fist, so as to leave no confusion about their anger or their defiance. Ariel may be tough in her own way; in fact, I know she is, but she isn't project-girl tough.

257

I've never been confronted by a naked girl before, especially THE naked girl. In all honesty, I'm confused about what I should do. I know she isn't really offering herself to me. I'm not that stupid. At the same time the ancient imperative takes hold.

You're damn fucking right, it's what I want.

Tired of my role as the simpering love-struck fool, I get up off the chair and take an aggressive step toward her. She shies away. That clinches it—I reach for the discarded blanket and gently wrap her in it.

"I would never do such a thing, I might think of it, I do think of it all the time, but I would never touch you unless you wanted me to. That's how I always think of it. I always hope you might want me to touch you. It was an accident when you fell. You have to believe me." There is no sense in telling her the whole truth, at least not now. I promise myself I must but at the right time.

She grabs the blanket from the inside, gathering it firmly around herself. She acknowledges my explanation with one of her nearly imperceptible nods. Her defiant, angry, naked, tough-girl act dissolves into trembling lips and welling tears.

She is hit by a memory; the way memory assaults her sometimes. Everything associated with this memory comes back to hammer her relentlessly. She remembers when she was a child, not so long ago, her father tucking her in bed at night, calmly and patiently dispelling her terror that he would die and she'd be left alone in the world. He would laugh and tell lies about never dying. She can right this moment, smell his after-shave. He hugs her so tightly and so gently; he is so strong. She believes his lies, Enzo the liar.

Now, the terror has come to pass. Now she is alone and there is no one to lean on but this strange boy. She has put off grieving for her father because she feels she did what she could to kill him and to mourn him would have been a lie. She knew she'd hurt him the moment she'd spoken her hateful words. If she hadn't intended to kill him with her words, then what had she intended?

She is unsteady and in danger of falling again, so I pick her up. She yields to me. I sit her down on my lap. She curls up in the fetal position, buries her head in my chest and proceeds to bawl.

She cries body-wracking sobs punctuated by attempts to choke out a word here and there. Her thoughts are confused. She is trying to say everything while unable to say anything. She gives up. Pressing her face into my chest, she howls a primal, wrenching expression of such deep pain I cannot begin to comprehend. It freaks me out. She is so far beyond the reach of the simple consoling platitudes that are the best I can offer. Nonetheless, I try.

"It's gonna' be alright," I find myself repeating, pretty sure that it isn't going to be—now or maybe ever. I stroke her hair and she let me. I'm very shaken.

I murmur what comes to mind. "I'm here......don't worry......It will pass.... what can I do......" I don't even think she hears me, she is so lost. Nonetheless, I steadily murmur my litany of supposedly comforting words, even if they comfort only me.

I would never wish this pain on her. However, she is turned so completely inside out it feels to me like lovemaking. This is a moment of such extreme and moving intimacy, I can't help it, I find myself wishing for its continuation. Now I can say to her, 'I've seen into and know the deepest parts of you.' I would gladly take the pain from her if I could. My anger and jealousy are forgotten. What kind of a person would I be if I just threw her off my lap and walked out the door without pity? This moment is like lovemaking in another way, that is, I have an erection.

Her tears collect into large tumescent droplets on her long, black eyelashes then break under their own weight to cascade down her cheek, across her nose, and onto my t-shirt. Her tears flow steadily. They smear her face, her face glistens. She dabs at her eyes with a corner of the blanket, but it is such a deluge that most of her tears find their way onto me. I don't mind.

She squeezes out a word then stops to sob and tremble, squeezes out a word, sobs and trembles. I try to concentrate on what she is saying, but can make no sense of it between the agony of anticipation as she tries to get out the next word and the fact that she is naked, wrapped only in a loosely knit afghan, and held firmly in my arms. I find the whole thing alarmingly arousing. I completely lose the thread, assuming there is one.

In reconstructing what I think she's said I come up with, 'He was riding a handsome horse in a car.' I know this can't be right but it's no time for clarification. I say, "yes, I know." This seems to be sufficient.

The unexploded bomb that had been ticking away inside her has blown away that carefully constructed wall of reserve she works hard to maintain. She reveals herself to me as someone hurt by life and by the world. We all get hurt by the world, I suppose. I have been, I know, but she really has been—so much more so, so unfairly so. She is so blessed on the one hand and cursed on the other. She teeters on the edge of the huge blast crater created by the bomb of her hurt with only her own failing strength and my weak expressions of solace to keep her from falling.

I am frightened for her. She shivers like a naked mountaineer in winter. It sounds funny, I know, but I don't find it even mildly funny. The intensity of her grief seems to be ratcheting upwards with each passing minute. The worse it gets, the worse it will get—at least, that is how it feels to me. A panic of helplessness grows inside me. I continue to stroke her hair, rub her arm and chant my small comforts like prayers. I kiss her, not on the lips but on her head, and she lets me. After about five more minutes of this inexorable ratcheting up, she breaks. She subsides in stages; first into ragged deep breathing and soon after that, she breathes more regularly. She remains quiet for a few minutes. I gently rub her upper arm.

I sense we are in the eye of the hurricane. There is an electric hum in the air. I have never seen a hurricane, but my father says it's the second half that brings the rain. She starts up again, forcing out the sentence "his nose was smashed" with all of her remaining strength. Her entire body tenses with the effort. She holds her breath as she says the words, like a weight lifter pushing too heavy a weight.

She resumes the wailing, crying and trembling with—as my father would have predicted—even more fury than before. If you had been through the first half of the storm, you would not have imagined it could get any fiercer. I'm helpless in the face of it and can only hold her and hope she doesn't blow away. I pray for the storm's abatement and continue to murmur my small comforts.

I lose track of time but after some while, she subsides again and begins to breathe shallowly and more regularly. I can feel what little strength remains drain away.

All the while she's been crying, I've been struggling to lower my erection. My cock is full hard and has popped out above the waistline of my pants. The texture of the blanket against the sensitive bulging head is driving me wild. The truth is, I'm close to orgasm. My mind has gone to DEFCON five. The klaxon is ringing and the order 'down periscope' has been issued. My crew of one is a disloyal mutineer with an indomitable brio all his own. DOWN, DOWN, DOWN, DOWN, I command my uncooperative other self. He scoffs at me.

What do you think, that I'm gonna' stand down just because YOU tell me to? You forget who's in charge here. It's gonna' be all right; I'm here, what can I do? You sound pathetic, why don't you give the girl what she really wants, which is me balls deep in her slutty little quim.

Slutty little quim!!? What the fuck? Where does he get this shit? I love this girl; you can't think about her that way.

I see what you mean. She is a sweet little thing; do you think I could go balls deep!?

Please forgive my other self. He is remarkably crude and a horrid boaster. He can think of this one thing and this one thing only. I bargain with him and we reach a mutually "satisfying" agreement that can be summed up this way:

I'll stand down if you promise to give me a massage later on. You see, I'm a little stiff, ha-ha. You will! Great, thanks.

She hasn't given any indication she is aware of my bulging penis, although she must be. *Because you can see me from outer space!* (There he goes boasting again, a thousand apologies.)

Her breathing becomes progressively shallower. She's exhausted the last drop of her reserves and falls stone dead asleep again. I wipe the tears from her face with the blanket. Her mouth is open slightly as she breathes through it. Finally, she is serene. I find her serenity astonishingly arousing.

I get up and lift her along with me in one smooth motion, finding the strength to do so from who knows where. Again, I lay her gently on the sofa. She rolls over on her side, facing the sofa back, and folds her hands under her chin. She must truly be exhausted, physically and emotionally. I know I'm almost done in, myself. I had left my apartment this morning supposedly ready for anything (sans underwear), but there was no way I could have imagined this, much less been prepared for it. There is only one way to relieve the pressure of this persistent erection. Ariel, asleep on the sofa, given the situation and even were she able, would be disinclined to lend me one or both of her beautifully expressive hands-never mind her slutty little quim. I have no choice. I adjourn to the bathroom and live up to my side of this hastily-made-though-mutually-beneficial bargain. Desperate times call for desperate measures and god knows, I'm a desperate desperado.

I come back into the living room feeling less desperate. Ariel is as I left her.

"Ariel, can you hear me," I whisper, and wait to see if she'll respond. She remains motionless and silent. I sit down on the floor next to her.

"Tough day, huh?" What does one say to a grieving, sleeping naked girl? I pause to think of something, "How about this, *I feed on sadness, laughing weep, death and life displease me equally, and I'm in this state, because of you.*[2] I love you more than Coleman ever could. How could you not know that?"

Fuck, it's not supposed to hurt like this, is it?

ii

Ariel awakens with a start to find Jax gone. She panics. She's been abandoned once again. Come back, her inner voice wails like the little boy at the end of that movie Shane. She hears him come out of the bathroom and her panic subsides.

She could never say why but she pretends to be asleep still. She hears his words and his stifled sobbing. They enter her mind like daggers. She has betrayed his innocent and constant longing and has used that betrayal today to make him jealous.

---

[2]

Petrarch: song #134

She knew immediately that Coleman could not have written that dedication. She didn't need a handwriting analysis to know. She even had an inkling that it had been Jax–a flash of intuition she wishes now she hadn't rejected.

The truth was; at the critical moment it didn't matter that she'd known for certain that Coleman hadn't written it. Coleman was there and he seemed not only kind but manly. He is neither enigmatic nor confusing. What he wants is what her own burgeoning passions crave. She cringes at her own shallowness, knowing this is the chief attraction: Coleman is so damn good-looking. She gave up her precious self to him. This precious self that she asserts so boldly to Jax that he should value more than his own life. The thing she herself valued so little that she gave it up like a bitch in heat, at the snap of his fingers, metaphorically at least sticking her ass in the air and welcoming his assault.

After Coleman's assault–that's how she thinks of it now–he dressed and stood over her. She remained naked lying on the bed, letting him look at her, thinking perhaps she had done something wrong. He did, he stood over her, seemingly savoring the moment, his looked changed to one of great disdain and he said, "Thanks for the fuck," delivering the verbal coup de grace in his long-planned-for and twisted revenge.

What had she ever done? She couldn't begin to imagine. She slapped him. It was galling because he was unaffected. She tried to smash his face. He was too strong and too quick, and wouldn't allow her to hit him again. He laughed as she tried. She had been standing on the bed while he stood on the floor. She tried to kick him but he easily swatted her foot away. Losing her balance, she fell over backwards rolling undignified, naked, ass over teakettle, and off the opposite side to the floor. She burns with anger and shame at the mental image of her naked vagina and everything else down there exposed to him for one last comic slapstick look as she slowly tumbles off the bed.

He left without another word, just laughter, which got louder as he descended the stairs, the image of her rolling off the bed becoming funnier and funnier to him with each step. She cursed him every step of the way with words she hadn't known she knew. She had run after him with the idea she would kill him. He was on her front walk. She was naked, but even so, charged out at him a few paces before retreating back to the doorway. This made her angrier. He challenged her to come out. "You want a piece of me Lirilinghi?" he'd taunted, crudely grabbing his crotch to indicate exactly which piece she could have. She threw her black swan rag doll, Muffin, at him, the little doll her mother had made in honor of the story her father had written. This is what she'd grabbed in her blind rage to 'kill' him with. Coleman took poor Muffy with him as a souvenir.

Muffy is gone now, along with all her illusions about love; dashed in their infancy like the head of a baby seal by a merciless blow from a polar bear just as it emerges through the ice to breath. He has since bragged to his buddies, using Muffy as a prop to demonstrate how she had rolled off the bed. His buddies make fun of the little sounds she had made by imitating them for her when she can't avoid them in the hallways, on the street or at the baseball games, to which she now can no longer go. "How about a little tumble?" they ask, and break up into howls of laughter. She confronts them (bravely if you ask me) but they are bold and she feels beaten. Thank god it will all be over in a few days and she'll be out of this prison she had loved until these last few weeks. She fears walking across the little stage to receive her diploma, the sounds she had made while he 'fucked' her raining down on her. The whole thing is blowing up in her mind to frightening proportions. How will she explain their shouted rude comments to her mother—and worse, her cousins? She will defeat them by raising that diploma, class valedictorian, summa cum laude. What has that asshole got but a few sycophants who aren't real friends, who probably secretly hate him and who will drift away as his glory days recede all too quickly. Or maybe she will poison him. She tells herself to quell these angry thoughts, they do her no good, they offer no catharsis. When he left, she had run to the bathroom in a panic to cleanse herself of him. She'd vomited, hanging on the toilet like an over-zealous frat boy driving the porcelain bus on a bad Friday night. How could she know that demons walk the earth and take such pleasing forms? She is terrified that love has been ruined for her forever. She will never be able to trust anyone again. How can she? One's first experience of love (she scoffs at the word in her head) lasts a lifetime, doesn't it?

Spinning in this nauseating sea of grief, confusion, anger and shame, she drifts back into that nether region between sleeping and waking. She prays intently like a child for redemption and forgiveness, for sweetness and innocence, for her father's love, for love. Her last thought before the ever-present exhaustion takes her again is that Jax will be there when she awakens. No matter how long she sleeps, no matter what she has done. He hurts enough to cry but has already forgiven her. How could she who prides herself on being so smart have been so wrong? The crystal shatters, blankness, blessed darkness.

She would never know what a stroke of luck it was that she had grabbed Muffy. Had she hit Coleman with something hard in his face, he would have pushed her back into the house and beaten her within an inch of her life. It is a grave mistake to think you can ever know what might set him off and an even graver one to underestimate what he is capable of. He doesn't know, himself. It was that close. She would never have recovered—even the strongest among us can take only so much. I'm glad our story doesn't take that turn. To see her shattered in mind and body would be more than I could stand.

While she sleeps, I wipe my eyes and venture into the kitchen. I make some more iced tea. I use the last of the ice cubes so I make some more of those too. There isn't anything in the fridge that I can stuff in my face to alleviate my hunger. I haven't eaten anything since a bowl of Life cereal early this morning before I left my apartment for the golf course. I'm dwelling somewhere between mildly peckish and dead from starvation. I drink a little of the iced tea and that does help some.

I use the bathroom, which by the way is very clean. I refrain from masturbating again. Instead, I douse my head with cold water under the faucet in the tub. My level of alert falls to DEFCON 2, maybe 3. I dry my hair with a towel that hangs there, a nice clean fluffy towel. I comb my hair and look at myself in the mirror.

I am not so unpleasant to look at by any means. Perhaps a little skinny like my mother says, but all in all, not so bad. I pose in the mirror, practicing being cool. I laugh at my reflection. It's funny, when I look in a mirror, I can still see that frightened, lovesick boy Sister Demetrius showed me. I don't feel very cool. I return to the chair and place The Doors of Dublin on my lap. I leaf through it slowly, imagining what secrets lay behind those doors and marvel that anyone could dream of publishing a book on such an arcane topic. Did they dream of it as a child?

She awakens with a start. She looks over at me and smiles a sheepish half smile while she stretches (taking care that the blanket stays in place). She seems to have emerged from her emotional cataclysm relatively unscathed. Her eyes are red and puffy and her mood is muted, but otherwise she seems fine.

"Oh my god, your shirt is soaked."

"It's almost dry, I did have to wring it out, though."

She laughs a little.

"Hold on." I dash out to the kitchen and pour iced tea for both of us and bring it back to her.

"Here, have some of this. I'm guessing you're a little dehydrated."

She laughs at this, too. "I'm sorry I cried all over you."

"Hey, listen. I'm glad I could be here," I raise my glass to her.

"To be honest, I'm glad you were," She raises her glass back at me.

We sit in silence for a few minutes. It isn't entirely uncomfortable to do so. I continue turning the pages.

"I hadn't cried for my father until today."

"I figured that out."

"You read the letter, didn't you?"

"Yes"

"I'm a horrible person, are you sure you want to be here?"

"You are not a horrible person. I think you're a very good person."

"You may think differently if I tell you what my last words to my father were. Promise you won't hate me?"

"I promise I won't hate you anymore than I already do!" She doesn't get the joke. Perhaps I'm a little cruel, considering her fragile state. "Ariel, it's just a joke." To know it matters that I might hate her makes me glad though. "No I will not hate you. I couldn't"

She breathes a long and ragged sigh, then proceeds. "I was leaving to go to the library. He was at the kitchen table writing. He had this idea about leaving something behind, about not disappearing into the void without a trace, however small. I think he was frightened by the idea. I said, 'Hang it up, Dad. You are never going to be a writer, you never were, you never will be, goodbye trash man,' to emphasize what he was and to let him know how I saw him and to really get him back for slapping me, that seemed so important. I slammed the door as I left. The next time I saw him..." She trails off.

"You can't blame yourself. There was no way you could have known those would be your last words to him."

"That doesn't matter. He would have found my words very harsh. I chose these words very carefully to hurt him...the words 'you never were.' I chose those specifically because he wrote stories for me when I was a child. To suggest that I hated those stories would have stung him pretty badly. One of my favorites was called Down on Muffin."

She becomes pensive as she lugubriously ponders what fate poor Muffy might have suffered or be suffering. "All he ever did was love me. If I ever felt like a princess, dark or otherwise, it was because he made me feel that way. I thank him by calling him a trash man." She pauses for a moment. She looks at me her eyes puffy, red and glistening with tears. "I have made such a terrible mistake." I have the feeling she's referring to a different mistake and isn't talking about her father. Her breathing is ragged and sobby again.

"We all make mistakes, even me. I know that's hard to believe, but I do." She tries to smile.

"Even now, you try to make me feel better...I feel so ashamed." Again, I have the feeling she isn't talking about her father.

"Maybe I understand." I resist asking, does Coleman? "Listen, you don't have to explain yourself to me," this upsets her. How could I know that she wishes she could? "Hey, if you're going to cry some more, can I run home and get another t-shirt?" She laughs and sobs simultaneously then makes a supreme effort to gather herself. I give her the time she needs and say no more.

273

Muffin returns

A small crowd is gathered in front of Ariel's locker. I push my way through. A black rag doll hangs from the padlock, a noose firmly tied around its neck. A little sign in red ink that reads: death to Muffin 3-7-77 is pinned through Muffin's fading yellow beak (I'm guessing the doll is Muffin). A garish vagina is painted with shocking pink nail polish between Muffin's legs. Muffin is a naked, tumbling Ariel hung in effigy. A crude fertility icon from a barbarous tribe.

Ariel makes her way through the little crowd, excusing herself as she passes. "Muffy!" she gasps. I take out my penknife and move to cut poor Muffin down. Ariel stops me, insisting I leave it. She immediately changes her mind. I ask the kids who've gathered, all freshman and sophomores, if they would please leave us alone. I ask very nicely. One wise ass wants to know if Muffy is a victim of the flood of '06. I punch him hard on his shoulder, full on in that place where the arm goes numb after a flash of intense pain. He leaves crying, mentioning his big brother. I tell him to ask his big brother about my big brother. The rest hurry away to their next classes, some not wanting to get smacked, some fearful of my big brother. I cut Muffin down. Ariel takes her and hugs her morosely.

"I don't know why I should care so much about a stupid rag doll." She says.

"Why is there a black swan rag doll with a painted vagina hanging from your locker?"

"Remember the story my father wrote, Down on Muffin?" She shows me Muffin, indicating that this is the Muffin of the story. I have to fight back the urge to say that it looks like someone went down on muffin. I desperately want to lift her from her moroseness, but I don't want to do it by making her angry. My mind is going a million miles an hour. "Muffy means better times to me. I feel like all the good times in the past?"

"No there are good times ahead, trust me." I say with as much conviction as I can muster.

"Really, what will we do?" 'We,' 'her' and 'I'. 'We' goes off in my head.

"Oh there's so much to do. We can go bowling if you like bowling." With more enthusiasm than bowling should generate in anyone.

"I've never bowled, but I'll try it."

"We'll go to the beach and the movies too of course and we'll listen to the music each other likes. We'll read the books each other likes and go to dinner and hold hands. We'll do everything. It's right in front of you, it always has been."

275

"That all sounds really nice, I feel better already." She reaches out for my hand. She leans into me and I put my arm around her. Someone should hang Muffy from her locker every day! "I love the beach." She says. "There's a beautiful place, a rocky beach, will you go there with me?"

"If I have to carry you..." I say. She laughs a melancholy laugh.

"I love the movies, too," she says, getting in the spirit. "I love sitting in a dark theater, entering another world. Sometimes I get so lost, it's a shock when the movie ends."

"Yes, I know, and we'll share popcorn, too."

"Oh no, I have to have my own popcorn," she blushes at this admission of eccentricity.

"Then you will have your own popcorn, as much as you can stand," I say, as though I were the great and beneficent Oz himself. She laughs her little laugh again.

"What else will we do?"

"Oh I know, here's a good one...I will write poetry for you. I will read them to you and you will tell me how beautiful they are. You will tell me I'm the world's greatest poet."

"Oh I love that idea!"

"You do?"

"Yes, very much. You must come to my house and read your poems to me—you must."

"I will." What had I gotten myself into? I had never written a poem before in my life. I had been caught up in the moment.

"Yes. A week from Saturday at my house! You must, I swear, if you don't, I will never speak to you again." The light has returned to her eyes. She is joking and serious at the same time. I'm really am not sure which she is right now. She holds Muffin over the wastebasket. "When I was a child, I thought as a child. Now I must put aside childish things." She drops poor Muffin in the wastebasket. She turns and walks away, waving goodbye to me, blowing me a kiss and insisting I don't follow.

She is mercurial, that's for sure. I contemplate rescuing Muffin from the trash, but decide against it.

The Angry Letter Carrier

The evening of the next day, Nancy Turner knocks on my apartment door. "Imagine my surprise," I say, trying to be nonchalant.

"Ariel asked me to give this to you." She hands me an envelope. "I didn't come here to have a pleasant chat with you."

"No, we've always been so cordial. Why would she ask you?"

"Believe me, I don't know, but she did and I said I would because it gives me the opportunity to tell you that I don't like you very much."

"Wow, tell me how you really feel."

"Alright, I think you're an asshole who's no good for my friend."

"Aaaaahhh, that was a rhetorical question. You're just mean, I've seen you be mean, especially to Ariel."

"You don't know anything and it's none of your business."

"Well, thanks for this." I wave the envelope. "I love your singing voice. If only the rest of you were so beautiful."

"Fuck you."

I really don't understand why Nancy hates me so much or how it is that she is Ariel's friend. She is resistant to explaining herself, especially to me. Would it help if I knew that to Ariel, she is as solicitous as any lover ever was? Would I change my mind if I knew that she feels for Ariel as I do? She's been fighting these feelings all her life. It is this that explains their periodic fallings-out and her rebuffs of Ariel's attempts at reconciliation. Would I sympathize if I knew it made her ill to hand this note to me and it had been so unfair of Ariel to ask her to deliver it.

278

Would I sympathize with her if I knew she wished she could choose another love or if I knew her dreams of Ariel are as fevered as my own. What would I say if I knew that the reconciling embraces I'd seen and imagined morphing into something more than friendly, had indeed been to Nancy a lovers embrace? Had I sensed something in that embrace that sparked my imagination. Would I understand that Nancy reenacts this embrace over and over in her dreams and lulls herself to sleep thinking of it because it had felt so nice too touch Ariel almost in all the ways she wanted to and that it sometimes makes her cry. Would I feel for her if I knew the effort she expends to restrain herself from reenacting that moment for real? Would I have sympathy for her if I knew that she knows her love for Ariel is more hopeless than my own? Would I feel for her, even as I prepare to write my poems, that she has written many, many love poems to Ariel? She burns them only after she's finished burning them into her mind. She's burnt them all even the ones that it breaks her heart to burn—Paeans to her longing, secret, Sapphic love that she must, at all cost, keep secret. She would be unable to stand having her poetry much less the emotion that compels her derided, as she knows it would be, viciously, perhaps even by Ariel. Would I feel for her if I knew that she feels cursed to have such a beautiful voice that she can't use to sing of her love to her love? I have no inkling of these things—to me, Nancy's motives are hidden, she just

279

appears mean. We part company and I honestly hope we never see each other again. Unless it is to hear her sing.

The Invitation

The letter has a strange power. To see my name written in her beautifully rounded calligraphy gives me a sharp emotional jolt. I have some idea what she must have felt when she discovered her father's posthumous letter to her and why she wasn't anxious to read it. I fear the worst. Will she thank me for being there for her in her hour of need? Will she say we will be friends and that I hold a special place in her heart? It will hurt all the more for being so trite and predictable, that she wouldn't waste the effort to write something—anything more original. These thoughts speed through my mind as I open the letter.

It is a card, not a letter. I slide it out. The card is handmade, folded once in standard folio. As soon as I see it, I know it's not a 'Dear John' letter and I curse myself for doubting. The front is painted in watercolor. A violet spiral winds its way outwards from the center, adhering to the golden ratio, an aesthetic necessity, pleasing to the eye and soul. The background is sky blue, turning the perfect spiral from geometry to an aerial phenomenon. In the upper right-hand corner is the silhouette of a bird. The two little brushstrokes that are the universal symbol of a distant bird in flight cross the upper left quadrant of the full moon. The moon looks like the real moon, shaded perfectly so that the man in the moon hangs in the sky looking down on the folly of humanity. In the upper left corner, there is the great pyramid of Cheops. The remnants of the cement casing that caps the point perfectly replicated. A large palm tree hangs over the pyramid as though the pyramid were being viewed from an oasis by ancient, weary Herodotus, to whom the pyramid itself is ancient.

I can't divine what any of it might mean, but that she had put a lot of work into it is readily apparent. How she had produced this masterpiece and done so in one day seems miraculous to me. I put it under the heading, 'genius is as genius does.'

I open the card, printed in her handwriting, which is severe when compared to her cursive, revealing perhaps a different facet of her personality, if you believe in claptrap. The right side is informational. It reads:

You are invited to read your work

at the first annual Ariel Lirilinghi

Poetry Contest

When: Saturday June 6th

Where: 19 Anselm Terrace (my house)

The left side of the card contains a personal message. This is in her beautifully rounded cursive. The voice is intimate and yearning.

Please come say beautiful words to me,

fill me with your dreams and your passion,

Say the words that only I can hear

Make me feel your heart in your words

if you can.

If you can, you may find

a prize I hope you will value beyond

any book or golden hind.

Including a little poem of her own is a nice touch. Across the bottom on the left side, she wrote RSVP. On the right, Formal Attire Only, which means another shoplifting expedition. My heart pounds with nervous excitement. I'm sitting at my kitchen table next to the open window. I look out at the parking lot, across to the overgrown patch of weeds that serves as a barrier in front of the truck junkyard that we have dubbed the truck factory. No trucks are manufactured there and so how it came to be called this is lost in the mist. It is rather an elephants' graveyard where the exposed bones of cannibalized trucks give themselves back to the earth.

How can I match the artistry of her invitation? Have I made a promise I can't keep? I have promised her better times. I have promised her poetry. I don't want to disappoint her right out of the chute, that would be awful. I envision her trying to hide her disappointment upon hearing my poetry and I cringe. I wonder vaguely if I can talk her into going bowling instead. I had promised her bowling, too, after all. Judging from the invitation, this is important to her. I have to try (plus the prize!).

My mother comes into the kitchen and reads the invitation. I had left it in the middle of the table while I mused, with my attention out the window.

"Who is Ariel Lie-ree-lin-gee?" She has trouble with Ariel's last name, as everybody does. I'm not quite sure if I'd ever heard that particular corruption though.

I snap out of my reverie. "Ma, it's not fair that you read that."

"I didn't know what it was, Johnny-poopy-doopy."

"Oh god, will you please not call me that."

"OK....Johnny poopy doopy!" It was kind of funny and I let it slide. "Be careful!"

"Be careful of what, Ma?"

"Of all the things you need to be careful of." This is as close as my mother would get to warning me about the dangers of premarital sex. "Be careful you don't get your heart broken. You're so sensitive. Are you going to write a poem for this girl?"

"I'm going to try, poems not poem. Poems." I leave out that my heart is broken, but I'm on the mend. I'm resilient, if nothing else.

"Poems, oh my, are you in love?"

"Yes, I think so. If love is a tidal wave of feelings that drives you mad, then I guess I'm as in love as anyone has ever been."

"Sounds like love...you're so young." She pauses. "You know your father wrote a poem for me once. I suppose it wasn't very good. I don't remember it specifically, but he was charming and nervous and swept me off my feet."

"You're shittin'!" I exclaimed, "not possible! Do you have it? I won't believe it unless I see it."

"No, I'm not shittin'. I'm sure it's long gone." It had once been as treasured a keepsake as this card would become for me if events beyond my control didn't intervene. My mother becomes sad. She, too, is mercurial. I don't have to tell her not to tell my father about me writing poems. I know she won't.

I leave my mother in the kitchen so that I might call Ariel. She picks up the phone and after a nervous exchange of pleasantries, I tell her I will be there. "I can't refuse your invitation especially since it is so elegantly rendered. How could I?" I leave out that I would have accepted if it was written on used toilet paper—no sense in being too honest. She tells me she can't wait. To be honest, neither can I. I'm highly motivated. If I fail, it won't be for lack of trying.

"I'm nervous."

"Why?"

"I hope you don't expect too much."

School is almost over. All that's left is studying for final exams. I'm not the best student, but I have a great head for facts. I remember things and am able to quickly recall them when pressed. I can name the capital city of almost any country in the world. I know the dates and places of all the battles of the Hundred Years War, the Civil War (American and English), and World War I. I know the names and order of succession of the nineteenth-century British prime ministers (backwards and forwards). My head is filled with all the arcana that passes for knowledge. I'm also supremely confident in my ability to baffle my teachers with bullshit when it comes to essay questions, their major failing being they believe themselves above being baffled by bullshit. Mr. Delaney had no idea and was such a densoid that he never would; my paper on genius was a work of fiction that I knocked off the night before and yet I got the best grade, of course Ariel said it was good too and she's no densoid, maybe I'm wrong about Delaney. I'll have to think about that.

The only subject I'm likely to have any real trouble with is physics. There is no bullshit in physics (until you get to advanced physics). Mr. Chisholm, our physics teacher is a priggish martinet who believes that once he's written it on the blackboard, I should know it in my bones. He is a terrible teacher. I devote all of the studying time I can stand to physics and things are actually becoming less murky. Otherwise, I devote every waking minute and many minutes when I should be asleep to writing poetry. That these poems wind up in a ball in my wastebasket is beside the point. The poetry prize weighs much more heavily on my mind than my diploma.

Driven to Distraction

Early on the next Saturday, following Ariel's emotional cataclysm, my father drives me to the golf course. He has an Oldsmobile Delta 88 coupe, black with a red interior. The engine is huge. It is the kind of car that when you step on the accelerator, it pushes you back in your seat and the needle on the gas gauge moves discernibly as the huge engine gulps gas.

My father makes it a habit of driving twenty miles over the speed limit—one hand on the wheel, one hand out the window with a cigarette (always a Camel) wedged between his index and middle fingers. My father has a large brown nicotine stain on these fingers. He expertly weaves his hurtling Olds through the narrow streets. I'm never nervous in my father's car even though he drives like a maniac. He is so sure of himself.

He takes a swig of whiskey from a flask and hands it to me. I can't tell if he's offering it or testing me. I decide it's a test and I say, "No Thanks."

"Pussy." I was right it was a test and I flunked.

My father is the kind of guy who beeps at old ladies stopped at red lights and yells, "Get outta' the way, old bat." I say, "Dad the light is red." He says, "shut up, I'm driving and if you don't like the way I drive, you can get out and walk." Then he threatens me with what he calls a backhander.

"What are you doing next Saturday?" He asks me as we speed by the cars lining the road that rises into Newton from the BC trolley stop.

"Why?"

He puts the cigarette in his mouth, switches hands on the wheel and threatens me with another backhander all in one fluid, catlike motion, not necessarily keeping his eyes on the road but maintaining a nice, steady twenty miles an hour over the speed limit.

"Don't answer a question with a question."

"I have plans." I can't think up a lie fast enough. I wasn't going to tell him about the poetry contest. If I did, he'd tell me that it just confirmed his suspicions that I was a little light in the loafers. If I tell him I know he had written a poem and was therefore possibly light in the loafers himself......well, who knows where that might end. If I tell him the prize for winning the contest is to make love with the most beautiful girl in the world, it wouldn't make a difference. He still would accuse me of being a little loose in the hips. My father is a notorious anti-intellectual. He has nothing but disdain for what he calls book learning and zero patience with my horrid vice of reading. He equates these things with effeminacy.

My father once 'caught' me reading War and Peace. I remember exactly where I was in the book: Petya Rostov had just won a scrum for a biscuit the emperor tossed from a balcony. My father tore the book from my hands and told me to "Go out and get laid and don't come back until you do." I kid you not. I sneaked back in later still chaste, much to my father's disgust. I never saw that copy of War and Peace again; I suppose it made its way to the incinerator.

There is no way I will share my poetry with my father. He would disown me and although technically there is no estate from which to be disinherited, I still need a place to live.

He announces, "next Saturday is the anniversary of D-Day and I have four little sapling birch trees we are going to plant in this place in the woods I found. One tree each for Ricky, Freddie, Tyrus and your Uncle Ray. We'll plant them and have a nice little ceremony."

Oh shit, how the fuck am I supposed to get out of this? The one day I can't be there in my whole life. The one day my father wants me around. I'm sure the only reason he really wants me there was so I can dig the holes and put the trees in the ground so he won't have to do it. I'd plant four trees in the woods and then go away and forget them, never visit them, never tend to them and neither will he. The little ceremony will be me digging holes and him drinking scotch.

"I don't give a shit about Tyrus or Uncle Ray." Bang. The world goes black and the stars come out. He lands the backhander square on my nose. I bleed. I throw my head back and check to make sure my nose isn't broken. We say nothing to each other the rest of the way. He stops in front of the clubhouse. I get out as blood spots my t-shirt, coagulates in my nostrils.

"Dad, I can't make it next Saturday."

"What the fuck is wrong with you? Your Uncle Ray died for you." He is super pissed, about to blow a gasket.

"Dad, I never knew him, He didn't die for me. If you want to beat me into going with you then go ahead, but I'm not going otherwise."

"Get the fuck out, and don't forget to bring all the money home. Don't buy a sub or a coke, if you do I'll be planting YOU in the ground." Always a pleasant drive with Dad. He tears out, tires squealing, spitting a rooster tail of sand and gravel at me.

A Poem Gets a Reading; Sort of

Nine hours later, after hauling a load of golf clubs that a mule should have been carrying for people who should have been banned from playing golf, I'm sunburned, exhausted and famished. I take some of the money and buy a large Italian sub with all the fixings. I say grace, which goes something like this: "Fuck you, Dad." I wolf down the sub, washing it down with two cokes. I know I've said it before but hunger makes things taste so good, I can't resist buying another one. I drink more cokes and head home, my stomach upset from eating too much too fast.

My walk home is a real trudge, T-R-U-D-G-E. I always spelled that word in my head. I take a number of rest stops. I finally make it to the top of the hill above the park. I'm almost home. I have one of my poems with me. I get to the bottom of the hill and take it out of my back pocket. I proceed to read it and recite it under my breath, concentrating as hard as I can while walking. I have this idea that I should memorize them so I can look at Ariel when reading the critical passages, so she may better feel my heart in the words.

Suddenly, the paper is snatched from my hands and I'm pushed to the ground. Coleman Curran stands over me. It feels good to lie down in the cool grass.

"Get up, faggot!"

"You knock me down then you want me to get up? Make up your mind!" He kicks me in the ribs, it really hurts. "I guess I'm getting up."

Coleman gets right in my face. "Stay away from Ariel. She has the sweetest, tightest pussy and its mine. If I catch you near her, you'll get more than a broken arm and a mouthful of piss. I will kill you."

"I won't stay away from her just because you say so and I know there's no way you could know anything about her pussy- so fuck you. He punches me hard right to my stomach. It not only really hurts, but it dislodges the two Italian subs. I go down on my knees and deposit my supper on the ground. Italian subs and cokes do not taste so good coming up, I can't really recommend it. Coleman has a laugh. He proceeds to read the poem to the audience of little kids who have gathered at a safe

291

distance. I roll away on the grass. He reads haltingly and tentatively. There is no rhythm to his reading, some of the words he is totally unfamiliar with, so he botches them. The sense is lost even to me. He doesn't get very far before he throws the paper to the ground and passes his judgment that I'm a puking faggot. He delivers another kick to my ribs and turns in disgust that I haven't put up more of a fight.

"Stay away from her or I will kill you, You've been warned." he says by way of a parting shot.

"I've heard this threat a million times and I've heard guys brag about fucking girls they hadn't fucked more than once. I didn't believe him for a moment, she never would fuck him. I don't even like associating that word with her. I believe her, how could I believe him over her. I lie in the grass and watch the hue of the sky change from pale metallic blue to azure. A vapor trail grows across the sky seemingly by magic, as the plane generating the trail is too high up to be seen. The air cools. A zephyr scented by the sweet and deep perfume of lilac wafts past. Calmness settles over me. The world is beautiful there on the grass. One of the little kids who'd been keeping a safe distance had retrieved my poem and brought it back to me.

"Are you all right, mister?"

"Yes, kid, thanks." I realize Coleman can't read. I mean he can read, he can look at a page and pick out the words. I know he's been cheating off other kids for years at school. He has to be able to read to do that, but it's a chore for him. He probably has never read a book in his life. How could he possibly. He can't escape the way I can. I almost feel sorry for him. I can't imagine Ariel, to whom the life of the mind is so important, tolerating this flaw in someone she might choose to love. She would see it as a grievous shortcoming. If there was or is a competition for her heart between Coleman and I, I mean if it were just the two of us, then I have already won. Coleman no longer seems so fearsome. The world is beautiful. My ribs do ache though. I have no idea that the issue had been decided by other means and that his desire to keep us apart has nothing to do with Ariel, but is just an aspect of his particular psychopathy. He remembers their tryst fondly, because he is crazy. My mind drifts back to being thrown hard to the floor. I cringe at the impact in my head. I remind myself of what else he did. He must never be taken lightly and to feel any sympathy for him is weakness.

.

The Chinese Philosopher Makes a Mean Coffee Frappe

One other thing of note happens before the poetry reading. I'm sitting in Rourke's drug store after caddying the next day. It is early afternoon. I had decided to do only one loop because I'm tired from lack of sleep and the emotional events of yesterday. I have a coffee frappe in front of me. It is awesome, so cold and thick. The door opens, the little bell tinkles signifying someone's entrance. I'm facing away from the door and don't turn around. Ariel's friend, Jeralyn, sits down next to me. I like Jeralyn, she is a nice girl.

"Hi," I say

"Hi," she says

"Why don't you turn around?" Jeralyn says while spinning me on the stool. Ariel stands there in the same beginning pose I saw the day she danced in the gym. She is wearing dark green shorts and a red tube top. She is like Christmas in July (even though it's not July). She hasn't got the full idea yet of how sexy she can be. The floor of Rourke's drugstore is polished marble, ideal for dancing. She dances the same dance she did in the gym, minus the grand amplitude maneuvers. She finishes differently. This time, while tiptoe on one sneakered foot, she reaches back and lifts the other leg behind and above her head, holding it in place with both hands. Her foot is above and slightly in front of her head. She spins slowly to a stop. I hold my breath while she does. I can see her underpants white with thin horizontal red stripes. I bite the inside of my cheek hard, hard enough to bleed.

When she stops, the man behind the counter bursts into applause. Ariel turns bright red, even her legs blush. Her legs, the blushing and the dance inspire a poem, which I hastily compose in my head (dance does rhyme with underpants). She puts a hand on my chest and says in her beautifully mellifluous voice, "you should believe your own eyes and what your own heart tells you."

"I will, from now on." No sense in spoiling the moment by mentioning Coleman. They move toward the door. "Will I see you?"

"If you look for me!" her eyes are gleaming. They run out the door laughing. Goddam it, she's a mystery. My hands are shaking when I pick up my frappe and the cold feels good on my bleeding cheek.

"Is that your girlfriend?" the man behind the counter asks.

"I wish." I answer, running my tongue over the torn skin inside my mouth.

"Don't be stupid," is all he will say in answer and would say no more despite my repeated demand that he explain himself. He stands there silently wiping down the fountain equipment. He finally allows that "a nod is as good as a wink to a blind man." He adjourns to the back room, annoyed by my insistence on an explanation.

"Who do you think you are, fucking Confucius!?" I yell after him. He doesn't come out of the room. "More like fucking

Confusedcius!" I mutter to myself. I finish my frappe and leave. Ariel is nowhere to be seen.

16. Poetic License

Thirty years ago, my father landed on Omaha beach. He dove into the sand and began as he puts it, digging his way to China. It was the most important and cataclysmic day in his life, a day more important and cataclysmic than any day I've faced or am ever likely to face the devil willing. I know the historical importance of the day. I know its importance in my father's and thus in my own life. I feel a pang of guilt, but I have a different life. I can't go forward and live in his past. I have my own cataclysmic and important days to live. If they can never be as cataclysmic or transformative I still have to live them. I can't live my days by helping him relive his. With luck my days can be as transformative without being so catastrophic or requiring so much bravery.

My father has always said I'm a lot like my Uncle Ray. Maybe I am. I like to think I'm smarter and would not stand up in a hailstorm of bullets. However, If I were as smart as I like to pretend to be, I'd know that my father has re-made Uncle Ray to be more like me in his mind, because he loves me in his broken way.

It's been a long two weeks of studying physics, exams, caddying, dodging Coleman, writing and anxious waiting. Ariel opens her front door between my first and second knocks (old Moses going through Missus' front door). I take it she'd been waiting by the door for my arrival. It's good to know she's anxious, too. The living room is to the left through an opening. It is the same room where she underwent her own, perhaps transformative cataclysm. It is strange to reenter; it seems smaller in reality than it is in my mind.

The room is arranged as it had been. The sofa is to my right, along the wall as I enter. The chair on which we sat while she cried is kiddie-corner opposite. The Doors of Dublin (old faithful companion) patiently awaits perusal on the table next to it. There are two additions to the room. A podium stands in the opening between this room and the dining room. A brown metal folding chair is in the middle of the room. This is where she will sit while I recite my poetry at the podium.

"Where did you get this?" I ask a hand on the podium. I'm glad to see it. I've worried about my stack of poems rustling like leaves as I nervously try to read. It's not cool to be nervous. Now I can place them on the podium and have one less thing to worry about.

"Oh, you don't know...I'm the class valedictorian. I asked Sister Cuthbert if I could use it to practice my speech and voila, here it is. She had Gary the janitor bring it. By the way, I think

Gary the janitor is kind of creepy." This was as much as she would ever say about her sleepwalking sojourn among the minor demons beneath St. Col's. She credits her sojourn to exhaustion, and has put it mostly out of her mind although she can't forget that she'd awakened naked except for the blanket her mother had covered her with. They have not discussed the incident. She has been sleeping better lately.

"Yeah, he's too friendly to be completely normal. But wow, congrats on being named valedictorian—that's a big, big deal. I should tell you that my money was on you. You beat out that snake in the grass, Julius.

"What do you mean, your money was on me?"

"I mean, I made five hundred on a twenty-dollar bet."

"Really?"

"Yeah, all the supposedly smart money was on Julius."

"I'm smarter than he is, how could the smart money be on him?"

"I know, that's why I put my money on you. Apparently he's been spreading the word that he's smarter than you."

She squints, eyeing me suspiciously. I'm usually pretty adept at weaving and putting across these little fictions. I had gone too far with the detail about Julius spreading the word.

How could that have any bearing on the outcome. She is more perceptive than most and sees I've made it up.

"Good One," she says and chalks one up for me. A gesture I taught her. It's awesome to see her so unconsciously imitate me.

I chalk up another one for me. "That's for me, too. If you're keeping score and it looks like you are, then you know I'm in the lead and pulling away."

"Oh no, I get bonus points for being valedictorian!" She starts drawing tick marks in the air with all ten fingers.

"I agree, but you get minus points for bragging about it!" I wipe her tick marks away with an imaginary eraser.

"I can't win, can I!?"

"Now you're learning!" I say, as I chalk up another one for me and she whacks me on the shoulder (a love tap). "Here, I'll give you back a couple for being valedictorian, now we're even." She seems pleased with my fair-mindedness. Am I wrong or did we just have fun?

"Have you practiced your speech?"

"Yes, I'm a little nervous. Do you have any suggestions?"

I can tell she's just asking to be courteous. "Well, I think you should start with a joke; they say it's always best to get the crowd on your side."

She looks doubtful.

"You're right, what do I know?"

I stand behind the podium. She stands across from me, bright eyed and expectant. She is dressed like a princess. My opinion as to what a princess should wear suddenly set in stone. Ariel is wearing it. She is a complete knockout. The dress is silken, a rich fabric that has depth. The body of the dress is sky blue. There is an elaborately stitched violet piping. The piping is a quadruple helix sewn from hem to collar, winding its way around her, accentuating the contours of her body to great advantage. It is made from a thread that reflects light to a greater degree than the dress. It catches the light at various angles causing Ariel to seem to always be changing direction. This affect mesmerizes me to the extent that sometimes I think it's happening in my mind. Since I had seen the invitation first, I marvel that she should have either made or bought a dress to match. It takes a minute for me to realize that of course it is the other way around. She had planned to wear this dress; she hadn't just donned 'this old thing,' as it were. The skirt is very short and her skinny, pretty legs are bare.

Her hair is done up in a complex intertwining of red ribbons and raven tresses, a love knot of such complexity I could lose myself. It is a crown befitting a dark princess. How she engineered this hairdo on her own, I can't imagine. I ascribe it to her genius, which exhibits itself in everything she undertakes. The hairdo pulls her hair off her forehead revealing her eyebrows. Her eyebrows are quite a striking feature, thick and black and stark against her skin. I can't fathom what it is about her eyebrows that I find so appealing but the truth is, I do. They are exactly the way I would have made them if I were the god of eyebrows. The hairdo also reveals the nape of her neck. Her neck is so delicate and feminine. I want to kiss her there so badly. I wonder if she'd like to be kissed there or if she'd find it strange.

She wears a pair of dangling earrings that I think of as gypsy earrings (she is my Esmeralda; I'm her Quasimodo). I remember that Quasimodo, as king of the fools, was captivated by Esmeralda's dancing as I had been by Ariel's. I get a lump in my throat. The Hunchback of Notre Dame is one of my favorite books, except I have a little trouble with the epilogue. It's difficult to believe that Quasimodo lies down next to his dead Esmeralda and waits to die. No one could love anyone that much, could they?

My eyes wander down her legs to her shoes, which are black leather and square toed. They are like Pilgrims' shoes, though more fashionable and without the buckle. She is slightly dink toed. She becomes conscious of where my eyes are and tries to square her feet. If only she knew how perfect and painfully endearing I find this 'imperfection'. The girl I know, beautiful as she is, has been replaced by this otherworldly sylph standing before me. She will shimmer and disappear if I reach out to touch her.

To see that she was serious about the "formal attire only" proviso makes me think that perhaps she is equally serious about the prize. I'm glad I took the attire proviso seriously, too. I'm not dressed formally but I'm dressed in all new clothes, right down to my underwear and socks. I had stolen the entire ensemble from Kings department store in Watertown. I had stolen clothes that I thought a poet might wear on such an occasion (and that were readily available to be stolen from King's department store, it not being renowned particularly as the favored outfitter of poets worldwide). My ensemble consists of black slacks (of reasonably good quality), black shoes (that pinch my feet a little), and a white shirt with French cuffs (I had no idea what French cuffs were when I stole it). I imagine that this is how a beat poet might wear French cuffs, with just the tips of his fingers extending beyond the sleeves. Also cufflinks symbolically manacle the poet to a societal norm and are therefore an impediment to free thinking and creativity, which is why I eschew the wearing of cufflinks (plus I don't actually own any). My shirt is not tucked into my pants, not just because I believe this is how a real poet would wear it, but it will also serve to hide the bulge that could at any moment press hard against my zipper.

All of a sudden, as though a trap door has opened beneath my feet, my confidence falls away. Is it because she is so beautiful and smart? Do I feel myself unworthy? Do I fear I will not be able to keep up with her and will fall short when the final tally is counted? Is it because I doubt my ability as a poet? Why am I so eager to hand my heart to a girl who I have reason to believe got "the shit fucked out of her" by my hated and sworn enemy? Why do I love her? Why have I always loved her? Why does anyone love anyone? Is it because she has nice eyebrows, or because she looks good in a short skirt, or because she's dink toed and cried in my arms? Do I love her because she can tell me her thoughts in that musical voice? I have no fucking clue why I love her; I only know I do. I want to believe she's told me the truth and that nothing happened between her and Coleman, but rumors fly at school. They are hard to ignore. I try to believe my heart. I try to believe in her. I try to be strong. Gorgon took great glee in my stricken expression when he too eagerly and too graphically apprised me of the rumor. I punched him as hard as I could right in his stupid face.

Who am I kidding? For god's sake, I've stolen the clothes I'm wearing in a pathetic effort to make myself worthy. Suddenly, I don't feel so good about that. Is being an accomplished shoplifter something to be proud of?

I live in a soul-crushing slum. I see it outside my window every day, a world where poetry doesn't exist. A world where life is nasty, brutish and sometimes very short (I have seen life be all these things). I would never ask Ariel to come to my apartment. I would be too ashamed to show her the relative squalor in which I live. My writing desk, the desk on which I've tried to write beautiful poems, is someone else's trash. My mother put contact paper over the writing surface in an attempt to dress it up. The contact paper is a sickening shade of green. The deep scratches on the writing surface cause me to puncture the paper I write on, as well as the contact paper beneath if I forget to back it properly. There is a matchbook under the right front leg. The desk wobbles like a leaky rowboat on a raging sea without it.

Where do I get the nerve to think I could write one single word that she might think is beautiful, never mind the string of words required to reasonably call something a poem? Most of what I know of the world is ugliness. The only real beauty I've ever seen stands before me now in this room, more beautiful than I have ever seen her even in my most beautiful dreams. The world eats dreamers like me.

"Are you alright?" she asks

"Not really sure," I answer. An iron band wraps around my chest. I can't breathe. I have to sit down. I sit on the brown metal folding chair. She comes and stands in front of me. I grab her and pull her to me as though she were my only chance at salvation. I press my face against her breasts; I feel their soft firmness through the dress against the side of my face.

"It's alright," she says. My own simple, consoling platitude used against me, so to speak. Her words soothe my emotional burns. Maybe my words did help her a little on that day.

"I've really tried," is all I can say, referring possibly to my poetry, possibly to everything. If I try to say anything else, I might cry… you know that feeling. I don't want to cry. I want to be a man, like my father is.

"You asked me if I ever remembered you being kind to me," she says tenderly. I can hear her words in my ears and feel them in her chest accompanied by her heart.

"Yes," I say.

"You lent me a pencil one day." she says. "Do you remember?"

"I remember," I say. "I remember everything, every moment of my life as long as you are in it." She wraps her arms around my head and strokes my hair with such a loving touch.

"I remember, too," she says, again very tenderly. "I'd did really well on that test."

"I flunked that test."

"Really!" she says surprised, Why?"

"That was my only pencil." I leave out the beating I'd taken for getting a zero. My father cursing me for being as stupid as my brother, the paragon of stupidity. She doesn't say anything for a few minutes; she embraces my head and strokes my hair. She leans her head atop mine. Finally, she says "Would you like your pencil back?"

"No, I want you to have it," I whisper.

"I knew that's what you'd say." She says so gently. I've never been spoken to so gently. She surrounds me. I grip her tightly around her hips and she does not resist. I love her with all my might. I tremble with this emotion. I have to grip her tighter to stop the trembling, I think I might cry, I think she's trying to make me cry. I think she wants to feel the emotion from me I felt from her. We stay like this, wordless, until she gently asks to be released, my grip too tight for comfort. It takes every ounce of will I have to let her go.

I adjourn to the bathroom to splash some cold water on my face and pull myself together. I come out into the kitchen. She has taken the time to make martinis.

"Here you go Mr. Bond, shaken not stirred just as you like it." She doesn't embarrass me by asking me if I'm feeling better. She knows I like 007.

"Thank you, Miss Lirilinghi," I say in my best imitation. I've never had a martini and have no idea what to expect. I raise it to my lips.

"Mr. Bond, aren't you supposed to say something clever before we drink."

"OK, how about this; bottoms up, Miss Lirilinghi," I say, trying hard to intone a suggestive double-entendre, as Bond would in a similar situation.

"Oh, Mr. Bond, you really are very naughty," she says, amalgamating every Bondian femme-fatale, playing along nicely.

"I'll drink to that!" we clink glasses and each take a larger gulp than we should, being the inexperienced drinkers that we are. My first thought is that her genius has found its limit. It tastes like gasoline, only not as good! I hold the liquid in my mouth and it burns. I can't imagine why Bond would choose to drink such poison. My body rebels against my brain's orders to swallow. Ariel solves this problem by spitting what she's gulped into the sink in neither very ladylike nor femme-fatale fashion. In a titanic act of will, I swallow. The liquid rides its fiery way to my empty stomach, hits and rebounds. I can feel the involuntary death mask grimace carved into my face. My diaphragm spasms as it tries to expel the alien substance. After a brief but intense struggle, I manage to hold it down. The delicious warmth spreads through my body. It isn't a bad feeling.

She raises her head from the sink. "Why Miss Lirilinghi, I take it your martini wasn't to your satisfaction?"

"No, definitely not."

"Strange, mine seems perfect."

"Really, then take another drink."

I do and it burns but is not as bad. I finish it in short order and feel pretty relaxed. She doesn't drink hers. The martinis were a brilliant idea. She is a genius's genius. I feel invincible and am ready to read my poems.

She sits in the chair. The short dress rides up and I can see her white cotton underpants stretched over the gentle swell of her Mons. I feel a tingle in my pants as my mutinous first mate rises from his slumber. I use the biting the inside of my cheek trick again and my penis resumes his tenuous hibernation. I take a swig of her martini, which stings this new laceration, further ensuring penile subjugation.

I look down at my first poem and am horrified. At the time I had written it I thought it was funny, a way to break the ice. Now, here with her, it just seems crass and crude. I resist a wild urge to apologize for the quality of the poetry. Don't do that, I tell myself. If she hates it she hates it, but don't tell her she should.

She applauds politely as though she were a real attendee at a real poetry reading. She squirms a little in her chair. Please don't do that I say to her, in my mind.

"Thanks for coming to the first annual Ariel Lirilinghi poetry contest. I may as well jump right into it since this is why you're here. I call this first work 'There once was a girl'." I clear my throat and grab the podium. I proceed, sure I'm about to ruin what had just been so beautifully repaired. I yell at myself not to edit what I've written while I read. Let go, god dammit!

"There once was a girl from St. Col's.

The smartest and prettiest in those halls.

I think of her all day.

And I hope by the way.

That someday she will play with my balls"

I brace myself against the barrage of invective and the retraction of the invitation I'm sure is coming. Is that laughter? It is. She is laughing. She applauds and says "Bravo! Author!" I step out from the podium and take a bow, as deep a bow as possible. I breathe a simultaneous and equally deep sigh of relief at her response. I resist the almost overwhelming urge to sneak a peek at her undies. Be cool, be suave, there is plenty of time I tell myself. It's a much better solution than eating my cheeks from the inside out.

It takes a minute or two for me to settle down. I pace back and forth, all jittery. I look at her and she looks at me. A spark passes between us. I take a sip of the iced tea she had placed on the podium (another nice touch).

She raises her hand to ask a question. I say, "Yes miss, what is your question"

While she asks I take another sip. Her question is this: "I was just wondering if the smart and pretty girl is strictly limited to only playing with your balls?"

I inhale the tea and launch a coughing fit through which I force out the answer, "It's a free country!!" I had perhaps wanted to shock her when I wrote this poem but she has turned the tables, which is why she is the valedictorian. I mentally score one for her. She is filling the air with tick marks.

My coughing jag subsides and I politely ask, "If the audience will please show proper respect for the artist, who has agreed at great personal cost to come here and let you feel his heart."

She puts her hand to the side of her mouth and in a stage whisper says, "Whew, that's a relief, I thought he wanted me to feel his balls." I break up laughing and she does, too. I would never have guessed her either inclined to, or capable of, such ribaldry. She would give my friend Owen a run for his money.

"Moving on, I call this next poem 'Ariel/Skinny/Pretty'

Ariel:

On skinny pretty legs she tries.

On skinny pretty legs she dances.

On skinny pretty legs she flies!

On skinny pretty legs she entrances.

On skinny pretty legs she cries."

She blushes, "My legs aren't that skinny are they?"

"Your legs inspire poetry, obviously. I wish my poem were as beautiful as your legs. The poem, however, isn't so much about your legs."

"I was just looking at my legs, though, and they're not that skinny are they?"

"They are also very pretty, don't forget."

"I know," she says ironically and smiles.

Something has come over me. I come around the podium and kneel in front of her. My heart pounds away in my chest screaming to be let out. I place my hands on her knees. "I can think of nothing better than to admire your legs for the rest of the day, I've spent many a day doing just that." She blushes pure red and so do I and thank god I'd decided to wear my shirt un-tucked. That was surely a stroke of genius. I gently stroke her

311

legs as far up her thighs as I dare, she doesn't flinch or push my hands away. We are close to the edge. "Should I stop reading?"

"No, I would like to hear them all." She says.

"Okay," I say pushing myself up from her knees and spinning as I go to keep my arousal hidden. I get back to the podium and shuffle my poems, my hands shake. I take a few deep breaths and she does too I notice. I explain the genesis of the next poem.

"I chased you up the stairs once. I sang to you; I don't know where I got the nerve. Do you remember?"

"I do, very much!"

"As you ran up the stairs ahead of me, I was able to see up your skirt, I mean as you ran and your skirt bounced. I saw your underwear with every step. I kissed you at the top of the stairs." She blushes at my remembrance. "It was the first time I felt desire so intensely. It was for me the moment when whatever drove me before became something else. I thought I would never feel anything so intensely again, I imagined myself jaded and worldly. I don't wish to ruin this moment, but, as I felt it then, so I feel now only more. I call this poem desire.

On skinny pretty legs

Her incarnadine mantle

Blossoms!

Scarlet vies with crimson

Cerise rings race Vermillion

Smudges

Across her skin.

She makes

Furtive attempts

To hide her

Red-essence

From misunderstanding eyes.

On skinny pretty legs

She runs.

(Have I said that before?)

Where she runs

I chase

Up the stairs

To the clouds

Bright innocence

Twinkles

Brilliant and shy from

Under her bouncing hem.

313

More brilliant than

The northern star.

She shines.

The cynosure

Of my terrifying

Beautiful-Silent-Voyage.

She is my siren on the rocks

Against whose lips I

Smash the fragile boat.

Of my psyche

Driven mad

By pure desire."

She waves her hand in front of her face like a middle-aged woman experiencing a hot flash (I'd seen my mother do just that).

"Wow, that's pretty powerful, I don't just like it because it's about me. I think anyone might say it's a powerful expression of desire."

I can't help it—I sneak a peek at her undies. She sees where I'm looking, she places her hands demurely in her lap ("please, no kind sir"). Intensely brilliant cerise rings and vermillion smudges race across her skin as I'm sure they race across mine. I look away as a 100-megaton blast of desire goes off inside me (a clear violation of the nuclear test ban treaty). I sip some tea and nibble my cheeks.

"It must be a heavy burden to have the power to crush someone with a word." I say when I finally recover from the blast sufficiently to say something. My mind is all over the map.

"Are you certain you haven't got that power?"

"Are you telling me I do?"

She doesn't answer. I don't press the issue.

I figure the best thing to do is continue like nothing is happening between us. "This next poem commemorates a very important day. It's called 'Fires'.

Tears of grief fall down

They soak me to the bone, my

Heart goes up in flames"

She is pensive for a moment.

"You don't like it?"

"No, I do, I like the paradox of the soaking tears setting your heart on fire.

"Yeah, I think it works."

"I'm not sure it's a real Haiku."

"Maybe not, does it really matter."

"No, I guess not. It was an important day for me too."

I let her have the last word.

"I call this next one 'Beatles or Stones!'

All you need is love

The Beatles say

Yeah yeah yeah yeah

It was a hard day's night

Yesterday

Hey Jude

Help me if you can

Down this long and

Winding road

Please, please me

She is just seventeen

If you know what I mean

If I fell in love me doo-doo

Would you love, love me do"

"I take it you prefer the Beatles."

"No, actually I prefer the Stones."

"So you're going for the irony thing."

"No, not really I was just trying to amuse myself. I laughed when I wrote 'If I fell in love me doo-doo, very scatological I realize and perhaps immature for that, I guess Wordsworth is in no danger of being displaced in the pantheon. I laughed when I wrote that, so I wrote the rest around that sort of."

"Oh my god I missed it, love me doo-doo, If I fell in love me doo-doo I get it now. Light dawns on Marblehead she says." It's great that she can denigrate herself, sometimes I had thought she took herself too seriously.

"Which do you prefer, the Beatles or the Stones?"

"I love them both."

"Oh come on. That's a cop out." I'm very passionate about music and am always ready to stand my ground against anyone who prefers the Beatles to the Stones.

"Why choose one over the other when you can have them both."

"Huh, I never thought of it that way."

She puts her hand to the side of her mouth again and says in her stage whisper, "Well, that comes as no surprise!"

"Hey! Please respect the poet and his delicate feelings." She puts a tick mark in the air for herself. She has, by my counting, taken a sizable lead.

"If you forced me to choose, I'd choose the Beatles," she says. "I really love George."

"I suppose that's as good a reason as any. Should I go on?"

"Yes, please do, kind sir." I smile at her use of that phrase.

"This poem is a different look at what eternal love might mean. What if it's true that people die but love doesn't? I call this next one 'Heisenberg's Love Song'. Close your eyes and open your mind to the fantastic possibility. She closes her eyes. I take the opportunity to look at her. She really is exquisite.

"Sounds interesting," she says. "You can go ahead and read it anytime now, I can feel you staring at me."

"*Early universe-from the fiery heart of the same star we're torn.*

We journey together over the great void of interstellar space.

Landing here, these intrepid atoms join to form your pretty face.

Those left over come together to make me and love is born.

When we die and give our atoms back is this the end of love?

I believe that love doesn't die and so herein, I speak thereof.

Suppose that we could be reconfigured by some cosmic chance.

Recombined by magic, luck or an all-powerful deity's plans.

Through all of these reconfigurations, we always remain true.

With times passing, I become again me, you become again you.

We will meet in the distant future in another place far away?

That circles a star like ours except that night always follows the day.

Where clouds sculpt themselves according to your every whim.

In the sky there am I and there you are, lightning flashes her to him.

In this strange and distant place, we will know. We'd feel 'us' in our souls.

We know us to the end of things when the time-space continuum folds

Until the end of things, we are joined by this nimble happenstance.

The atoms of me to the atoms of you in an endless quantum dance.

We pass through infinite iterations in this atomic brew.

Finally, I become the better me and you become again just you.

We kiss and are happy together on a tiny distant point of light.

That circles a star like this one but the day always follows the night.

Under the moonlight, we feel the force that binds us hand in glove

The strong force isn't the strongest force; the strongest force is love.

I hope my strange theory is true and not just crazy science fiction stuff.

Because to give you all the love I have, one life will not be enough.

"You can open your eyes."

"Oh my god" she says.

"What? What's wrong?" I nervously sip some tea.

"Nothing, it's fantastic, it's such a romantic idea, such a beautiful sentiment. Maybe Wordsworth isn't safe. I never would have guessed you were such a romantic."

"I'm not real sure how to take that," I say a little ruefully.

"Don't be mad."

"How could I be mad?"

She says nothing for a moment then gently changes the subject. "You make me believe it's possible. You make me want it to be possible"

"It is true that every atom in our bodies was created inside a star, very likely the same very massive star. When that star exploded, these atoms," I indicate our bodies "were sent out into the universe. Atoms never die. Who knows what's possible."

"Are you a scientist or a poet?" she asks jokingly.

"I prefer to think of myself as a poet/scientist rather than a scientist/poet." I say. "Science makes living possible poetry makes life worth living." I assert as though I were an authority on the subject

"Is that the finale then, the magnum opus?"

"I have one more."

"Please." She says, turning one hand palm up. The other stays in her lap blocking her undies from view, my cheeks are not as badly mauled as they might otherwise be for this. She is amused by my attempt to conjure a reasonable scientific justification for my romantic notion and my view on the ascendancy of poetry.

"I dedicate all these poems to you. Were it not for you, I could never have written them. You are my muse and my inspiration."

"Thank You." She says.

"*Your tender lips draw from mine a gentle kiss.*

The juice of your forbidden fruit flows

Gently I push you to the abysmal edge

In the last moment when you whisper no

You fall into the throes of petit-mort

And germinate in me love's dormant spore.

Which grows and grows and grows and grows some more.

For your sweet love I sing this mad refrain.

When lost alone in darkness and in pain.

You turn your light on me so I might see.

You've filled my empty soul with this belief.

Where no belief has ever lived before.

That your love will be mine now and forever

And our love's bonds no earthly force can sever."

She stands up and smooths her skirt. "To be honest, I wasn't sure what to expect. I didn't expect anything like this. You promised me poetry and you delivered on your promise. You have a real talent with words." She is effusive.

"I'm really glad you like them."

"Well, since you delivered, I guess it's my turn. I'm going to get your prize." She heads out to the kitchen. I'm a little confused by this because I had convinced myself she would get naked and offer herself as the prize. That was my all-consuming vision of these past two weeks. I guess she can get undressed in the kitchen. But wait, shouldn't I undress her? I would love to do that.

I sit down. I hear her banging around getting plates and silverware. I wonder if I should get naked and get this ball rolling. The man should be the one to get things started. Fortunately, I don't. She comes back, still fully clothed, carrying a cake. It is a fancy orange cake with orange frosting and the words 'World's Greatest Poet' in blue icing across the top. I do my best to mask my disappointment, although she must have seen it flash across my face.

She cuts two pieces from the cake, puts them on separate plates, hands me a plate and takes the other one for herself. I take a bite. It is delicious. I tell her so.

"It took me over two hours to make," she twirls her fork.

"Are you sure you put enough TLC into it?"

"I think I did."

"Yeah, I think you did, too." I say trying to be cheery and breezy, trying to hide my disappointment. It hits me. What a great thing she has done. She has really made an effort, an all-out effort. This whole thing, the invitation, the cake, the hairdo, the martinis, the sexiest dress ever, even the ice tea, is all for me. She gave me a podium, literally from which I could unabashedly express my very deepest feelings for her. The podium wasn't for her to practice her speech; she didn't need that. I had fallen so completely for her little fiction. This whole thing is her stroke of genius, not mine. I had thought it was all for her and it wasn't. I had thought she had backed me into a corner to write poems for her, but it turns out they are as much for me

324

as for her–they are ours. It turns out she had backed me into an entirely different corner. The put up or shut up corner.

No one has ever made me feel so good, no one has ever tried (my mother doesn't count). I cringe that I had felt disappointment. She has shown me so much love, yet like the blind cretin I am, I've almost missed it. I could not imagine myself worthy and yet here she is telling me I've won the prize, that indeed I am worthy. All the emotion I've ever felt for her compresses into this moment like a dying man's vision of his life in the instant before dying. I want to tell her how I feel about what she's done, but I can't speak. I can't find the right words and I couldn't say them if I could find them, so overwhelming is the storm within me. I feel the need to run. I need to get up and run as far and as fast as it takes for me to drop from exhaustion. She grabs my hand; she won't let me run.

She leads me to the base of the stairs in her front hall.

"Jackson, Jackson McNamara?"

"Yes," I say, in the haze of a dream.

"You know I'm only just a girl right?"

"Are you just a girl?" I say; not sure I believe it.

"Yes, I don't want you to be disappointed. I think sometimes you think I'm something else."

"So you are just a girl and I'm just a boy." That she could disappoint me seems the most ludicrous of ludicrous propositions. My heart is fluttering

She proceeds up the steps and is three steps ahead of me. I'm frozen momentarily at the base of the stairs. As she proceeds up the stairs, she leans forward slightly, revealing the back of her thighs all the way up to her bum, like the day I wrote the poem about, my heart swells with how long and how much I've loved her. She doesn't fully understand her own power. My heart beats even faster. I have never imagined anything beyond this point even in my dreams. I have felt desire for her as keenly as a knife. Yet I have never actually fantasized about joining with her. That is, I have never seen in my fantasies my penis inside her. I think now how strange it is that perhaps my own mind conspired against me to suppress my hope. However, I have fantasized endlessly about this moment, the moment just before.

I come home to her after a hard day's work. She is there in white, always white, waiting. Sometimes she wears a simple sundress, but most times it's a flowing gown, diaphanous and elegant. She has made a light supper of cantaloupe slices and avocado. I have never tasted avocado. I suppose that's very symbolic.

The house we share is a hacienda somewhere in the tropics. I'd seen just such a house in one of my mother's architectural magazines. Warm breezes flow through the house, for the house is built to encourage these breezes. They stir the folds of her dress. The dress flows around her in the breeze, clinging to the places I want to touch, suggesting her naked body. She is tantalizing, spellbinding, mysterious. The breeze dances over my naked back (I always come home from work shirtless). There is piano music from another room, a melancholy ballad full of love and loss. A tune I know. It clings to the edge of my mind. Its name eludes me. She leans back hands on the table and throws her head back wordlessly commanding me. I kiss her delicate jaw. She puts a foot on the chair and raises the flowing dress to mid-thigh, I kiss her knee. She turns and bunches the dress at her waist, I kiss her buttocks.

I wake from this very dream with a painful hard on, so stiff and seemingly permanent. I lay in my too-small, sagging childhood bed trying to conjure the vivid images of my dream. I ease my pain. Sometimes I ease my pain twice or thrice as necessary.

"Why are you stopping, don't you want to come."

She proceeds up the steps and I follow. I walk slowly, my heart pounds, my senses heighten. She had slipped off her little pilgrim shoes when I wasn't looking. She has little feet with little toes that no one should ever step on.

I notice the pictures on the wall; I hadn't really looked at them the last time I was here. There is one in particular that grabs my attention. It is an eight-and-a-half by eleven in a bronze frame that has falling leaves in the lower right-hand corner. The picture is of Ariel as a young girl, maybe four or five, smiling. She has lost her two front baby teeth. Her picture is crudely cut to make her appear to be riding on a hand-drawn pink horse. Painted around the picture are the words: Ariel Rides the Pink Pony. It doesn't really say that does it? I look more closely to make sure my mind isn't playing tricks on me, and yes that's what it says. I want to remember the details; I want to remember it all.

My heart is beating so fast and my breath coming so quickly it is actually an effort to climb the stairs. I have to stop again before I reach the top. She had already turned into her room and has to come out to see what is keeping me.

"Jax, what's wrong? My mother will be home around 5:30."

The practical considerations of the real world intruding, "Isn't your heart beating fast?"

"She comes over and takes my hand and places it on her heart, just below her left breast, I feel the curve of her breast in the crook of my thumb and forefinger. My heart beats all the faster. Her heart is beating fast, too, and that feels good. I make her put her hand on my heart.

"Can you feel my heart now?" I say gently, thinking myself suave and clever.

"I feel it." She says.

"Don't break it." I say, my suave evaporating.

"I won't." she says simply.

We stand there in that embrace for a moment looking into each other's eyes and feeling each other's hearts. She pulls me gently to her room.

We stand next to her bed; it is frilly and feminine. We are caught in that moment of indecision that happens in life whenever you're about to cross a line that can't be crossed back over.

She had been nervous just like me when we came up the stairs. She is tentative now, like me, as we stand by the bed. She turns away from me and signals that I should unzip her dress. I do and the dress falls to the floor. She doesn't wear a bra and thus her back is naked. I kiss the nape of her neck while my hands go where they must. She doesn't think it strange at all. On her back, there is a pattern of freckles arrayed like Cygnus in the night sky. She is the swan! I kiss each freckle/star. I kneel down and kiss the freckle that is Deneb in the small of her back.

I pull her underpants down, slowly, savoring the unveiling, she steps out and I throw them on the bed. She is beautiful beyond imagining, I kiss her everywhere I have in my dreams. My breath comes in short bursts.

She is disarming, playful and shy as she takes my clothes off. She smiles a Mona Lisa smile at my rigid penis, I have no idea what that smile means. She studies my penis closely. This is so like her. I make it waggle and catch her by surprise. She jumps away, startled. It's pretty funny and I put a tick mark in the air for myself. She laughs.

I pick her up to lay her on the bed, like Rhett did to Scarlett. If my senses weren't so heightened I would have missed these signals. Terror flashes over her face and she stiffens like someone anticipating an attack. If my mind weren't racing so fast I would not know what these signals mean, but my senses are heightened and my mind is racing. I know immediately that whatever had happened between her and Coleman had been bad. I suppose I should be glad about that, but I can't be. No one knows better than I do what it means and just how bad it can be. I have been plagued by similar bouts of nostalgia. Momentary shots of fear that strike like lightning. I don't know where or when they might happen, or what will trigger them, just that they are frightening. She has lied to me. Something happened between her and Coleman. I have a choice to make, the choice of my lifetime.

If I knew the details of what she'd been subjected to would I see how brave she is, what a reaffirmation of life this is. Could I love her all the more for it? She never in a million years will beg me to stay, that just isn't her way. She owes me nothing. I have the choice. I can be a fool and a coward or I can try to be as strong as she is.

I try my best to kiss away her terror.

She stops me. "Jax" she says.

"Yes."

"I'm so glad about what happened between Coleman and I."

"Really!" I say, completely taken aback and ready to bolt, thinking I've made the wrong choice and have blundered my way into being the brunt of the most vicious of high school pranks. I expect Coleman to jump out of the closet, disbelieving still that what is happening could really be. She holds me tight though and won't let me bolt.

"Yes, because now I know for certain what a real loving kiss feels like." She whispers, a silent plea in her eyes. I was wrong she would beg me to stay.

She pulls me to her and she kisses away my terror. She breathes her gentle orange-scented breath of life into me. We embrace and kiss in a frenzy of passion. Our naked bodies melt one into the other. She is so soft and so warm and so willing and so everything. We are a tangle of naked limbs as we try instinctively to find how we best fit together. Our hands are as insatiably curious as our minds. Her slightest touch suspends me between ecstasy and bliss (or perhaps the other way around, I'm too happy to think about the hierarchy of happiness). I don't have to tell you; you know how it is.

By this time in my life, I had seen many a shadow play of love. Although the shadow players could never tell me what love feels like, for they do not know themselves, their antics are useful from an instructional point of view.

I assume a position from which I may adore her. She, without question or reserve, allows me to arrange her into a position from which she might be readily adored. Her smell, at once sweet and pungent surprises me, though I do not let on, nor am I deterred. Rather, her "display" of obvious excitement spurs me on. I don't know how I know what to do, I just do, and I do it. What I lack in experience, I make up for with ardor, tenderness, and my lifelong desire for this very moment. I feel these things so strongly; they make me faint as my heart beats a hummingbird's thread of a heartbeat. She feels these things too and knows they are true. She rewards me with the sweetest nectar—that is all I can taste, smell, and be intoxicated by. She resists being pushed over the edge, mentally digging in against relinquishing control. Her mind splits in two. I've learned this

332

might happen, that she might be afraid to let go (I wrote about it in my poem). I lovingly continue pushing (with a love only she will ever know). I gain her trust and she hurls herself headlong over the edge, rewarding my persistence with an unforgettable vision of pliant, ecstatic beauty and a symphony of sounds. There are no curses or shouts at god, only the beautiful call of a beautiful bird, freed from all restrictions, in full flight. The beautiful call falls to a paroxysm of silence in the moment. I don't know what Coleman heard, but I know in my heart he never heard this silence. The nectar flows, too much to drink, even for one as mad with thirst as I.

   She comes back from where I've sent her. She is different in many ways, not the least of which is that her terror is gone. Her eyes are so deep and filled with wonder. She draws me into her eyes. She lovingly wipes my face with her underpants. When she realizes what she's doing, she laughs and laughs until she can laugh no more.

   She won't let me feel confused or hurt by her laughter. She holds my feelings in her hands. I don't penetrate the mysteries of love so much as she envelopes me in them. In her warm envelopment, she lifts me and shakes me. I collapse within and die my own little death. I catch a glimpse of heaven. She is there, it could not be heaven otherwise.

No one imitates her little sounds. An unspoken agreement abides at graduation.

Ariel stands at the podium on the little elevated stage on which she'd trod her whole life. As a dancer, entertaining King Herod the night he orders the slaughter of the innocents. As an angel, quieting the audience so the newborn baby Jesus may sleep. As a bobbysoxer in Bye-Bye Birdie, "We love you Conrad oh yes we do!"—a song I first heard her sing so long ago (was it second or fourth grade?) and later in the senior class production of that play that she, more than anyone else, brought to life. Now she is the class valedictorian—a public recognition that she really is the brightest among us. Despite the darkness all around, she remains in the light. She is the light.

Even though I had nothing to do with it, I'm so proud of her. This is such a moment for her, such a victory, such a vindication almost no one in the room could understand. That no one has tried to spoil her moment is a relief. She has trouble restraining her emotions. Maybe others couldn't see behind the reconstructed wall of reserve, but I see. She's accomplished something, no small feat, and she is deeply satisfied.

The class is small; one hundred and five of us are graduating. Nonetheless, there are some other very smart people. Her accomplishment was not a one-person race. There

334

is Julius (the "favorite" among the bettors); Carlo Cence; Tim Hart (a math genius, who later worked for NASA); Nancy Turner, sharp as a whip and not afraid to wield it; Susan Darwin (almost all the girls are very smart); and dare I say it, me! Not that I really should be included among these people or had any reasonable shot to be the one, but hey, I consider myself valedictorian by association.

She begins her speech

"Someone very close to me recently suggested I begin by telling a joke in order to get the crowd on my side. I prefer a more direct approach. Is there anyone out there who isn't on my side?"

No one says anything

"Whew that's a relief," she says wiping her brow with an exaggerated gesture. A smattering of laughter and applause ripples through the crowded gymnasium. Pretty classy, to begin with a joke without beginning with a joke.

Someone yells from the back "I'm with you Arilly!" It's Buddy Merrill. Buddy is a sort of local mascot. He is slow-witted and has a pure heart. The crowd erupts with laughter.

"Thank You, Buddy, you're very kind," Ariel says.

She speaks about overcoming adversity and the trials placed before us. She speaks about keeping one's heart and one's eyes open to love. "Love—the most passionate, enduring love of your life—may be and may have always been sitting next to you."

Her mellifluous voice hypnotizes the crowd.

She thanks her cousins for coming up from New York to see her. As valedictorian, she was given extra seats and her Aunt and cousins fill them. She thanks her favorite teachers, all of them through the years, some who have passed. She shocks me by naming Sister Demetrius. Mr. Murphy also makes the list. He blushes so ferociously; I'm surprised his head doesn't explode. "You can't take the Wisconsin out of the boy," she quips and his blush deepens. She thanks her favorite teacher who she says is teaching her what love might be. "The lessons are ongoing," she says and she hopes they will continue for a long, long time. "It's a difficult subject." This elicits a chuckle from the cognoscenti.

She pauses before continuing, quietly she says, "David." Just that, her little prayer of devotion. The crowd murmurs about who David might be, even some of our fellows have forgotten. She looks at her mother. "I love you, Mom." Her mother is crying; it is a very powerful moment. She has not said these words to her mother since long before her father's death, and their relationship has been rocky.

She pauses for a few moments to gather herself, starting and stopping a few times. The quiet in the room is supernatural and the suspense is difficult. It seems like she might not be able to continue. I'm rooting for her so hard. "It's alright, Ariel," someone says. She looks to see from whither this supporting voice comes. Some of my classmates raise their voices in support. They are as it turns out, with the noted exceptions, decent people.

"Thank you all," she says struggling hard against her emotions. "It means a lot. Please bear with me."

"This is a celebration; life at its beginning; life at its most hopeful, passionate, and beautiful. I have felt all these things recently. I would, however, like to take a moment to look back at someone special in my life. Some of you may not know that my father died earlier this year. Many of you came to be with me at that time. If I didn't thank you then, understand I was a little out of it. I want to thank you all now very much."

"I never said goodbye to my father, he died so suddenly. He told me often: 'the most important thing is the life of the mind.' He imbued in me a thirst, I hope an insatiable thirst, for knowledge. I stand here humble, realizing were it not for him, I would not be. He would be proud of me no matter what, but would have been so proud of me today." She is sobbing a little, not a lot. She twists her hands under her chin. She looks up to the ceiling. She is not predisposed to dramatic gestures and I

337

can tell she's amended what she is going to say, cutting it short before she blubbers again is how she would put it.

"Goodbye, trash man," she says, and then runs from the stage to the seats where her mother, aunt and cousins sit. She hugs her mother tightly.

"I didn't kill him, did I Ma?" she whispers

"No sweetheart, no," her mother whispers back. "Don't ever think that."

Her Aunt and cousins hug them both. They hug for a long time and the ceremony comes to a halt for them. She makes her way back to her seat. People reach out to touch her because she has moved them. She is seated in the row in front of me. This time, she doesn't ignore my solicitously extended hand. She almost pulls me over as I lean as far forward over the seat backs as I can. Those seated there part to give her room. She grips my neck as though her life depended on it.

"You've made peace with yourself?"

"For today," she says, then releases me and goes back to her seat, running the gauntlet of knees and seat backs. She sits down and looks back down the row of chairs and smiles at me. What have I done to deserve to feel so good?

The ceremony is over. High school is over. I feel the relief and the trepidation. Little crowds are milling around, students

338

writing in each other's yearbooks, throwing their caps in the air, stripping off their gowns and having to put them back on so their parents can take pictures. Some have already gone off to get drunk or high. I'm standing with my parents when Ariel comes over.

"Mom, dad, this is Ariel Lirilinghi. She is the smartest and prettiest in these halls. Ariel, these are my parents." Ariel raises a hand in a small gesture of greeting and smiles.

"Oh sweetheart, we're so sorry about your father. We didn't know him. Why did you call him trash-man?" My mother says. I can tell she is nervous. My mother is high-strung in public.

"Thanks, it's a very long story," Ariel says. "You know Jax has really helped me a lot."

"He is basically a good boy." My mother says. Thanks ma', I think to myself, please don't call me Johnny-poopy-doopy. I'll kill myself after I kill you. Too late, my mother's social anxiety lets the cat out of the bag. Ariel can't help herself, she sputters the phrase "Johnny-poopy-doopy." We laugh ourselves silly about it together. Thank god no one else heard and that I wouldn't have to be locked up here with them if they did. Everything has changed.

Ariel places her hand on my father's forearm and looks at me

"Is this your dad?"

"That's him. Dear old dad." My mother and I share a laugh. I can see my father is pissed but he contains it because Ariel is here.

"Jax, you didn't tell me your dad was so handsome." I can see my father sort of melting.

I shrug my shoulders. "Geez, I didn't know." My mother and I share another laugh and my father stops melting.

"Sign my yearbook," she says. There is a full-page picture of her, which people are signing instead of their own little pictures. It was one of the perks of being valedictorian. Others have signed: to Ariel, a great kid......from Goo-Goo; to Ariel, good luck from Dr. Cluck; Ariel, you are the best......from The Goog.

"Are Goo-Goo and the Goog actual real, live people? Are they two different people or the same person? They just graduated with us?" I say, with great amusement.

"I'm a little embarrassed to say, but I haven't been keeping track."

"Alright, then." I write: to Ariel: precious love, more valuable than life, remember Antarctica has two C's in it......J. Max "I won't sign it Johnny-poopy-doopy."

"Thank god for that," she whispers so my mother won't hear her, then she smiles. "Aaaaahhh, thanks for cluing me in on the Antarctica thing."

"You don't remember do you? I'll tell you later? It's a cute story."

She signs my yearbook: Darkly Passionate: Love, Ariel

"I love it." She kisses me on the cheek.

"If you can come by my house, please do, kind sir," she says, whispering seductively. I have told her everything. She touches my arm and runs off on her skinny, pretty legs yelling as she goes how nice it was to meet my parents. Shit, I forgot to ask her who was teaching her about love.

"Oh my god, you're all grown up!" my mother says.

"What in god's name is that girl doing with you?" my father asks, with real incredulity in his voice.

"That's funny. I've asked myself that question about you and Ma!"

"I've asked myself that very question, too!" My mother chimes in.

"Oh shut the fuck up, both of you!" My father says. We all share a laugh. Things really have changed in the blink of an eye. My father is already thinking about kicking me out if I don't get a real job. My mother has gotten me a stay of execution because

I'm her favorite and she doesn't want me to suffer too much. My father thinks that if I suffer, it will be good for me. He was a little less than a year older than I'm now when he landed on Omaha beach where Freddy, Ricky, and Tyrus were killed, and Uncle Ray died in his arms with a bullet in his brain.

"Hey Dad, I'm sorry I missed the tree planting and I'm sorry about what I said."

He looks at me. "Don't worry about it, your brother and I had a nice moment."

"I'm glad."

"Congratulations, son," he sticks out his hand and I shake it. "I'm proud of you." He says. Whether he is proud that I have graduated high school or that he finally has some reason to believe I'm not a little "loose in the hips" I can only guess. I shake his hand and he of course proceeds to try to crush mine, as he always does, everything is a test of manhood with my father. I try in turn to crush his. We reach a stalemate.

At Ariel's house later, we get high with her older cousins right in her backyard under the stars (I had mowed the lawn yesterday). Almost everyone from school comes through her backyard just to say a few words or exchange a hug. She is more well-loved than she knows. We sit in the same chairs we sat in three weeks ago. She laughs and cries as her cousins regale her deep into the night with funny and poignant stories of

342

both David and Sonny (as they call her father). Her cousins take turns embellishing each other's memories, interrupting each other constantly to fill in a new detail, while never missing a beat in the story, like maybe only real New Yorkers can. They make a huge deal out of Ariel and they are terrific.

We celebrate our passage between the two worlds, our childhood and what's to come. I learn just who is teaching whom about love. If anybody asks about to whom she was referring, we will say the answer is Jesus, of course! That's why she is the valedictorian.

18. The End of Things

I loved you, and I probably still do,
And for a while the feeling may remain...
But let my love no longer trouble you,
I do not wish to cause you any pain.
I loved you; and the hopelessness I knew,
The jealousy, the shyness - though in vain -
Made up a love so tender and so true
As may God grant you to be loved again.

-Alexander Pushkin

I walk home from Ariel's house the night of the graduation. I want to stay, but her older cousins express some discomfort with this idea. She walks with me to the corner, holding my hand. I give her the little graduation gift I've been holding in my pocket for the right moment. My gift is a small charm with a Picasso-like representation of an angel on both sides of a flat sterling silver disc attached to a thin silver chain.

"Now you have a guardian angel," I tell her, blushing in the darkness at my corniness and my eternal wish to be her protector. We agree we will see each other tomorrow. She kisses me sweetly.

"I love you." She had not said these words before. How I had imagined her saying these words didn't matter now. It only mattered that she'd said them, quietly but with conviction. To hear them proceed from her lips was magical. I saw them rising in the light of the streetlamp under which we stood to be written in the sky. The spell she had cast on me that first day was made permanent. I leave her under that streetlamp.

My head is in the clouds; I'm so happy. I'm walking through the park, almost home. I have reached the spot where Coleman snatched my poem from my hands (was it only two weeks ago?). I feel the first blow cleave my skull. I go down. If I have a choice, I guess dying happy is what I'd rather do.

I am dead by the fourth blow. My death doesn't stop him.

You may think I'm outraged as I float overhead while Coleman pounds away on me with a heavy iron bar. You may think I'm mournful for the loss of my bright and loving future with Ariel. I had waited my whole life (such as it was) for what has taken place in the last few weeks and it has been mercilessly torn from me. Instead, I feel bad for Coleman, who wears himself out with all these unnecessary blows and his constant maniacal chanting, "I told you to stay away from her."

Poor chap.

It's different over here. The things that concern everyone so deeply over there seem to matter very little to us. I have crossed the one line that no one has re-crossed. My one and only remaining earthly concern is for Ariel, that she should not be sad for me or for herself.

As for me, I have loved she who I was meant to love. I have held and kissed her hands, her cheeks, her lips. I have held her and said with all my heart, "I don't want to let you go, I love you." I have heard from her those very words. They were the last words I heard before I passed through. I have seen love in her eyes. All our moments together burn within me now and though fleeting, in each I live a thousand lifetimes.

Time doesn't matter here. I'm able to go back and forth from the moment of my death to the end of eternity on a wish. I

345

wish myself away from the scene of my murder. I find myself in Ariel's bathroom. I stand behind her while she brushes her teeth. She is in her underwear getting ready for bed. While she brushes, she hums a tune. The tune she hums is the song I sang to her when I chased her up the stairs all those long eons ago.

When I'm sad she comes to me.

A thousand smiles she gives to me free.[3]

She is fifty-four years old, a beautiful accomplished woman, a doctor of letters, respected in her field, a professor of Comparative Literature at her Alma-mater and the author of many books on that subject and others.

She has three children, twin boys who are in their first year of high school. You may think they are very young for a fifty-four-year-old woman. However, it took her some time to get pregnant. She has an arrhythmic cycle, that sometimes occurs as Infrequently as twice a year, since onset. This made conception more difficult. More importantly it took a long time for her to love again

Her husband is a good man and he loves her.

_____

[3]

Jimi Hendrix, "Little Wing"

Ariel's oldest child is a thirty-six-year-old woman, as much a sister as a daughter. She looks like Ariel. I would have loved her with all my heart had I been able to hold her on the day that she was born. I love her anyway. She knows about me.

Ariel's sons are Paolo and Luigi, named for Enzo's fellow trash men who were a big help to Ariel and Kathleen in their hour of need. Paul felt so good about helping out, he even restrained himself from asking Ariel for a "nice tit shot," even though he really wanted one. She honors her father with her sons' names as well, and is now very proud of her heritage, her childish wish to be French long forgotten.

Ariel's daughter is named Moira.

Moira is named for the character in my talent show story. Strangely, like Moira in the old city, as a child she ran around naked everywhere she went until finally her mother laid down the law. The other choice for Moira's name was Muffin. As much as Ariel loved Muffin, Moira won out.

Moira never took her husband's name because she was already well established professionally at the time of her marriage. She is a world-renowned concert pianist noted for her sensitive interpretations. She wrings tears from the piano. I love to listen. I don't have to be there to hear her, I can be anywhere; here and there, then and now have no meaning. When she plays, I hear it.

Moira single-handedly launched a revival of the French composer Erik Satie when she scored a movie with his music. Satie's music is full of love and loss. It clings to the edges of your mind and plays in your dreams. You can't recall its name or where you heard it.

The movie is about a boy who loves so much and dies too young. Ariel cries when she sees it, a lot of people cry. Finally penned a real tearjerker, eh old trash man! Yes, that's right. He's around here somewhere.

One of the wonders of being here is that I can see what would have happened had I not been killed. We would have left Brighton and hit the road. I would have sustained us as best I could by any means necessary. I would have done things I would not wish to do. Even so, the rigors of the road would have proven too much for both Ariel and Moira. Ariel would have died giving birth to her stillborn daughter on the dirty steel floor of a railroad car somewhere in Eastern Montana. This is the ignoble, anonymous end to which I would have dragged them.

I would have jumped from that train car in despair as it passed over a trestle. I would have flown with the birds for a moment, but I would have hit the ground at about ninety-five miles an hour, smashing myself to pieces on the creek bed below. Whenever I get down and wish things had been different, when I wish that I could have touched her and been touched by her just once more, I replay this other ending.

I can see Ariel dead, stripped of her grace and dignity, her mouth hanging open, her pants covered in her own and her daughter's blood. I see this and can be glad things happened the way they did. I can even thank good old Coleman and praise his name. It's all about forgiveness over here.

It isn't easy for Ariel. She is the one who suffers the most from my death. How much can one person take? You can try to imagine the weight of so much tragedy and so much darkness in the life of a person who dances in the light. She went to her beautiful place in Gloucester one August day the summer after our graduation. If one has to die unhappy, it's best to die in a beautiful place.

She summons me with a quiet word, my name spoken in a desperate whisper. She leaves her shoes and my little charm on the rocks. She enters the cold ocean off the rocky East-facing beach below Atlantic Avenue. She is pregnant and fears beyond reason that the baby is Coleman's. This is the last thing she can stand. She swims out quite far, she cannot make it back. I enter her mind for this one and only time. I show her that the baby is mine. My memory of what I saw while she played at naked tough girl, that white and slightly corkscrewed string becomes her memory. I exhort her to swim for the shore and she does. She almost doesn't make it and would not have but for the life growing inside her. She never again thinks seriously about killing herself. If being a hero is saving someone else's life, then I guess I finally got to be her hero after all.

We are here in this beautiful place together. The wild ocean meets the wild shore, the ocean constantly trying to drag the rocks away. There is no surf here, for the rocks plunge deep below the water. The dark ocean swells and falls here like a beating heart. The sun splashes silver flakes across the water as far as one can see. I had promised her I would be here with her. I linger inside her by the water while she dries shivering and crying on the rocks. I have been given such a gift. Ariel and I entwine our memories and dreams. That she is even more beautiful on the inside makes it hard for me to have to say goodbye. I must say it though for I have come to the end of things.

She will always remember me.

She will always be with me.

Love never dies.

God is great.

The End

The idea for *The Mythology of Sylphs* came in the mail. I received a card inviting me to attend the thirty-third class reunion of Saint Columbkille's High School in Brighton Massachusetts. This would have been around June of 2008. I didn't attend that high school. I did, however, attend the grammar school through eighth grade. During my time at the grammar school I had a long standing and very intense crush on a girl, with whom I barely exchange two sentences. After I left the eighth grade I did call her once to ask her for a date. That did not go so well, I was nervous and perhaps she was too. When she said no I was both hurt and relieved. Her name was on the card as a "committed attendee"

As I held the card in my hand, I realized the emotional hold her name (If not her) still held on me. Her name is a very unusual name, so unusual that she may be the only person in America so named. The last name of my heroine is an anagram of my grammar school crushes last name. I'd long been looking for a story to write and the idea of that boyhood crush becoming something more sprang to mind. I began writing in earnest and the project took on a life of its own.

The Mythology of Sylphs is my first book. I have never written anything before. I hope, if you get to this point, you're surprised by that. I wrote and wrote and wrote from about November of 2008 until November of 2011 when I was struck by a horrifying revelation. That revelation was this: everything I'd written was total crap. I had written as many as a million words. You would think I had written something that could have been preserved in the finished product, even by accident, like the typing monkeys who eventually reproduce the works of Shakespeare. No such luck for this primate, there really was nothing. It had all been such a colossal waste of energy.

In desperation, I reached out to the woman who inspired my main character. I told her I was writing a book, she was flattered and it turned out very nice. She agreed to read my output. I had backed myself into the same corner Jax had backed himself into. Art imitates life in this instance. I was inspired though. Over the next couple of months, the outline of the story, largely as it is emerged.

It turns out those first three years were not entirely wasted. The ability to spot crap in your own work is the single most important thing a writer can learn. If you think what you've written is good because you put it on the page and it is free of grammatical and spelling errors, then it's very likely that you either suck as a writer or you are a freak of nature and I bow to your astonishing prowess.

I worked hard for another two and half years. I engaged an editor (for a flat fee) and published through amazon in July of 2014. I made the mistake of believing it finished and I rushed to publish. I had been working so hard for so long I could no longer see the forest for the trees. I should have put it aside and let it ferment a bit.

I have surely done that now. I am releasing this new version in the firm hope that the story is finally finished, that is it will no longer call me back to make more changes.

The story stands largely as it was when I first published it. I've given more background to Ariel's parents. I added a chapter called; *In the Forest of Thorns*. This chapter had previously appeared as a sub-chapter in the chapter called *Occurrences*. I thought it should be expanded and was more appropriately placed earlier in the book. Also it is now presented as the dream it always should have been. This gave me the chance to present Ariel as beautiful through other eyes and to see some tenderness amidst the terror besetting her. It also adds literary allusive and intertextual elements (assuming I understand those terms). Ariel is sleeping beauty, her tragedy and her horrific dreams are the forest of thorns behind which she sleeps. Her awakening is not a gentle kiss but a cataclysmic explosion of emotion.

The Mythology of Sylphs is also about writing. Enzo writes his letter and his silly short stories, Jax writes his short story, his paper, and his poems, Ariel writes her paper. The book is about my journey to becoming a writer as much as it's about anything else. I hope that's not too sub-textual to see.

I am with time and distance able to divorce myself from the whole thing. I was, but am no longer married to every word and would change everything if I believed I could improve the story, while leaving it fundamentally the same. I feel this is another huge stride in my development as a writer. Before coming to this enlightenment I had felt the need to defend everything I'd written vigorously against even constructive criticism. I took it so personally. I no longer feel that. I take a more pragmatic view and have a different conception of what artistic integrity really is. In rereading the book with an eye toward improving it I found numerous places to say what I wanted to say in clearer more impactful prose, places that before I would have deemed sacrosanct. I made a lot of changes to previously sacrosanct passages, starting with the very first paragraph. Most of these changes were additions, some were subtractions, all hopefully are real improvements. I'm sure if I came back to the book tomorrow I would find more such places, perhaps even the places I've changed today. There were also places that struck me upon rereading as nearly perfect. The ability to see what's actually good in your own writing and leave it alone is as fundamental to being a good writer as spotting the crap and perhaps more difficult.

This afterword is my personal acknowledgment that *The Mythology of Sylphs* isn't perfect even as I've worked very hard to try and make it so. No human endeavor can ever be perfect.

September 5th, 2016

Northborough, Massachusetts